I0819913

El Niño

El Niño

A Novel

Bryan Buchan

RESOURCE *Publications* • Eugene, Oregon

EL NIÑO
A Novel

Resource Publications
An Imprint of Wipf and Stock Publishers
199 W. 8th Ave., Suite 3
Eugene, OR 97401

www.wipfandstock.com

PAPERBACK ISBN: 978-1-5326-5969-0
HARDCOVER ISBN: 978-1-5326-5970-6
EBOOK ISBN: 978-1-5326-5971-3

10/17/18

In loving memory of my parents
Thomas Summers Buchan
Darlene Jensina Buchan

Contents

1.

TORONTO

I WAS PART OF it from the very beginning. Well, maybe not the very beginning—there were rumors out of both Barbados and Botswana that perhaps the boy had already been at work, but no one has ever been able to verify any of those early reports. My own story was documented in minute detail, pored over, studied and reported in textbooks. I was the "Toronto case," the template for all the others that followed.

Not that I was aware of anything at the time, mind you. I was only a toddler then. It didn't look as if I would ever make it past the toddler stage, because I was unconscious and hooked up to all kinds of medical devices, right here in Toronto, in an institution then known as the Hospital for Sick Children, which at the time was still a gleaming centre of edgy research. Little patients arrived from across the province and from around the world to be treated for any number of problems. The family-friendly layout softened its somewhat discouraging name. That was a time when children often became sick, when there were medical problems that couldn't be solved, when children even died from their illnesses.

My parents were in the room with me, more or less twenty-four hours a day, because the end could come at any time. I had been born with a heart defect, a tiny u-shaped hole that leaked blood from one chamber to another. The surgeons were successful in repairing the hole, but later, when I was just over three years old, a virus infected the heart tissue. At first, it looked like I had a minor respiratory ailment—labored breathing, a slight fever, loss of appetite, lack of energy, the type of infection many parents used to deal with regularly, but within hours, my breathing grew worse, the fever spiked, and my parents took me to the emergency department at the hospital. I was tested, poked, scanned and admitted to the hospital.

The next day, my condition became critical. The infection resisted all the medications the pharmacy threw at it. The doctors prepared my parents for the worst; my heart function steadily deteriorated.

Of course, I was in no position to observe any of this, much less remember it, but my mother told me the story so many times that I came to feel as if I had been another presence in the room, watching myself rapidly losing the battle.

On the day she died, almost twenty years ago now, my mother smiled as she retold the story for the hundredth time or so. My sister and I sat on either side of her bed, each of us holding one of her hands.

"You looked so small and defenceless, Daniel," she whispered. "I've never been so afraid in all my life as I was that day. There seemed to be nothing we could do." No matter how many times she repeated the tale, Mom's voice always faltered a little when she spoke this part.

"Your father was crying quietly, trying not to let me see. He was turned toward the window, looking out at that gray November rain as the day wound down toward evening. Beads of moisture were sliding down the pane, reflecting tiny sparks of color from the traffic below. I had every light in the room turned on as if that would somehow keep the darkness away from you. I was refusing to cry, because it seemed that tears would mean we had really and truly lost you, and I was doing everything in my power to prevent that from happening. Still, the numbers on the machine kept dropping as your blood pressure sank. You were perfectly still, barely breathing, very pale. I had one finger in your open palm, stroking it in hopes that we would have a miracle.

"And then, there he was, standing on the other side of your crib, looking into my eyes with a solemn expression on his face. He seemed about twelve years old, dressed in very ordinary clothes and wearing his hair straight and shaggy, as was the fashion at that time. I thought he must have wandered in from one of the other wards - after all, this was a Hospital for *Sick* Children - and I immediately panicked. What if this boy were a patient with an active infection? What if he were even now shedding millions of microbes into the air you were breathing?

"Before I could shoo him out, however, he gave me the faintest of smiles and spoke quietly. Your father turned around and glanced from the boy to me. He wiped at his eyes, but said nothing and sank down in the chair beside mine.

"'I can help,' said the boy. 'But many things will change.'

"'What do you mean?' I asked him, but your father simply said, 'Yes. If you can help, do it.' Your dad was always the practical one." My mother smiled wistfully.

"I sucked in my breath as the boy reached in and lightly touched your forehead, then withdrew his hand and smiled again. I still had my finger in your hand, and after a few seconds you curled your fingers around mine. It was the first movement you had made in days.

"'Now he will get stronger,' said the boy. Within minutes there was a change in your blood pressure and the numbers on the machine started to climb. Your father began crying again, and I joined him, this time with relief, as color came back into your face and your pulse became more regular.

"The boy looked into my eyes and seemed to be about to ask me a question. 'Yes,' I said. 'Please.' I had only the vaguest sense of what I was agreeing to, but the boy reached over and touched my forehead, too. At once I felt all the fear and pain draining out of me, replaced by a calmness such as I'd never experienced before. Your dad leaned forward and the boy touched him as well. We've treasured the memory of that feeling, of that moment, all our lives.

"I realized we both had closed our eyes. When your dad stood up we found the boy was no longer there. We hadn't even thanked him."

"I think he knew you were grateful, Mom," I said. She just nodded. She was looking beyond me at some other point in the room. She closed her eyes and seemed to fall asleep, her hair spread lightly across the pillow, a quiet smile on her lips. I felt her fingers gently close on mine. She lay back, breathing softly. Rachel looked across at me and smiled. As we sat watching, Mom's breathing became slower; minutes later she turned her head slightly toward Rachel and then she was gone.

That was the story of my first connection to the boy, some two years before the events in Uruguay brought the world's attention to him and the media began calling him El Niño Milagroso, the Boy of Miracles. Now more than eighty years have gone by, and although I have spent a lifetime researching the El Niño phenomenon, I'm still finding the truth elusive. I've followed his strange odyssey all over the globe, and back here to Toronto; I've collected wild tales and eyewitness accounts; I've seen the impact of his actions as they transformed so much of the world; and I've tried to counter the skepticism of those, especially in the early days, who felt my interpretation of events was just wrong-headed. The track is muddied and has brought me to many dead ends, but the search even now calls me on.

My mother held firm to her story for sixty years, and the details never changed. Her belief in that miracle in Toronto has played a part in my own determination to find answers.

The answers, of course, have never been as numerous as the questions. In the case of my sister and me, the questions began early.

There was no reasonable explanation for my recovery at Sick Children's, and the doctors were left grasping. The fact that they didn't accept any part of my parents' story frustrated my mother especially. It wasn't that they called her a liar; they simply suggested she was overwrought and emotionally in no position to judge what had actually taken place. In her desperation for a cure, she imagined some sort of miraculous intervention, just as a perfectly explainable (but unexplained) change in my condition occurred.

As it turned out, this was the beginning of what at the time were many strange developments. After my near-death experience at the hospital, I was never sick again. No colds, no childhood illnesses, no allergies: nothing. Now as I approach my eighty-fifth birthday, I can say I have been in good health ever since the boy came to my hospital room. The same was true of my parents—never sick, even for a day, aging without any apparent loss of physical or mental fitness, dying quietly and calmly, my father at eighty-nine, my mother two years later at eighty-eight.

When my sister Rachel was born, a year and a half after my time at Sick Children's, the birth was completely without incident. My mother was the envy of all her friends, with a problem-free pregnancy and very brief, painless labor. Today this would be unremarkable, but at the time it was almost unheard of. Rachel was a perfect baby, Mom always proclaimed, eating well, sleeping soundly, smiling at everyone. As children, we were best friends, Rachel and I. Neighbors would comment on how "nicely" we played together, as if it were somehow unnatural.

Rachel, too, has never had to endure any illness. She fell off her bicycle once when she was ten, breaking her wrist, but the fracture healed quickly without complications or even much discomfort.

Both of us, however, were slow to mature physically and, I later realized, emotionally as well. When I started secondary school at the age of thirteen, I was the same size as most of my friends had been at ten. The first signs of puberty didn't appear until I was seventeen. Until then I had my little-boy voice, and no matter how much I stretched and exercised, I remained stubbornly and substantially smaller than my classmates. No facial or body hair, either. We were taught the signs of puberty in our health classes, but I was missing all the benchmarks. This was cause for some apprehension on my part and a certain amount of teasing; at first I avoided the showers after gym and the change room at the pool, but eventually my friends and I got used to the way things were.

Rachel had it worse, it turned out. She attended a different school because she was in a French-language stream and I had chosen the English.

"You weren't there when I was in high school," she once complained to me, not that her underdeveloped brother could have done much by way of shielding her. "Girls my own age treated me like I was some kind of doll or stuffed animal. I kept waiting to be discarded when they outgrew me.

"They were always talking about this boy or that, and I didn't start to notice boys until I was almost finished high school. So much for being part of the conversation. I could at least chime in on topics like makeup or hair styles, but there really wasn't much drama in that, and drama was a big deal for most of my friends.

"But the real hassle was with that idiot Bradley Trent and a couple of his buddies." The exasperation in her voice, even so long after, was rather out of character for her. "They were always cornering me in the hall, asking if I had started to grow boobs yet, or if I'd had my first period. I'd tell them to piss off, and they'd gasp in feigned shock and say little girls shouldn't use bad language. Sometimes my friends would intervene, but it never stopped Trent. I know I should have reported him, but he was more of an annoyance than a threat. It was a relief when he moved away in Grade 12; his sidekicks sort of forgot about me after that."

"Sounds to me like he was secretly in love with you," I suggested. "That used to be how guys showed affection." Rachel looked at me in disgust.

Our late development provoked much interest but few theories in the pediatricians' office, and it wasn't until I had almost finished high school that the numbers started coming in from around the globe. Then it became clear that thousands and thousands of us were experiencing the same slowing of the biological clock. Researchers began to take an interest. Intensive study revealed a dramatic genetic shift and an enormous strengthening of the immune system. The condition even acquired its own acronym: SIGMA—"Stress-Induced Genetic Mutation Acceleration". Rachel snorted that it must have taken months of research to devise a catchy enough name, but in fact, the label fell out of use within a couple of years, to be replaced by a simpler term: "the mutation," or just "the change."

My parents, of course, were still standing by their belief that the boy had given me the gift of life. "He told me," my mother said, with a touch of awe in her voice, "that a lot of things would change if he helped you. Maybe this is part of the package."

Her opinion was reinforced by the many reports that came in over the decade after my recovery, reports of a boy appearing in many parts of the world. The first time he made the world news was in the Uruguay prison crisis, of course, which is why he became known as El Niño, but his appearances soon after in Asia and Africa generated much greater coverage. And it was in Asia and Africa that entire multitudes of children first began growing up much more slowly.

"It's not stress," my mother insisted. "Stress may have been present in your case, Daniel, but it wasn't in Rachel's. And surely these thousands of kids in Africa can't all have been stressed. I tell you, it was the boy, the same boy, El Niño. Something happened that we will never understand unless we accept that."

Once I asked my mother what the boy looked like. She had to think for a few moments. "He looked a little bit like your friend Aaron," she said.

"Aaron Lim? The boy was Korean?"

"No, no. I said he looked a little bit like Aaron. His hair, at least, and the color of his eyes. He was about Aaron's size and build—not thin but certainly not overweight. He also looked a little bit African, except for the hair. I don't remember how dark or light his skin was. It's his eyes I remember most—they were so black, so big. In them, there was a sort of profound sadness, though, until he smiled. Then the sadness seemed to soften."

I've heard many descriptions of the boy since then, from people all over the world, sometimes conflicting in details, but never in the remembering of his eyes. Dark, deep, sad. Until he smiled. I never saw the boy, but I can picture his eyes as though he were standing right in front of me today. In some ways, he is.

2.

MONTEVIDEO

I'M SURE AS HELL not proud of the way I've lived my life so far. I'm not even twenty-one yet, and I've lost track of the times I've fucked up completely and the people I've screwed over. Some days the shame almost makes me crazy.

I don't even have anyone to blame it on. Lots of guys like me end up getting a pass because their childhoods were so crappy. Yeah, well I had a crappy childhood too, but it was me that made it crappy. My parents tried everything to get me to straighten out, and I fought them all along the way.

My mother is a veterinarian in Las Piedras. She worked for a few years as an agricultural vet, checking up on the cattle and sheep that Uruguay has always been famous for, but now she works mainly with small animals - dogs, cats and other pets. Papa is an electrician and works most of the time in Montevideo. It's on account of me that they've been tied to home so much. When I was younger they had to keep a close watch on my activities, and when I went into Punta de Rieles, they wanted to be near enough to the prison to visit every week. There were so many times when they could have just walked away and forgotten about me, but I'm thankful they've never given up.

Even though Mama is a veterinarian, we never had any pets. I guess they were afraid I'd hurt or even kill any animal I came in contact with, but that was the one thing I wouldn't have done. I liked animals; in my own strange way I liked people, too. I would never have hurt anything that way, like physically, you know. I just couldn't help myself when it came to doing stupid, nasty things. I broke stuff deliberately and mouthed off and glared at my parents when they caught me. Mama didn't believe in what she called "corporal punishment"—another word for beating the crap out of me—and I doubt if it would have made any difference even if she had.

By the time I was five, I couldn't be allowed outside on my own. I threw rocks at the neighbors' windows, I smashed the plants in the garden, I swore at people walking by on the roadway.

School opened up a whole new world to conquer. Papa had taught me to read before I went to kindergarten, but there was no way the teacher could let me do any activity on my own when the others were learning their letters. I threw paint, snapped crayons into pieces, pulled the heads off dolls and smashed trucks into each other.

Teachers learned quickly not to trust me, and word passed from one class to another about the animal that wouldn't be tamed. I didn't give a damn about anyone's opinion; I had no friends and any enemies I might have kept their mouths shut just in case I decided to pound the shit out of them. I went through a whole army of counsellors. Some tried to be my friend; they were the easiest to get around and they didn't last long. The ones who were strict always gave up eventually and said I was "hard to serve"—as if they had any intention of serving me anyway. There was one woman who stuck it out longer than most—she at least had a sense of humor and never got mean, no matter what I had done. I kind of liked her, but that didn't stop me from doing the same things to her as I did to the others.

Although adults generally were careful about keeping an eye on me, there was a time when I was nine that the teacher was called out of the room. Everyone else was busy making pictures to go with the stories we were supposed to be writing. I got up from my table and went to the teacher's desk. I opened a drawer and pissed all over the papers it held. Then I got up on the teacher's chair, dropped my pants and took a shit on the seat. The other kids were so stunned that they just stared; I could almost hear them breathing. I wiped myself on the cloth we used to clean the blackboard, and was just about to pull my pants back up when the teacher came back into the room.

She looked like she was going to cry. "Miguel, what are you doing?"

I pulled up my pants. "I had to crap. You weren't here to say I could go to the toilet." In fact, I wasn't allowed to go to the toilet on my own anyway—someone from the office always came to take me to the little room next to the staff lounge.

This little stunt ended my school career. The director said I was a "moral hazard" to the other kids and I wasn't allowed back in class. My mother gave up her practice and began to home-school me, but it wasn't too much of a success. I wasn't exactly stupid, and I could read and write as well as kids much older than me. My math was okay, and my parents had tried to keep me interested in current events. I just didn't give a damn.

Always being kept at home, never going out without one of my parents tailing me the whole time, got to be a real drag. So, I started to escape whenever Mama had her back turned. Many times I was brought home by the police; Mama had to sit through a lecture about controlling her kid whenever this happened, but it didn't stop me from sneaking away the next time the opportunity was presented.

Eventually my behavior led to the child welfare people taking me into custody. At twelve, I was placed in foster care with a couple who were both adolescent psychologists. This lasted just long enough for me to set fire to the drapes in the bedroom. I ended up being charged with arson; the psychologists said I was lucky it wasn't attempted murder. I never even met the youth court judge who convicted me.

They stuck me in a group home with a half-dozen other troubled youth, all of them older than me. There was a staff person on duty at all times, keeping an eye on us inmates, as well as a cook and housekeeper. We were expected to do most of the meal prep under supervision, as well as help with cleaning and maintaining the house. The older kids sort of fell in with this routine, and I was afraid enough that I toed the line as well. We had a couple of tutors who came in to the house every day to get us through the curriculum.

The other kids were all in trouble with some mental issue or other. They would have days of normal behavior, then all of a sudden there would be a huge breakdown with screaming, crying, hitting out. The staff on duty were not always the biggest and strongest, but somehow they always managed to keep a lid on whatever violence was going on. I think now that the kids never really wanted to be out of control, and went along with the house parents. They'd made their point and blown off the steam; no advantage in pushing too far and risking transfer to a stricter institution.

My roommate was a fifteen-year-old guy named Andreas. He was a really weird kid. He almost always had a hand down the front of his pants, and he wet the bed pretty much every night. You could smell the piss on him in the morning. A lot of times he would have a nightmare and start yelling and thrashing around in the middle of the night. The staff on duty would come in and get him all calmed down again, but an hour later he'd be repeating the performance. Some nights he would crawl into bed with me and start crying. After a while the sound would stop and Andreas would move up against me and fall asleep. I was too afraid of him to push him out and I was always worried I'd get a black eye from his flailing around, or worse, that I'd end up lying in a puddle of his piss. I tried to make myself as small as possible, hunched against the wall until morning. It turned out, though, that these were the nights when he didn't have bad dreams and when he managed to stay dry.

Although he was three years older than me, Andreas was studying the same stuff with the tutor as I was, so we were stuck with each other for most of the day. He was my partner for cleanup and cooking, too, so I was spending like a hundred percent of my time with him.

One day we got taken on a trip to Punta del Este. I think I had been there with my parents when I was little, and I remember running in the waves at the beach. This time there were no parents. Because I had a reputation of causing problems, there were two staff members assigned to me; since Andreas was hanging with me, that really meant there were three house parents keeping track of my every move.

We parked the van near Brava Beach and wandered down to see La Mano, the big sculpture of a human hand rising up from the sand. Andreas and I and a couple of the others started climbing and got hauled down by the supervisors. We weren't allowed to go in the water, because it would be too difficult to keep an eye on us, so we ended up hiking along the beach and then back to the boulevard Artigas. This is a town with lots of money, and it showed in the shop windows - all that jewellery and high-class fashion stuff.

"As soon as I'm old enough," said Andreas, "I'm coming here to live."

"Me too," I said. I doubt if it dawned on either of us just how expensive it would be to rent a place here. Our only hope might be to work in one of the hotels and get servants' lodgings or something. There were a hell of a lot of luxury hotels, so maybe it wouldn't be too tough to get a job.

Eventually we walked over to the Rio de la Plata side and up as far as Mansa Beach. Andreas kept up a steady chatter about the women in their bikinis, about the big yachts anchored in the Plata, about the fancy cars that drove by on the Rambla Claudio Williman. He wanted to come back to play the casinos once he was "free" from the group home. Even I knew he wouldn't likely ever have the cash to live out these fantasies, but the dreaming seemed to make him happy.

I spent five years in the group home, finally learning to control my behavior so that I got more privileges. I even ended up going back to my parents on weekends and staying out of trouble for the most part. Still, there was always a whole lot of tension in the air, as if Mama and Papa worried that anything would set me off and they'd be left to pick up the pieces. Besides, I missed the other guys from the home; my mother and father weren't much for hanging out and doing the kind of crap we kids did.

During that time I still got into scrapes every now and then, but there were some things I never did: I wasn't into booze or drugs; I didn't even smoke. Living with a bunch of boys and being under supervision twenty-four seven meant that I was still a virgin. I broke loads of stuff, but I never stole anything. I never used violence against living things, although I sometimes felt like it. My small size and the age difference in the home may have had something to do with that, I suppose.

Andreas left the group home when I was almost sixteen and I was surprised at how much I missed having him around. I was teamed up with a new guy two years younger than me, but we never hit it off. He always seemed to be down on everything and dragged me down with him. Andreas may have been weird and unpredictable, but I realize now that was part of the attraction; the new boy, Julián, was totally predictable. He was sent to the home because his family couldn't cope with his depression. He spent days on end just sitting, without talking, and almost had to be fed with a spoon. Not my job, I decided.

In the two years I lived in the same room as Julián, nothing changed. He was in his own world most of the time, and I wasn't allowed in. I stopped trying to get along and just ignored him. The staff kept encouraging me to "be friends" with Julián, but I blew them all off. They were the experts, and it was them getting paid to fix Julián, not me. Losing Julián and his black cloud was one of the things I was most looking forward to when I turned eighteen and could leave the group home.

When the day finally came, however, I found I was kind of sad to be leaving. There was no way I would ever consider the staff at the home as my family, and Julián sure as hell wasn't much of a brother, but the place had been home for almost six years. My security blanket was worn thin, but it was still in one piece.

I went home to Mama and Papa, back to the strain and the sense that both of them were tiptoeing around my moods, worrying that the old Miguel might return to bring chaos back into their lives. Mama had established her own veterinary clinic by then, and Papa was often away from the city on construction projects. I guess I was just another problem they had to schedule around. They wanted me to enrol in the trades college and apply for an apprenticeship in electricity, but the tutors at the home had taken me through the second cycle of the pre-university program and I had none of the technical stream credit. Papa thought that I could bypass the secondary certification if my father was a licenced electrician, so I made the application.

Before I heard anything about getting the apprenticeship, though, I was in the old city, near the Palacio Salvo, just wandering around. Papa wanted me to learn about the city so I could find places when I was working on different electrical jobs. As I was crossing Plaza Independencia, someone called my name. Of course, there could have been a hundred Miguels in the plaza at that moment, but I turned around. It was Andreas. He trotted over to me, grinning like an idiot.

"Hey, chico. How are things? Did you break out of the jail?"

"Nothing so cool, Andreas. I graduated, just like you. Now I'm trying to find a job—or at least an apprenticeship. My father wants me to become an electrician like him."

"That what you want?"

"I guess so. I haven't got any better ideas. Besides, I think electricians make good money."

"Yeah, and they also get into people's houses and have a chance to poke around. Check out the doors and windows, if you know what I mean." He still had that stupid grin on his face; it was getting kind of annoying.

"Yeah, man. I get what you mean. Nothing would be smarter than to steal things from a house where you've been the only visitor all day. No way they could ever trace the crime to you, is there?"

"Asshole. You don't steal anything. You just make a map of the easy ways in and out, pass it on to someone else, and they do the stealing. You have a great alibi because you go somewhere else and make sure people notice you. You get a cut of the profits."

"Great idea, man. Is that how you're getting your cash these days?" He had stopped grinning and was looking at me kind of funny now.

"No. I'm working the plaza here. Lots of tourists, mostly from Argentina. They've got fat wallets. I've got fingers. None of them are likely to stick around to lodge complaints as long as I just take the cash. I don't try to use the credit cards. I toss the wallets into a mailbox when I've lightened them up a bit; I don't know if they get them back. Maybe the mail guys take the credit cards—all the better to throw the cops off my tail."

"How much are you making off this?"

"Depends on the season. Tourists don't like the really hot weather or the rain. Some days I get twenty thousand pesos, some days only a few Argentine or American bills. It's enough. I go from one part of the city to another so no one gets a chance to notice me hanging around."

"Where you living? "

"A little room in La Unión. You should drop by some time."

"Yeah. What's your address?"

"Not telling. You want to hook up with me, you can usually find me where the tourists are." So much for dropping in on him in La Unión. Not that I was even considering paying him a visit.

We said goodbye and I thought that would be the end of it. Andreas didn't seem as weird as he once was, but I didn't think his new occupation was an improvement. Not that I was one to judge, I guess. I had the criminal record and he was clean, at least on paper.

Cuando el diablo no tiene que hacer con el rabo mata moscas. When the devil has nothing to do but swat flies with his tail . . . Within a week I was back in Plaza Independencia, pushing my way through the crowds, looking for Andreas. I couldn't explain why, but it was something I felt I had to do. He wasn't there, and I didn't find him the next week or the week after that.

Then I got lucky. He was leaning against a palm on the edge of the plaza, watching the people. I edged up to him.

"Hey, Andreas." He jumped a little.

"Oh, it's you, chico. Come for a lesson in fishing?" He was staring at a middle-aged man in front of the Canadian embassy. "I think that old Chileno over there might have a few pesos to spare."

"No thanks. I'll just watch you. You going after him?"

"Not yet, chico. Too many security cameras where he's standing. I want him out in the plaza, but with people around. There's a police guy over there, too, not in uniform. You can always tell the fuckers, though. They have a certain look. It's hard to keep an eye on everything without looking like you're keeping an eye on everything."

Andreas walked out into the plaza, heading toward the statue of Artigas. I trailed after him, and he kept up a stream of chatter, like we were two buddies in from the country, excited by all the big city had to show us.

When we were only a few metres from the monument, Andreas stopped and looked at his watch, which was one of those expensive ones, or a good knock-off. He smiled at me.

"The Chileno is heading this way. He's going to have to go through that crowd of tourists."

"How do you know he's from Chile?"

"Saw him earlier with his tour group. The guide had a Chilean flag."

Andreas was drifting off toward the same crowd the Chileno was heading into. I followed, but not too closely. If anything went down, I didn't want to get dragged in with Andreas. As far as I knew, he was still the same weird guy he'd been in the group home.

A woman on a motor scooter buzzed across the plaza, taking a shortcut past the statue and forcing people to jump out of her way. The cop and most of the tourists stared after her. So did I. I kept watching the cop, but he didn't make a move, even though the woman was cutting dangerously close to the pedestrians.

I lost track of Andreas, and it took me a few seconds to find him already on the sidewalk just east of the embassy. He was walking along as if he was checking out the sights like any other visitor to the city.

"Hey!" I yelled at him, but he took no notice. I realized how dumb it was to call out and bring attention to myself—and to Andreas—so I turned and walked back toward the statue, letting the cop see me wandering the plaza. Even if he decided to question me, I had nothing to hide that couldn't be hidden. Maybe he wasn't the only cop in the plaza; Andreas was probably better at figuring out this kind of thing than I was.

Within minutes, I had no idea where Andreas was, and I decided to head back home. Maybe in another couple of weeks I'd find him back in the plaza. I wasn't sure why I even wanted to find him again. Must have been because he was the closest thing I had to a friend.

I walked up Florida and turned right onto Colonia, walking against the traffic. As I passed the Holiday Inn, Andreas was suddenly right beside me.

"Don't ever yell at me like that, you asshole. You want people to remember you, go ahead, but don't make them look at me." This was rich, coming from the guy who called me by name last time.

"Sorry, Andreas. I wasn't thinking. Too bad you got stopped. That bitch on the scooter made a mess of things."

"What are you talking about, chico? She was a great distraction." Andreas flashed a wallet at me and pulled out a wad of bills. American dollars, lots of twenties. He handed me a couple and stuffed the rest into his pocket. He tucked the wallet into the waist of his jeans, inside his shirt. "Too far to the post office. I'll leave it on the seat of the bus if there aren't too many passengers. Now, how be you go home and let me get on with my day?"

He wasn't fooling me. He didn't care if I went home, just as long as I didn't see where he went. He never asked me where I was living, and I don't think I would have told him if he had asked. I said so long and headed up to Calle Mercedes to catch a bus.

I waited a couple of weeks before going back to the plaza Independencia. The apprenticeship approval still hadn't come through, and I was beginning to think it never would. I had lots of time on my hands, but never seemed to have enough cash to do anything. My father gave me a couple of hundred pesos every so often, but it didn't last long. Even bus fare was a problem at times.

That Tuesday, Andreas was in the plaza. "I'm not working this area today," he said. "If you come on Thursday to the cathedral, I'll be there. Maybe I'll go to confession." He grinned at me. It took me a few seconds to realize that he was planning to harvest a couple more wallets, or maybe break into the poor box.

Two days later, there I was, standing under one of the big trees in front of the cathedral. People were constantly crossing the little square with its fountain, coming and going in and out of the arched entrances of the church. Some of them—the old ladies in country clothes - seemed to be worshippers heading for prayer, but most of the crowd were tourists. The cathedral wasn't one of those soaring high buildings, like the ones in Europe I'd read about. Uruguay is a small country, and it's probably fitting we have a small cathedral, with two ordinary little towers. I noticed that the clock on the left-hand tower was showing the wrong time.

I waited for about an hour before Andreas showed up. He came out the left-hand doors of the cathedral; I never even thought to check inside for him.

"Okay, chico. Here's the deal: you're going to start across towards the fountain, but when you get to that little bench there, you're going to bang your knee on it and fall down. You don't need to scream or anything, just act like you're hurt. Don't overdo it, and tell people right away that you're fine. You don't need help. This will only take a few seconds."

I did as I was told, and actually did bang my elbow when I fell down. It hurt like hell, but I was pretty sure nothing was broken. A couple of women helped me up and asked if I needed to go to the clinic, but I said I'd be okay on my own. Just a little bruising, nothing serious. Thanks, ladies.

Andreas was nowhere to be seen. I sat on the little bench for a while, then got up and went into the church. It was the first time I could remember ever being inside a church. The place was amazing. The ceiling seemed to go up forever, and the light was somehow much different from the light outside, although it was the same light, coming in through windows high up in the ceiling. From outside, the building looked much smaller than it did from the inside. It didn't make sense to me.

I wandered around the church, looking at things, following what I now know were the stations of the cross, but being careful not to touch in case someone called the cops. No use drawing attention to myself.

Andreas still wasn't around, and I realized he wasn't likely to stick near the church. I headed off down Sarandi and once more he quietly joined me as I passed the Missiones intersection. He handed me two thousand pesos.

"Good work, chico. There's a football game at Estadio Centenario tomorrow night. Meet me there at seven. Doesn't matter where you wait; I'll find you. There's always a good harvest when the fans have been drinking." Andreas was already walking away when I said I'd be there. He got on a bus heading up Buenos Aires Street. I knew better than to get on the same bus.

We made a great team at the stadium. Too much beer and not enough caution made easy marks of the football crowd; we didn't even need to go into the stadium itself. There were lots of half-drunk guys outside, but Andreas wouldn't touch them until they'd paid for their admission ticket. No point in having them notice too quickly that their wallets were gone. My job was to ask the guy a question, usually about which team he was going to cheer for. It was incredibly easy to distract him, even if he had a bunch of buddies alongside. Andreas would slip in behind and lift the wallet. As soon as I saw Andreas turn away again, I would wish the guy luck and head on out from the crowd. Then Andreas and I would move on to a different part of the stadium and repeat the process. Andreas said we should never get greedy; he had a limit of three wallets a night, even if there were only a few pesos in each.

We carried on like this for about a month, then one day Andreas asked me if I remembered the time we went with the kids from the group home to Punta del Este.

“That’s where the big money is, Miguel. We should try a few jobs there.”

I wasn’t as eager. “But we don’t know the city at all. Don’t you think we’ll stand out more? People will notice us.”

“It’s a tourist town, chico. Everybody stands out so much they blend in. I’m thinking we should get real jobs there—hotel jobs, maybe. Then we’d be sure to learn something about the place—and about the tourists.”

I protested that I was waiting for my apprenticeship.

“Yeah, chico. You’ve been waiting for that for how long now? Do you really think they’re going to come through for you? I bet they’ve read your files from the group home; they’ll have labeled you trouble and tossed your application. Let’s go to Punta.” Andreas put into words the thoughts I was having myself. There were going to be all kinds of questions people would think but not ask out loud.

My parents weren’t too happy about the plan. I didn’t say anything about Andreas, and they worried that I’d be on my own and more likely to fall off the wagon. In the end, though, they gave me their okay, as long as I promised to keep in touch every day, or at least every few days.

Andreas got us the bus tickets, and we left on a Tuesday morning. We settled into a couple of seats at the back and Andreas promptly fell asleep, even before we’d left Montevideo. The ride took us eastward along the coast, stopping only a few times to pick up more passengers or to let someone off with their shopping bags from the capital.

It took about two and a half hours to reach the Maldonado Terminal in the outskirts of the city. The terminal bays looked like a forest of mushrooms sprouting up from the concrete, ugly as shit, but everything was clean and the air, even in the bus terminal, smelled fresh.

What we didn’t realize was that the terminal was a long way from the hotel district. Andreas thought we could easily walk downtown, but it turned out to be a few kilometres. We hiked down avenida Roosevelt to boulevard Artigas, and by the time we reached the big casino we were hot as hell, covered in sweat and sore from lugging our sports bags.

There was a temporary employment office near the corner of Gorlero and Calle 17. We dragged our butts into the air conditioning and just stood for a few minutes. There wasn’t much of a line-up, and when we got to the counter the agent quickly took down our information and gave us a couple of addresses to try. Both of the hotels were an easy walk, she said. I wasn’t sure any walk would be easy; I had blisters on my heels because my shoes were just a little too big and kept rubbing on my skin.

It turned out the first hotel was only too eager to hire a couple of young guys. We had the choice of working on their grounds crew, doing the landscaping and maintenance, or in the laundry, cleaning the hotel linens and stuff, or in housekeeping, mopping floors and doing deliveries. Andreas picked the mopping. I would rather have done the outdoor jobs, but it made sense to be able to check out rooms all day.

It turned out that wasn't part of Andreas's plan. "We can't pull any jobs here in the hotel, chico. We need to be as far away as possible so no one recognizes us. We'll spend a couple of days, maybe a week, just getting to know the city."

We didn't get much time to case the neighborhood, though, because our shifts were ten or twelve hours long, six days a week. I wasn't used to the heavy labor, and neither was Andreas. At the end of our day, we basically just flopped down on our bunks in the staff quarters and fell asleep, then woke up in the morning to do the whole thing over again.

"Maybe this wasn't such a great idea, Andreas. I don't have the energy to keep on running supplies to all the linen cupboards. I think I pulled a muscle in my shoulder yesterday, lifting the garbage barrels in the kitchen."

"Just another couple of weeks, chico. We should be able to pick up a lot more cash from the tourists here than in Montevideo. Three hits and we'll have enough money to rent our own apartment; then we can tell this place to screw off."

It was almost a month before we managed to do anything outside the hotel other than walking up and down the beaches or checking out the streets around the downtown. Andreas was getting antsy; I was just tired, but I kept up with him on his little scouting trips.

"We should stick to the Plata side. That's where the Argentines have their yachts moored. Those guys live on the boats—they're not as likely to run into us at the hotel and start putting things together."

Our first couple of hits went smoothly, too smoothly, maybe. Andreas had a thing about not robbing women; he always zeroed in on some middle-aged guy near the waterfront. We changed our method; instead of me talking to the mark, Andreas would move in close, then I would jog up from behind and sort of run into the guy. While he was yelling at me to be careful, Andreas would lift the wallet. I would just keep jogging ahead. Even if I were cornered by a cop and searched, I'd be clean. I never turned around or said anything, so the guy wouldn't see my face or hear my voice. Andreas would walk calmly back the other way, and the mark wouldn't even know he'd been robbed until he got back to his yacht.

We scored quite a few times with this method. Andreas stuck to his rule about no more than three a day, and we moved around the city so no one would get too suspicious.

By the middle of January I wanted to go back to Montevideo. The work at the hotel was exhausting, with a lot of heavy lifting, and the heat bugged me. The little business Andreas and I had going had brought enough money for us to live pretty well back home. Andreas thought I was nuts.

"Just one more month, chico, then we can go back. Look how busy the marina is. We can't pass up that many chances."

We should have passed them up. Late one afternoon we targeted a guy on the Muelle de Mailhos. As usual, I jogged up behind him as soon as Andreas was in position, nicking him with my elbow as I went by. A few seconds passed, then all hell broke loose. Two tough-looking guys came at me from the right and another from the left. I tried to run faster but they cut me off. I turned to go back and saw that another couple of men had grabbed Andreas. One of the guys yelled at me to stop, and I did.

In no time at all, they put handcuffs on us both and fished the wallet out of Andreas's pants. That was when I noticed they were wearing the lapel recorders that the police used. Even the guy we'd robbed had one.

They had two unmarked cars waiting on the rambla, and we were each shoved into one of them. Soon we were headed downtown to the marina area. That's where the station is.

It didn't take them long to get us fingerprinted, photographed and thrown into separate cells. They took away everything I had except my shirt and pants. I'd heard lots of stories about guys being beat up in police stations, smacked around until they confessed, but these cops treated me okay. There was no one else in my cell. I sat down on the cot and breathed deeply; I was afraid I would start crying, but I kept it together. I wondered where they'd put Andreas, and how he was handling this.

I guess I was in that cell for about an hour before a cop came along and opened the door. "Come with me, please." I got up and followed.

He took me to a small room with a desk and two chairs. He sat in one and told me to take the other. "Okay, Miguel, you're in big trouble here. We know what you and your friend have been up to. We have evidence on a number of security cameras and can document your thefts many times over. No, don't say anything. You don't need to confess yet. I will suggest, though, that once we get you in front of the magistrate, your lawyer should tell him everything. That will make it easier on you. I can guarantee you'll get a shorter sentence if you come clean on this. Do you want your own lawyer, or shall we ask for an appointed counsel?"

"I don't know. I don't have any money. What's Andreas doing?"

"He no longer concerns you. Listen, Miguel. You're young, in good health. Do the right thing here and you'll spend a little while in jail, then you'll get a chance to go on with your life. Were these thefts your idea or your buddy's? No, don't answer that yet. But when you make your submission to the magistrate, tell the truth. I'm betting that your buddy started this and you got sucked in. Think about it. I doubt if he'll stick with you—probably he'll screw you to save his own skin." The cop looked at me closely. I felt my face grow warm as I realized I likely couldn't count on Andreas not to stab me in the back. I was such an asshole.

"Okay, Miguel. I'm taking you back to the cell. Get some sleep and we'll take you up to Maldonado to the courthouse in the morning. There'll be a lawyer there to advise you."

Get some sleep? It wasn't happening. I spent hours trying to imagine what Andreas was telling the cops. Thinking about what my parents would say when they found out. The cop who talked to me had been so polite—was that a trick of some kind?

I didn't see Andreas the next morning. They must have been deliberately keeping us separate, in case we cooked up some story line. I heard that the cops would try to get you to contradict yourself, make a mistake in telling the story. I went handcuffed in a van with no windows, and ended up at the courthouse. Still no sign of Andreas.

There was a lot of confusion, people going back and forth everywhere. I could smell a faint whiff of vomit, and wondered if it was my own. Some of the guys were like me, in handcuffs and looking pretty down. The cops said something to a woman at a desk, and she nodded towards a hallway. The cops took me down there to a room with a big desk.

"Okay, Miguel. You get a chance to talk with your lawyer, without us listening in. Then you and your lawyer will talk with the magistrate. We're right outside the door and there is security inside, so don't try anything stupid. You're lucky; there are no other prisoners beside you right now." They took the handcuffs off, which surprised me. The older cop patted me on the shoulder and they both left the room.

My lawyer was an older guy, half bald and kind of paunchy. He had really heavy eyebrows, as if the hair that was missing on the top of his head had slid down over his forehead and come to rest above his eyes. In addition, he had really droopy eyelids, so that he seemed tired or bored with the whole thing. He ran through the papers the police had given him, then stared at me for a while.

"So. They've got eight video recordings of you and your friend pulling the same little pickpocket routine. Did you know that one of your victims was a member of the Representantes? That's not going to go over well with the magistrate. At least two years if you're found guilty." I didn't say anything, and he went on.

"Because this is your first offense and because you are just past the age of majority, I think the magistrate will want to treat you generously. On the other hand, robbing a member of parliament isn't going to sit well, and the video evidence shows repeated robberies. Who knows how many of them weren't recorded? Any ideas, Miguel?" I shrugged.

He went on. "A lot, I'm guessing. What's your friend's name?" I told him Andreas's first name and realized I didn't know his last name.

"Do you think he might try and make you into the idea man, the one who conned him into the life of crime?"

"Andreas wouldn't do that. He's the one who can pick pockets. I never learned all that."

"So, you're ready to testify against him?" I shook my head. "Anything else I need to know? Abusive childhood? Mental illness? Coercion? Anything that will get you a little sympathy?" His voice was filled with weariness.

"No." I was feeling more and more hopeless, thanks in part to the lawyer's tired tone of voice.

The door opened and the magistrate came in. The security guards and court officials took their places. My lawyer stood in front of the magistrate along with the prosecutor. My mind kind of went blank, and I wasn't paying attention to what they were saying. It was like the court people were talking at the end of a long tunnel, and all the sounds were jumbled up. I don't know how long we were standing there before my lawyer—I never did learn his name—took my elbow and said, "Sorry, Miguel. They're going to keep you in custody until your trial. You're being transferred to Montevideo, to the prison at Punta de Rieles. They don't usually grant surety if the crime is punishable by more than two years, and there are no mitigating circumstances."

I didn't know what "mitigating circumstances" meant, but I sure as hell knew what prison meant.

"But I can't go to prison. I haven't even had a chance to talk to the magistrate."

"You don't get a chance until the trial. Even then, most of the magistrates don't want to hear your voice. They want everything in writing. That's partly why it takes so long to get to trial. I imagine you'll be in Rieles for a year or so."

I felt the floor moving and thought maybe I would throw up. A year in that hell hole? "No!" I yelled. "I can't go there! I never stole anything—I just helped." The lawyer tried to shut me up, and I realized how stupid it was to say anything about helping. What an asshole I was.

The police, or maybe it was security guards, came and put the handcuffs back on, and I was taken to a van outside the back of the court building. The guards pushed me into the back and one of them clicked the handcuffs into another set of cuffs on the wall of the van. I started to kick at him, and he slapped me across the face. "Keep that up and we'll cuff your feet, too. Then you'll be really uncomfortable." I stopped kicking.

"Good boy," he said. "We have a two hour drive to Montevideo. I'll be in the back here with you. Try anything and you'll be restrained. Behave yourself and things will be a lot easier for us both."

"Where's Andreas?" I asked. I wanted to know if he'd screwed me.

"Not my problem, kid, or yours, either."

The doors were slammed shut and I noticed there wasn't any way to open them from the inside. I leaned back against the wall, but that position hurt my wrists so I ended up hunching forward instead. By the time we got to Montevideo I was bent sideways and aching from my shoulders to my fingertips.

The van stopped, then started again. Voices called out and my guard moved a little closer to the doors. When the van stopped again, he got up from the bench and unlocked the handcuffs that tied me to the wall. "We're here."

The doors opened and a couple of guys grabbed my arms and almost lifted me out of the van. I couldn't really get a look at the building as they were taking me in, because we were right inside the place already. We went through a couple of doors that opened automatically and then we were in a small room. They unlocked the handcuffs and told me to take off all my clothes and put on the outfit they handed me. I thought they'd do a body search, but they just watched closely as I stripped and got dressed again. My old clothes were bundled up and stuffed into a bag, then I was taken to be photographed and fingerprinted all over again.

The blocks were crowded, with at least six or eight men in most of the cells. It looked like it would be hard to lie down, maybe even hard to sit down, in some of them. When all my admission details were finished, I was led to one of the cells and put inside with four other guys. All of them seemed to be about my age.

"Welcome home, kid," said one of the guards. He locked the cell door behind me. For some weird reason, the place actually did feel more like home than the jail in Punta or the court house had. I tried not to make eye contact with the other prisoners, but I knew they were staring at me.

"Hey man," said one of them. "What's your name and what are you in this shithole for?"

I told him my name, but I wasn't stupid enough to admit to anything. Who knew which of these guys was a plant, feeding information to the police? "They think I was a pickpocket in Punta del Este. I'm supposed to stay here until my trial."

"Well, you'd better make yourself at home, man. The waiting list for trials is at least two years. I've been waiting for over eighteen months now for mine. All of us are here waiting; nobody has been found guilty of anything. Sometimes the waiting is longer than the sentence the guy gets."

"This place is really crowded. How come there are so many guys in a cell?"

"What were you expecting—a five-star hotel with a spa? This is a medium security joint, but we've got a whole lot of tough guys in with us right now because there was a riot again at Comcar and they've brought a whole bunch of those guys here. Last time this happened they were here for half a year before Comcar was cleaned up. The worst part is that all of us now are stuck in the cells except for a few minutes outside once a day. And meals. We only get a shower once a week."

"You talk too much, Felipe," said one of the other guys. "Shut the fuck up and leave the new kid alone. He'll figure things out soon enough."

"Don't tell me to shut up, you jerk. Who keeps us awake all fucking night complaining about the floor being too hard to sleep on? Anyway, Miguel, Mariano is right; I do talk too much and you will figure stuff out. We just need to stick together so the Comcar guys don't get at us."

"Go on, Felipe," said Mariano. "Scare the shit out of the kid."

"Just warning him, you idiot. What are we here for? Waiting for a trial for car theft or break and enter. Those guys are already doing their years for murder or armed robbery."

The other two guys in the cell hadn't said a word all this time. They didn't even seem to be paying attention. One was sitting hunched on the floor in one corner, staring at the wall opposite. He looked like he might have been a bit crazy. The other was lying stretched out on the cot. It dawned on me that there was only one cot for the five of us, and I was the new guy. I'd probably get the part of the floor nearest to the toilet, which didn't seem to have been flushed lately.

In fact, though, they gave me the cot the first night. It was like they felt sorry for me. Like them, I was looking at a couple of years in this place before my case even came up for a hearing. Shit, I felt like crying.

The days went slowly. We spent most of the time locked in the cell, with only twenty minutes in the mess hall to eat our meals. The food mostly came from the guys' families, since the prison menu was really bare: rice or bread, sometimes potatoes. Once a week or so, a boiled egg or a little bowl of stew. I hadn't told my parents anything, but they got word of what had happened and sent me food parcels every few days. No one was allowed in to visit because of the Comcar guys being here, but the food parcels got through. Maybe the kitchen staff took a little off the top of each one; I don't know.

Once a day we got out into the courtyard for what the prison called exercise. This usually meant standing around in little gangs, watching to make sure no one caught you off guard. I hung out with Felipe and the other three guys from my cell. I didn't smoke, but we were allowed to have a drag if someone brought us cigarettes. Only Antonio ever had any.

It wasn't until the third day that I was called out of the cell to have a shower. I guess I stank worse than the other four, because they were left behind. As I was leaving, Mariano whispered to me to watch out for the Comcar guys.

The shower room was like hell. The floor was slippery and the air was full of steam. Soap scum ran across the tiles. There were about thirty shower heads, and the same number of guys standing naked under them. The biting stink of some kind of disinfectant stung my nose. I stripped off my prison outfit and found a shower that wasn't being used. The water wasn't hot; I don't know what was making the steam, but it sure wasn't the temperature of the shower.

As I was lathering up, the big guy next to me kept watching. He was older, maybe forty or so, heavy but not fat, his head shaved. If you threw in a couple of tattoos, he'd look like your standard street hood in Montevideo. He reached over and grabbed my dick. No one had ever touched me there before, and it was a total shock. I squawked and jumped back and almost fell on my ass on the slimy floor. The guy laughed, showing a mouthful of big teeth, and the guard at the door yelled at him. "Leave the kid alone, asshole, or you'll be downstairs again."

He just laughed again and growled at me. "New chicken, eh? When I get you by yourself, without your mother over there, we'll see about assholes." He turned around and spread his cheeks. I felt like puking. No one else in the room looked at us; it was as if they were all afraid of the guy. Quickly I finished the shower, toweled off and got dressed. My hands were still shaking. The guy stared at me the whole time. He didn't seem to be in any rush.

Later that day he was coming into the mess hall as Felipe and I were being taken back to our cell, and I whispered to Felipe. "That's the guy that grabbed my privates in the shower."

"Oh, God, Miguel. He's one of the Comcar guys. I don't know his name, but he's the one that fucked Matías when they first brought the men in from Comcar. Matías hasn't been right in the head since." That explained why Matías sat hunched in that corner most of the day, never speaking.

I didn't have to face the Comcar rape guy in the showers again. We seemed to have separate times after that first day, and I only occasionally saw him in the mess hall; he was never in the yard when we were outside.

Life went on like this week after week, month after month. Antonio's trial date came up and he was taken off to the Palacio de los Tribunales, a huge grey stone building I knew from my wanderings around Montevideo. He didn't come back, and we figured he must have been given a sentence equal to the time he'd already been in Punta de Rieles. No one took his place in our cell. Mariano's trial also came up, but he returned. He was found guilty of dealing drugs. Use of drugs was legal in Uruguay, but selling them, or "trafficking" was not. Mariano had tried to convince the police that he was carrying drugs for his own use, but the magistrate didn't believe him. He was back in our cell and would be here for another four years. "Fucking assholes didn't listen to a thing I said," he complained. "How could I be dealing when I only had a hundred tabs on me?"

One day Matías was taken out of the cell and didn't come back. We guessed he must have gone to trial, but no one ever told us anything and Matías himself didn't seem to know what was going on. That same afternoon another guy was put in our cell. He said his name was Rodrigo, and he was waiting for his trial on a charge of stealing from the store where he worked. "I turned off the cameras," he said, "but someone must have turned them back on, cause they say they've got me on video." My first impression was that Rodrigo wasn't too bright.

Felipe and I had become buddies, and it looked like both of us were going to have to wait the full two years or more for a trial date. We agreed that whoever got out first would make sure the other wasn't forgotten in the prison. For the first time in my life I was beginning to care what someone else thought about me. Felipe wasn't nosey, but I found myself telling him things I had done. He just listened and told me it would be all right in the end.

It took a year for most of the Comcar guys to be returned to their high-security prison. Things went more smoothly at Punta de Rieles after that, although even so it was crowded. We did get more time in the yard and had daily showers instead of weekly. Visitors were allowed again, and I saw my parents for the first time in eighteen months. They came every week and brought me magazines or paperbacks. No e-readers were allowed in the prison, so the books got passed around until they fell apart. My father dropped off food every day on his way to whatever job site he was working on.

Our block also got a new guard, a young guy named Artigo. I imagine he was named after José Artigas, the general who freed Uruguay from Spanish control. It was weird that someone named for a liberator would be a prison guard.

Artigo wasn't like the older guards. He didn't have a big belly; his hair was full and dark. He looked healthy and didn't have the standard prison scowl that so many of the other staff wore. He laughed a lot and was always ready to listen to the prisoners, even when most of the talk was just complaining about the fact we were in prison. Artigo always spoke to us as if we were human beings; he almost made the place bearable. I kept asking him to find out when my trial was scheduled. My mother was trying to get the same information, but neither one of them could give me a date.

Then it all fell apart again. There was another riot at Comcar and the prisoners once again were moved, many of them here to Punta de Rieles.

Visits stopped and even the books and magazines were banned. Just my luck, the guy who'd raped Matías and grabbed my dick was brought here. I saw him once as we were going out into the yard, but I don't think he recognized me.

Things tightened up. Artigo was working days and got the job of taking us regular inmates down to the mess hall or out to the yard. No more trusting us to find our own way. It was our bad luck that we had to pass the cells where some of the Comcar prisoners, including the guy who scared me shitless, were kept.

It was fucking awful going down that corridor. Those guys were bad news, not just for us, but for the guards too. They jeered at Artigo every time we got near.

"Hey, Arti, boy! Come on in here and join us. We'll pound the shit out of you and fuck your ass."

Artigo would pretend he didn't hear and just hustle us past. We didn't want to hang around there, either. On the second day, I learned the Comcar guy's name was Mano—like the sculpture of the hand in Punta del Este, probably a kind of nickname for "Manuel", but I thought it was pretty fitting, given that his hand was the part of him that I had the most trouble with.

The threats never let up. Every day we heard how Mano and his buddies would kick our heads in, or worse. I was damned grateful we didn't have to share the yard, the mess hall or the showers with them. The prison director was keeping them strictly away from the regular inmates, except for that trip down the corridor we had to make too many times in a day.

One afternoon we were sitting in our cell, waiting for Artigo to come and take us down to the yard for a break, when we heard shouting from the next cell block. The alarms went off. Within seconds we could smell smoke, the kind of stinking chemical smoke that comes from burning plastic or rubber. We pushed up against the bars to see what was going on, and a minute or so later one of the senior guards came and opened our cell.

"Get out of the range and go down to the yard. The four of you stick together and get ready for roll call. Don't stop for anything." He didn't have to tell us twice. The smoke was growing thicker, and seemed to be coming from further up the corridor. The guard moved to the next cell and opened it. We could hear him giving the same instructions to those guys.

"Stay low to the floor," said Felipe, and we ran sort of hunched over. My eyes were stinging. I tried to hold my breath; the fumes from the smoke were sickening. As we passed the cells where Mano and his friends were housed, I noticed the doors were all open. No one was in the cells, and I had a sudden pain in my gut; those guys must be out in the yard, too.

At the end of the corridor, in the open area next to the mess hall, we stopped short. The smoke wasn't thick here, and we could breathe, but the breath stuck in my throat. People were yelling and laughing. There was a tight circle of guys standing in the middle of the corridor. As we came up, the wall of bodies parted slightly and we could see what they were watching. Artigo was lying on his chest, unmoving, on the floor, his face turned to the side and his head in a pool of blood. His pants had been ripped off and there was blood smeared across his ass, too. He looked like he was dead. Mano was there. His pants were down, and he had blood on his legs and crotch. I knew it wasn't his blood. His eyes scanned the four of us and locked on mine, but there was no flicker of recognition. My fear must have made a connection, though, and a mocking smile spread across his face. Where the fuck were the guards? How come no one was coming to check?

"Hey," Mano yelled, looking at us. "More chickens. Your turn, boys." He jerked his head at us, signalling to his buddies. A couple of them moved towards us, fumbling with their pants. I felt panic rising in my chest, spilling into my throat. The first of Mano's guys, a stupid-looking ape almost as big as Mano, was shuffling straight toward me. I stepped backward, into a clutch of other prisoners. There was no retreat. The guy reached out his hand to grab me and I felt his grip on my arm; then he halted. His expression shifted from the leering, eager smirk to confusion and hesitancy. The laughing and shouting stopped, and the sudden quiet reminded me of a time long ago when my nine-year-old classmates had been shocked into silence. Mano and his gang were looking past us, and I turned, expecting to see a bunch of guards with weapons drawn.

Instead, right behind us, between Rodrigo and me, there was a boy. Not an older teenager or someone our age, but a young boy, about twelve years old. Among all us prison inmates, he looked tiny and vulnerable, but there was a strange presence as well, one that stilled all movement in the corridor. For a few long seconds, he just stood there in the quiet, then he walked toward Mano, who was standing over Artigo's body, looking like a total asshole with his pants down around his ankles.

"No, wait, kid," shouted Felipe. "Don't go there. You'll get hurt." The boy paid no attention, and walked right up to Mano. Mano looked stunned. The boy stared at him for a few seconds, then looked at Artigo.

"I can help," he said. He knelt down, turned Artigo's head gently and touched him on the forehead. Artigo let out a great sigh, and I almost cried with relief that he wasn't dead. Mano was pulling up his pants, and more and more guys began piling out of the corridor beside us, all of them stopping to stare at this boy. The boy kept his eyes focused on Mano, then reached up and touched him on the forehead. Mano shook as if he was going to have a seizure, then sat down heavily. His buddies looked like they were hypnotized. The first guy, the one who had reached for me, nodded, and one by one they came to the boy and he touched their foreheads, just as he had done with Artigo and Mano.

A change came over them. Their muscles seemed to loosen, their expressions lost the grimness of prison. One of them took off his shirt and used it to cover Artigo's nakedness. Another one took his shirt and wadded it up, lifting Artigo's head gently and lowering it onto this makeshift pillow.

The boy turned to face us. I couldn't imagine how he had gotten in to the place, or what he was doing. He looked sad, as if bad things had happened to him or to someone he loved. Those eyes seemed to see beyond, to reflect an understanding of things I couldn't even begin to grasp. I felt somehow as if I knew him, but of course that was impossible. He looked just like a normal kid, except for those sad dark eyes.

"I can help," he said. "All of you." I wanted that help, but I sensed that things would never be the same if I got it.

Felipe went first. He stepped forward and knelt down in front of the boy. The boy reached out and touched him on the forehead, and Felipe uttered a soft groan and seemed to relax. Other guys were going forward and the boy was touching them, too, and I was pulled ahead by my own need.

I bent forward to his touch, and felt a coolness flow through me. There was a pain that I hadn't realized I had, and now it was gone. All the anger left me, and the fear. I glanced at Mano and felt only sadness at what he had done. Mano looked like he was asleep, but there were tears running down his cheeks. I felt the same wetness on my own face.

"Come on," said Felipe, "let's go to the yard."

To my surprise, Mano picked up Artigo like he was a little child and carried him out. Someone brought a bunch of towels from the mess hall and we all walked silently down the corridor and out into the sunlight. As the quiet spread through the crowd that was already in the yard, guys began to head back in toward the mess hall, and soon there was a stream of inmates coming and going from the corridor. I could see guards, too, many of them with tear-streaked faces. The whole place was deathly still.

Against the wall I could see Mano still cradling Artigo, who was now conscious, looking tired but stronger. He was smiling slightly.

By now the fires were out. Some of the guards went back in to check on the situation, and soon inmates were also heading back to their cells. The boy was gone from the place he had been. No one spoke, but as we passed the cells we saw that Mano's buddies were already quietly sitting inside.

That night it was Mariano's turn to sleep on the cot, but I didn't feel the concrete floor that I lay on. The smell from the toilet didn't bother me, and I slept better than I remembered ever sleeping before. In the morning there was none of the pain or stiffness. My lungs seemed to be full of something lighter than air, and things looked somehow more real than usual. I knew this was because of the boy.

At the same time, though, there came a towering wave of shame at what I had done—to my parents, to people who had tried to help me, to the guys Andreas and I had robbed. This was a totally new feeling, and I didn't like it. I did, however, like the idea that I could feel what other people felt, that at last I could think like other people.

When the guards opened the cell door to let us down for breakfast, they seemed calmer, less nervous, and I realized they too had been changed by the boy's touch. As we passed Mano's cell, there was none of the panic I normally felt. Mano looked up from where he was sitting on the floor and spoke. "Sorry for everything, kid. I won't hurt you." I actually smiled, and he smiled back.

We learned later that out of the two thousand or so people in the prison, only a handful had not been touched by the boy. Just one of the guards had been missed. Even the prisoners who were in the hole downstairs had seen him, and he had somehow managed to touch each of them.

All this went down months ago. The Comcar guys have gone back to their own prison and things at Punta de Rieles have been easier. Lots of news reporters have been in, asking questions. I didn't think any of them would believe us, but my father said that the story was all over the web and in all the other media, too. His voice was filled with awe; I understood.

The government has been investigating. Punta de Rieles is getting lots of attention because everything is so different from before. There are prison psychologists coming in here all the time, not just from Uruguay, but from Argentina and even from the United States.

And me? I feel better than I ever knew I could feel. No pain, no more being afraid about stuff. No more urge to do anything stupid. I think about that boy a lot; I wonder where he came from, where he went, how he did what he did. I wonder about the look in those dark eyes. He changed my life, and the lives of a couple of thousand other guys in this place.

Andreas and I were idiots, I know now, a couple of chicken punks pretending we were real thugs. I've never been able to explain, even to myself, why I used to act like I did, but it's over.

I'm still waiting for my trial date, and so is Felipe, but now we don't worry. We know that when the magistrate passes sentence on us, we'll be ready to face it. What's more, we'll be ready to go back out into the world and try to make up for all the years we've wasted.

I want to be an electrician who makes my father proud.

3.

BRAZZAVILLE

My name is Corinne Lissunga. I am a medical doctor, a physician, with advanced training in epidemiology and tropical medicine. At the time of the Central African pandemic ten years ago, I was the World Health Organization's Regional Director for Africa, based at the WHO Africa head office in Brazzaville. Brazzaville was my birthplace, and I grew up there, finishing my secondary education with a D level certificate from the Lycée Générale and doing my basic medical training at Université Marien Ngouabi. I graduated at the head of my class and went on to do post-graduate studies at the Université Paris-Sud.

It was in Paris that I met my husband, Alain—Alain Saint-Jour. I was active at that time in the university's African Students' Union. Alain is Canadian, born in Montréal, but his parents were from Haïti and he was interested in exploring his African roots. We were drawn to each other almost immediately. I was charmed by his easy manner and readiness to laugh, his instinctive ability to relate immediately to others. He was the perfect extrovert, the youngest of four siblings—and the only boy—in a very active family.

What did he see in me? I was always the methodical, rational, serious one, absorbed in my studies a lot of the time. I was an organizer, a list-maker, an analyzer. People complained that I threw out words like "iatrogenesis" and "karyotype" without explanation, as if everyone should know what they meant. Alain always claimed he admired my mind—a joke about the way in which other young men were attracted by a woman's appearance. As an only child, I had never learned how to give and take until I started school; the joking and sheer physicality of childhood and especially of adolescence I found stressful at times. Alain helped me loosen up and enjoy student life in Paris.

Soon we were spending every free moment together and within four months I had moved into his small apartment on the second floor of a house on the avenue du Maréchal Joffre, within an easy walk of the university. The landlady, a smiling French lady whose husband had run off with another woman, leaving her, as she put it, "free of chains", was welcoming. She looked on Alain as a son, and was glad to see him "settled". She bought us chocolate croissants once a week and left a bottle of white wine at our door from time to time. We always paid the rent two days before it was due.

We were married during my second year of graduate studies. My mother and father were unable to make the trip to Paris, but Alain's parents and sisters were there with us in the little chapel near the university.

Alain finished his doctorate a year before me, and was offered a position in the European office of the École des Hautes Études Commerciales de Montréal, doing orientation and some teaching for international students wanting to continue their studies in Canada. It was not a permanent appointment, but it was a foot in the door.

Affairs moved quickly after that. Alain attracted the notice of several administrators and was recommended for a teaching position at HEC's main campus in Montréal. We debated the pros and cons for a week before Alain accepted and I applied to continue my graduate work at McGill University in Montréal.

McGill had two big advantages, besides allowing me to be with my husband: it had a top-level medical school and it would allow me to improve my admittedly unsteady knowledge of English. I had been working on English studies, but living in Brazzaville and Paris didn't give me much opportunity to use the language. Montréal was the best of both worlds: a work environment where I could use my new language and a community where I could fall back into French. McGill already had a number of programmes in tropical medicine, with field work in India and central Africa, and I was able to secure a position as research assistant while I completed my doctoral degree.

The greatest part of my time was spent not in the beige stone structure that housed the McGill School of Medicine on rue de la Montagne but in various hospital laboratories in the city, most of them not too far from McGill. I was working on tropical epidemiology, looking specifically at hemorrhagic fevers like Marburg and Ebola, terrifying infections that caused severe internal and external bleeding; Montréal was a major point of entry for immigration from French-speaking Africa, and both the Québec Ministry of Health and the World Health Organization were supporting the research. The basic genetic research on the diseases had been done decades ago, and my thesis was focused on the changes that had occurred in the genome over that time. This meant studying tissue samples brought in from the occasional outbreaks in Cameroun and Gabon. I was guaranteed a role in the research after my postgraduate degree was completed.

Alain's office at HEC was on the opposite side of the Parc Mont-Royal from McGill, and on bright days we would try and meet in the park at lunch. Sometimes we went instead to Notre-Dame-des-Neiges Cemetery, next to the park. This was a pleasing contrast to the noise of the city that surrounded it.

On the day I passed my orals and earned that PhD in epidemiology, I also learned that I was pregnant. I was worried that it would be difficult in Montréal to support a child, but we were both happy with the news. Alain was ecstatic when the ultrasound revealed twin girls.

We decided that perhaps my laboratory work with tropical diseases posed too much risk to the unborn babies, and I requested a leave of absence. Instead, my supervisor offered to let me do the online aspects of the research, avoiding not just contact with tissue samples, but with the people who handled them. I did this until the day before the twins were born.

They were healthy little girls, not identical, but very much alike in appearance and temperament. We named them Hélène, after my mother, and Éloïse, after Alain's grandmother. Alain was enchanted with them from the moment he first held them, nervously balancing one on each arm and cooing softly to each in turn.

When we brought the twins home, it was Alain who changed their diapers and sang them to sleep, who got up in the night when it was time for feeding and brought them one at a time to me. Every week he would come home with a new outfit for one or both.

They made few demands on our patience, eating well and sleeping through the night within four months. They wasted no time in thoroughly charming Alain's parents, especially his father, and eventually the twins spent most days with their grandparents and I went back to work.

The work was becoming more essential, with Ebola on the rise in what was left of the Democratic Republic of the Congo. Although this country shared its name with my native land, my Congo had survived the civil wars of four decades ago and emerged as a relatively stable and free nation. The other Congo, sadly, had been ripped apart by unremitting conflict, stoked frequently by the large multinational mining operations that profited from weak central government. Especially after the failure of the Zimbabwean state, the south of Congo was ruled not from Kinshasa but from foreign financial centres. The collapse of state institutions meant that health and educational facilities were often in a state of crisis, shuttered because of lack of funding. The NGOs working in the country were strained to the limits, and even the World Health Organization was finding it difficult to cope with the demands. Two years earlier an outbreak of influenza had killed almost eighty thousand people in the southwest, and each month seemed to bring some new crisis. Now flare-ups of Ebola were occurring frequently throughout that part of the land, and my research in hemorrhagic fevers brought many questions to my inbox.

When the twins were two years old, Alain was offered a position at the European University School of Business in Geneva. We considered the option carefully and decided not to uproot ourselves and take the twins away from the life they shared with their grandparents. It would also have disrupted my own research and perhaps delayed some of the solutions my team was developing for the problems in Kasai province of Congo.

Before Alain called to decline the offer, though, a second message came from Geneva—not for Alain, but for me. The World Health Organization had been following my research and wanted me to head up an international team to undertake a region-wide study of the hemorrhagic fevers and investigate possible prophylactic measures that were practicable in the conditions in Congo. They had been in touch with McGill, and the university was willing to collaborate on the project.

"Corinne, this can't be coincidence," Alain told me. "The WHO wants you so badly that they've twisted arms at the European University."

"Or perhaps McGill is anxious to send me to Europe?" I smiled.

Alain's parents were supportive, although we could tell they wanted the girls to stay. "Both of you have so much to offer," Alain's mother said. "And the experience in Europe will be an advantage in your careers. Maybe we can visit you in Switzerland, and of course you'll come to Canada during your vacations, won't you?"

Of course we would. I was feeling somewhat uneasy because we had never taken the girls to visit my parents in Brazzaville. My family home was in a clean, safe neighbourhood of the city and Brazzaville as a whole was one of the best-run cities in equatorial Africa, but I confess to being nervous about exposing my daughters to even that slight risk. Kinshasa was right across the river, and conditions there were much more dire.

After much discussion and many changes of heart, we accepted both calls and went to Geneva. Alain was teaching undergraduate classes at the university and I was given a small office and a large laboratory at WHO.

The assistant director-general for tropical diseases, a Dr Nakamura, conducted my orientation himself. "Dr Lissunga, I have to tell you that we are facing a major problem, and that is why we have asked for your assistance. The incidence of Ebola in southern Congo has increased year by year, and the disease seems to be infectious for longer periods. As you know, many of the hemorrhagic fevers appear suddenly and flame out quickly because their high mortality rate and rapid onset do not allow sufficient time for the disease to spread quickly. What we are now finding with the newer strains of Ebola is that they take much longer to become symptomatic, while remaining contagious right from the early period of infection. It is true that the symptoms are somewhat milder and the mortality rates are lower, but we are concerned with the prospect of a disease that remains silent for the largest portion of its infectious stage."

"I have seen some subtle changes in the genome of the samples we've had from Cameroun and from southern Congo," I replied. "We also have similar changes in samples from wild primates in Cameroun, although Congo hasn't given us any wild primate tissue."

"We have funding for a very thorough study, Dr Lissunga. You will have a team of specialists whose research complements your own. Several of them are based here in Geneva, but you will also have collaboration from researchers in Africa, working out of our regional office in Brazzaville. You will wish to travel to Congo on a regular basis to consult. I understand you have family connections in the city?"

"Yes, I grew up there and my parents still live there. I'll look forward to the trip."

"Excellent. Now let us go over the resources we have ready for you and your associates."

There wasn't a lot of time to spend preparing. We plunged right into the project, and started to coordinate the various strains of the virus with the localities in which they were prevalent. I was surprised that this basic step had not already been undertaken, but soon we had moved on to deeper examination of the directions in which the virus seemed to be evolving.

Dr Nakamura was correct. Although the virus seemed to be much more adapted to spreading through the population, the symptoms were less severe and the death rate lower than it had been in the last few decades. People were surviving the fever in greater numbers, and internal bleeding and organ collapse were infrequent. There was some indication that the virus was replicating at a different rate and perhaps even in a different manner. It was demonstrably slower and seemed more selective in the cell-surface receptors it attached to.

New outbreaks of conflict in southern Congo disrupted several strands of our research, and by the time we were able to once again access the region, most medical facilities had been severely degraded. Equipment had been looted, medical personnel had fled or been killed, and sanitation was virtually non-existent. Surprisingly, though, the incidence of the Ebola-like illnesses had declined almost to zero. This was perhaps a result of the war disturbing the bat colonies that we believed were the reservoir for the virus; certainly the disease was still occurring in other regions.

It was in Geneva that Alain and I learned to play bridge. His colleagues at the university had a regular evening of bridge and we were invited to join in. We welcomed the opportunity to get together in a less formal setting and to share some of the more personal aspects of our lives. Two of the other teachers had little girls the same age as Hélène and Éloïse and we began to spend a couple of hours each weekend with the children together in the parks near the lake—the botanical gardens and Parc la Grange. In the warmer weather we went to Genève-Plage with its stepped swimming pool.

Alain and the twins formed a circle of mutual adoration. They loved to perform for him, and he was a thoroughly appreciative audience. His patience was bottomless—no matter what the girls were doing, he was willing to play his part. I sometimes felt that he was a better mother than I was. I loved the twins and enjoyed spending time with them, but often found my mind wandering to some problem I had in the lab, while Alain would be completely focused on his daughters.

In addition to my work in epidemiology, I was being encouraged to become familiar with public health issues in general. My contacts at McGill were useful in this respect, and I also found many resources in WHO's general offices. It was clear I was being groomed for a greater role, although no one spoke about what that role might be. I was flying every two months to Brazzaville to meet with staff at the regional office there; I got to know them quite well. Often they would invite me to their homes, and I was able to return the courtesy by hosting small dinners at my parents' house. Twice a year I would take the girls with me so they would get to know their Congolese grandparents as well as their Canadian family. They were shamelessly spoiled in Brazzaville, even more so than in Montréal.

After two years of research work, I was assigned as chief aide to the Assistant Director-General for Polio, Emergencies and Country Collaboration. This involved travel throughout much of Africa and southern Asia, along with occasional visits to research facilities in the United States, Canada, and Australia. I was beginning to feel uncomfortable about the amount of time I was spending away from home. Alain was very competent in caring for the twins, but I missed them while I was out of Geneva. If I were being honest with myself, I would also confess to a certain amount of jealousy that their governess was growing more central to their lives than I was.

As if the director was reading my thoughts, she summoned me one day in March and asked me to take on the role of aide to the Assistant Director-General for Health Systems and Innovation, a post that would keep me in Geneva for much more of the time. This was a welcome development as the girls began kindergarten at the International School. Alain had wanted the girls to attend a regular Swiss school where they would be taught in French, but I persuaded him that learning English from the very beginning would be an advantage to them in their future careers. Alain wasn't quite ready to think about their future careers—they were, after all, only five years old.

I found my work with Health Systems and Innovation challenging and exciting. Although infectious diseases were still a major issue in many countries, we were making great progress in organizing the health systems around the world to cope with several of these sicknesses. A major breakthrough in the control of malaria meant that hundreds of thousands more children throughout the tropics and subtropics were growing up free from the illness and vaccines had recently been developed for Dengue and yellow fever, diseases closely related to the Ebola I had been studying for so many years. Perhaps a vaccine for the other hemorrhagic fevers would soon be available. My department was charged with setting up the programs that delivered the vaccines to the field.

Then came the shocking news that the regional director of WHO for Africa, a woman I had come to know quite well during my time in Country Collaboration, had been killed in an automobile accident in Brazzaville. I was sent to represent the director at the funeral service, and for once

Alain accompanied me. We left the girls with my parents and drove to the Cathédrale Sacré-Coeur at the end of Avenue Maréchal-Foch, a squat yellow-brown brick structure with airy white latticework on the front and the motto "Dieu est Amour" written prominently above the entrance. Mme Dr Sengwo had been respected and well-liked by her staff, and there was a large turnout for the service. The archbishop himself conducted the mass, and the president of the republic was in the pews.

At the reception following the service, many of WHO's African office staff came up to greet me, and we shared memories of Dr Sengwo's devotion to her employees and to the people of Africa. Although I didn't realize it at the time, there was no mention of possible candidates to replace her as director. Alain and I flew back to Europe three days after the funeral.

When I returned to the office, the director called me into her office and asked me to take on the post of regional director for Africa, assuming Dr Sengwo's role. It occurred to me that perhaps I was the last to know I was even being considered for this promotion. It was a tremendous honor, but it carried a heavy load of responsibility. I went home to confer with Alain, but even then I knew I would accept.

Alain, of course, was more than supportive. He joked about being a stay-at-home father in Brazzaville, but I knew he would have no difficulty finding a teaching position at Marien Ngouabi. His English was approaching native fluency, and the university was trying to attract students from outside Congo—he could teach business courses in either French or English. The twins were excited about going to live near the grandparents who doted on them, and I felt a sense of peace at the thought of homecoming. My only reservations were due to my lack of administrative experience.

The director dismissed my doubts. "You managed the research team here in Geneva, Corinne. You acted as administrator in two of our major departments. I've heard nothing but praise from your colleagues here and in Brazzaville." She delivered the final bit of persuasion: "Dr Sengwo herself asked if you might come to Brazzaville. She felt you would be a wonderful deputy, and I think you're the best person to assume her responsibilities."

It didn't take long to close up our life in Geneva. After the quiet farewell gatherings at the WHO and the university, we flew to Paris and then on to Brazzaville. We landed in a torrential rainstorm, and just walking the few metres to the airport transport bus left us completely soaked. Hélène found this very amusing, but Éloïse wasn't at all happy. "I wanted to be perfect for meeting Grandpapa and Grandmaman," she complained. "Now my clothes are ruined."

The Brazzaville office arranged for accommodation for us until we found housing, and within the week the girls were in school, Alain was busily looking at real estate with my parents, and I was getting the requirements of my new position in hand. The sudden death of Dr Sengwo had left most of the staff dazed, and I was treading softly. If anyone in the regional office was resenting not being chosen as Dr Sengwo's successor, he or she was keeping quiet about it; everyone in fact seemed to be quite willing to help me learn the procedures and protocols. Parts of Africa were still in considerable turmoil, unrest was brewing in the northeast again, and although some areas, Ghana, Benin and South Africa, for example, had established high-quality health care systems, the ongoing civil disturbances in the other Congo and in Zimbabwe were setting back any progress from the past three decades.

Still, most of the continent was optimistic. The agreements of the World Trade Organization had led to increased economic development throughout the equatorial zones, vaccines had brought malaria and AIDS under control, the effects of climate change—so devastating in southern Asia and the Pacific—were less severe in much of tropical Africa, educational levels had risen to acceptable standards and the long-standing issues of corruption had been addressed with some success throughout the area. The regional office was staffed by Africans with outstanding medical and administrative expertise.

Alain surprised me by suggesting we accept my parents' invitation to move in with them on a more or less long-term basis. The house was not exceptionally large, but there was enough space for all. We would have our own cooking and living space as well as the bedrooms. The twins were overjoyed, and my mother immediately set to work cleaning the already spotless rooms. Alain was especially pleased with the large mango tree that had been planted right outside our window on the second floor; he could reach out and pick some of the fruit from our room. We had a small grove of plantain trees at the end of the garden, and orange and lime trees as well.

Our home near the Route du Djoué put me close to the WHO offices, and as expected Alain made his way to the university. After several rounds of interviews he was hired for a temporary position lecturing in the business school. This did not go as well as he had hoped. He was of course accustomed to hearing my African French and had no difficulty understanding the Congolese with whom he worked, but his students were not used to Canadian French, and several of them complained loudly about Alain's "terrible accent". He persevered, learned a few of the local idioms, tried to imitate my intonations, and eventually reached a point where his students accepted his foreign version of their language.

On weekends we often went to the area north of the university, where the girls could visit the recently upgraded Parc Zoölogique and stare at the giraffes, their favorite animals. We wandered through the grounds of the National Assembly, watched soccer or basketball or whatever other activity was taking place at the Massamba-Debat Stadium and occasionally made it all the way down to the river. We were happy.

One day during my third year in the Brazzaville office, the Cameroun national director contacted me to report an outbreak of Ebola-like illness near the eastern town of Batouri. This was very unusual, as Ebola was normally associated with more heavily forested parts of the country. We inaugurated the monitoring procedures, requested blood samples and alerted Geneva.

Two days later, Cameroun again called to report the disease was something new. Like Ebola, it caused severe internal bleeding and organ failure, but it was accompanied by the breakdown of subcutaneous tissue and bleeding from large areas of the skin. Patients in the advanced stages of the disease appeared to be dissolving in their own blood. The local health facilities were overwhelmed and bewildered; people were starting to panic. The Cameroun government imposed quarantine on the entire town, fearing that anyone fleeing might be carrying the virus to other parts of the country. Geneva ordered samples sent to Europe and to Atlanta.

By Saturday it became clear that the original quarantine had not been effective. The disease apparently had a long infectious period before becoming symptomatic, and three patients exhibiting the signs of the disease presented at hospitals in Douala and Yaoundé. All three had been in Batouri, but had left the town six weeks earlier. If they had been infected during their time in Batouri, this meant the incubation period of the disease was asymptomatic for over a month. Police in Eastern Cameroun reported that family members of the original patients were falling ill, and the number of deaths had risen to over a hundred. The disease had both high morbidity and high transmissibility. Sanitary conditions in Batouri were reportedly quite adequate, and the few medical staff in the town suspected the disease was airborne. Cameroun ordered isolation of the patients in Douala and

Yaoundé, but it was likely that hospital staff had already been exposed; few intake personnel wore masks as a regular precaution. There was also the question of other patients who had come into contact with the infected individuals in the hospital.

The samples arrived in Brazzaville and were sent off to Geneva and Atlanta for analysis. We discussed a ban on air traffic in and out of Cameroun, but Geneva and the Cameroun government opted to hold off, fearing the risk of panic. The hope was that like other highly contagious outbreaks in the past this one would burn itself out after an initial period of infection. When I reminded Geneva that those previous eruptions had flamed out because the time between infection and the appearance of symptoms was extremely brief, a characteristic this new disease did not seem to exhibit, the director general agreed, saying she would review the situation on a daily basis.

By the following Monday, we had analysis from Atlanta. The virus was a mutation of the Marburg virus, but included material from other viruses, probably both measles and influenza, that had the potential to cause myopathic conditions. That same day, the Cameroun health authorities reported an outbreak in the general population in Yaoundé. Air traffic was halted throughout Cameroun, and other forms of transport were monitored.

We had been searching desperately for some diagnostic procedures that would allow us to isolate and treat patients before they had a chance to infect others. The only signs that seemed to be consistent occurred late in the incubation: a reddening of the sclera of the eyes and a darkening of the tissue under the fingernails and toenails, both likely caused by bleeding near the surface. Unfortunately, by the time these indicators emerged, the patient was only a week or two away from the full-blown manifestation of the disease. None of the traditional treatments for Marburg or Ebola seemed to have any effect.

All the governments of tropical Africa were on alert for any signs of the disease in their jurisdictions, and for a week after Cameroun was closed off, we were hopeful the spread had been contained. Geneva had been frantically tracking all travelers who had left Cameroun during the past few months and none of them were showing signs of infection. It was too early to declare the disease confined to Cameroun, though, because those who had left the country in the past month might still develop the symptoms.

It was with great dismay, then, that we received the reports of further outbreaks in Nigeria and Gabon. The *cordon sanitaire* was expanded, with all travel in and out of these countries, plus the Central African Republic, my own Congo and Equatorial Guinea banned. Schools were closed across equatorial Africa, and sports events cancelled. Special flights were authorized to import masks and other protective gear to bolster our own regional stocks. We debated extending the ban to the other Congo, Angola and the West African nations as well, but this was vetoed from Geneva.

Military surveillance flights continued, operating out of three regional air centres. The travel ban was generally being observed, with railways at a standstill and road traffic very minimal. A few river boats were still operating, but most of the movement was police or military deployment.

Morbidity from the disease approached one hundred per cent, and by the third week of the outbreak we lost contact with the hospital in Batouri. Air surveillance of the town and surrounding area showed no activity other than a number of cattle wandering across a field. It was difficult not to make terrible assumptions.

When the disease was detected in Kinshasa, the travel ban was extended southward all the way to Zimbabwe and eastward into the mountain regions, South Sudan and parts of Kenya and Tanzania. The order to shut down rail lines and ports in Congo and Angola brought protests from the international resource companies and pressure on Geneva from the governments who backed the corporations. The director-general held firm, and the ban was proclaimed. It was soon apparent, however, that railways and port facilities were continuing to operate at normal capacity, with freighters leaving Lobito in the usual numbers. The big mining corporations held powerful sway, not just over the governments in Congo and Angola, but over their home governments as well. I was angry that safe in their offices in Shanghai, London and Toronto the officers of these companies were risking the lives of their employees and thousands of other Africans, but Geneva held out little hope of changing the situation.

Cameroun was imploding. The disease was spreading rapidly in Yaoundé and Douala, and the military and police were failing to stop the exodus of people from the cities. Within weeks the entire country would be exposed. Things were little better in Nigeria, where the president and other leading government officials had flown their families out of the country in defiance of the ban. It was unclear how landing permission had been obtained, but when the news leaked out it caused deadly riots in Kano and Ibadan.

We lost contact with the WHO national office in Gabon. The Gabon military were unable, or unwilling, to investigate what had happened.

Geneva gave permission for experimental treatments of the disease to go ahead without clinical trials, but nothing seemed to stop the progression of the pandemic. New cases appeared in Ghana and other parts of West Africa, and the first outbreaks occurred in my own country. Soon we were registering patients right in Brazzaville.

Alain was growing more concerned each day. He came to see me at my office. "Corinne, we have to send the twins to Canada. You know it isn't safe for them to remain here, now that the disease is in Brazzaville. My parents will take care of them until the epidemic subsides."

"Alain, I can't do that. There's a travel ban, and Canada won't grant them entry anyway."

"You know you have the influence, Corinne. You have the authority to override the ban and issue the clearance. The Congolese government will issue the travel documents if you request them. Your Geneva office will intervene with the Canadian immigration people. No one is going to deny entry to two little girls and send them back. The worst that can happen is that they'll be put in isolation until the medical people are sure they aren't infectious."

Everything Alain said was true. I could get the twins on a military jet to a secure airfield in Europe. They could be put in quarantine in Switzerland or Germany, which had high level biohazard containment facilities. I could even send Alain with them. Nigeria had shown it was possible.

But I knew I wasn't going to do it. I had a responsibility to the people of Congo and the rest of the continent. Sending my own family to safety would be a betrayal of that responsibility, and risk spreading the disease farther.

"Corinne, listen to me. You have to do this. You can't let your sense of duty, some perverted idea of *noblesse oblige*, kill your own daughters. Éloïse and Hélène have their whole lives ahead of them. You and I can stay here, but you have to send the girls to safety."

Alain's words cut me, in large part because they hit close to the truth. Deep down, I knew I was putting my own daughters at risk, that I was more willing to sacrifice them than their father was. Alain would have broken every rule in the book to keep the twins safe. I was angry that I wouldn't —angry at myself for being so rigid, and at Alain for pointing it out to me.

"Do you imagine, Alain, that I haven't realized the danger we are all in? I've studied this disease in all its horrible details. Do you think I don't know that there are millions of children here, all of whom have their whole lives ahead of them? Am I to fly all of them out to Montréal too? And what if the flight crew are already infected? Do you want me to open the door to the pandemic in Canada?"

Alain was unmoved. He looked at me steadily and spoke without raising his voice. The ice in his tone warned me he was near the point of rage. "Military jet, Corinne. Crew of two. Refuel and return, leaving the twins in Montréal. Do your trick with biohazard outfits, whatever it takes. You can play Mother Teresa if you have to, but don't gamble with our daughters' lives."

"Moving them increases the risk. The safest thing is to keep them isolated. Your classes are cancelled, you can stay with them at home. Keep them inside; keep yourself and my parents inside, too. Don't answer the door. I'll stay here in my office. I can have food delivered to you; you don't need to go out in the street."

"Corinne. You have the authority. You can't sacrifice the lives of your own children on the altar of some god you call duty. Any god that demands such an offering is not worth worshipping." I said nothing.

Alain just stared angrily at me for a minute. Then, with a look of defeat, he turned and walked out, without saying a word. His eyes told me something had broken in our relationship, that we would never be the same.

Send the girls to Canada until the epidemic subsides. If only I could be sure the epidemic would subside. There was no further word from Geneva or Atlanta on possible treatments, and we were losing medical personnel every day. Even in the WHO offices here in Brazzaville people were failing to show up, whether because of fear or infection, we did not know.

The reports coming in were discouraging. Surveillance flights over Gabon showed some activity still going on in Libreville and several other cities, but much of the countryside appeared deserted. There were only a few reported cases in Brazzaville, but the streets were mostly empty. Church services were being broadcast so people could pray together without sitting together. Shops were still open, but the staff always wore masks and gloves.

When the disease was recorded in Nairobi and then in several cities in South Africa, we knew it had gone beyond its tropical origins.

I spoke with Alain, the twins and my parents every day on the phone. My mother and father were as cheerful as they had to be, and the girls were their usual bubbly selves. Only Alain was distant—polite but remote. The news was mixed. They were doing well, although there had been disturbances not too far from the house. The high cement wall around the garden would keep out some trouble, we hoped, but anyone determined to get in could do so. We could only pray that the neighborhood would be spared any serious violence.

I had been staying in the small apartment that was part of the WHO office; after a week, the water supply shut off. There was plenty of bottled water, but hygiene was going to be an issue. We still had electricity and the phone towers were operating, but internet connectivity was intermittent.

Suddenly, things changed. One of the few surveillance planes still flying—fuel was becoming scarce and we had cut back on flights—reported something happening in Bangui, far up the Congo River to our north. It looked like the roads were full of traffic and crowds were everywhere in the streets. The pilot flew as low as he dared to get a better look, and it did seem as if people were out in vast numbers, and more were coming in from outside the city. I tried to contact the Central African Republic government, but no one was answering the lines.

Finally, we got through to the air force command based at Bangui M'Poko Airport. I spoke with General Mbaye himself. They had one helicopter that should still be in service, and I asked them to investigate what was happening in the city. The general, though, surprised me.

"We already know what is happening in the city. Everyone is going to the Université Palais des Sports. I have been there myself."

"I beg your pardon? Is there no risk in large gatherings? What is so important that you ignore the recommendations from our office?"

"There is a boy, Madame Doctor. He cures the sickness."

"What are you talking about? There is no cure for the sickness."

"Ah, Madame Doctor. You mean you have no cure. Your modern medicine does not know what to do. But this boy, he has the magic. He makes the people well. Even those who are ready to die. I have seen it myself. The army is telling everyone to come to the Palais. They have sent trucks and buses to bring people. It is a miracle."

"This is not possible. There is no such magic."

"Come and see, Madame Doctor. I will take you there myself."

"I will have to report this to Geneva. They will not be happy with your government's decision."

"We do not care. We are happy with our government's decision. We are no longer sick."

In a daze, I flicked off the phone and set it down on my desk. That was when I noticed my fingernails. The tissue under the nails was dark—very dark. When I took a few steps to glance in the mirror, my eyes were red, as though I had not slept in days. I picked up the phone again. I was going to call Alain, but changed my mind. I entered the number for the air force command in Brazzaville. If I was infected, there was nothing to lose by going to Bangui; perhaps I could learn something that would help the struggle against the disease.

"Colonel Obengu, please. This is Dr Lissunga at the WHO office." I waited for almost three minutes before the colonel came on the line. "Hello, Colonel Obengu. Dr Lissunga here. Can you arrange a flight for me to Bangui, as soon as possible? There are urgent developments there that I must investigate. The pilot need not remain in Bangui."

"Doctor, we know about the activity in Bangui. We do not think it wise to travel there. We are not even sure the airport is operating."

"It is essential that I go to Bangui. To go by river would take much too long. I must beg you for a flight."

"Such a move is very dangerous. There is a large gathering of people in Bangui, in contravention of your own instructions. The disease is known to be present in the city. I cannot ask my pilots to expose themselves to the risk."

"The risk will be no greater than in Brazzaville. The pilot need not leave the plane. He can let me out and return immediately to Brazzaville."

"Doctor, let me call the president and get authorization. Does the WHO make a formal request?" I knew he was referring to the Geneva office, but I chose to understand that he meant the African regional office—my own branch.

"Yes," I answered. "It does." What was I doing? I had spent my entire life being the sceptical scientist. I had always demanded proof, irrefutable evidence, empirical investigation. Yet here I was, grasping at a wildly unbelievable story. It was not as if I was throwing myself in harm's way, of course; harm was already part of me, in the form of my red eyes and darkened nails. I wasn't sure what I planned to achieve in Bangui. I simply needed to go.

Two hours later I was in the air, fully equipped with biohazard clothing to protect the pilot from my own infection. I wore sunglasses to hide the redness of my eyes. The green of the Congo Basin flowed beneath us, kilometre upon kilometre of forest, with occasional settlements. I saw no activity in any of the towns we flew over.

Within an hour we were approaching Bangui M'Poko Airport. The pilot radioed to the control tower but got no response. Air traffic was banned and there was no need to operate the tower unless a surveillance flight was going out. Apparently no one had called Bangui to say we were coming. The runway was clear, however, and the pilot simply came in and landed. He opened the cockpit for me and I climbed out and lowered myself to the tarmac. The place seemed deserted.

I waved the pilot off and began to walk into the terminal building. As I reached the gates, my jet roared off down the runway and was gone.

A soldier came towards me as I crossed the arrivals area of the deserted terminal. "Madame Doctor?" I nodded.

"You will not need the suit, Madame Doctor. I am Denis. I am asked to drive you to the Palais des Sports whenever you are ready to go. The general said you would be coming soon." I peeled off the protective coveralls and face mask, but kept my sunglasses on.

He led me through the terminal to the main entrance and out to the parking area, where he had an army jeep waiting. Soon we were driving quickly along the avenue des Martyrs towards the city centre. The further we went, the more people we saw, most of them on foot or on bicycle, moving in the same direction as we were, but occasionally coming against the traffic. There were military and commercial trucks packed with passengers, some even clinging to the sides.

Eventually we slowed almost to a stop. The crowds were so thick we could only nose our way through.

"Let me out here, Denis," I suggested. "I can walk the rest of the way, just like everyone else."

"But General Mbaye said I was to drive you right to the Palais," protested my chauffeur.

"It will take forever to drive through this crowd. It will be easier to walk."

"Then I will go with you, Madame Doctor. I will take you to him."

"To General Mbaye?"

"Oh, no, Madame. To the boy. Is it not he you have come to see? He can cure you. It is like magic." Denis looked at me expectantly.

"Yes," I said, "To the boy." As I said the words, I realized that in fact that was the real reason I had come. Like all the thousands of others crowding into the sports field and arena, I wanted to be cured.

Denis gently wove his way through the masses of people. Everyone was strangely quiet; the only sound seemed to be the footfalls of the people and the rustle of clothing. Dust was everywhere, making it difficult to breathe without sneezing. There was no breeze; the air hung humid in the stadium. Overhead the African sun blazed uninterrupted by even a hint of cloud.

We had gone about a hundred metres when I noticed I was holding Denis's hand. He seemed to accept this and I was somehow grateful. Although he was probably ten years younger than I was, he took on the role of older brother.

The heat was oppressive and I was sweating by the time Denis stopped. In the centre of the crowd was a small clear space, and in the space stood a boy, about twelve or thirteen years old, dressed in a yellow shirt, brown shorts and a pair of worn-looking sandals. His hair was long and quite straight, not at all African, but his face was Congolese, I thought.

As people came up to him, he was touching them gently on the forehead. They stiffened slightly and then relaxed. Most of the people who came to the boy appeared healthy, but in some cases, the signs of the infection were shocking, with bleeding from the pores of the skin and a terrible sunken look to the face. Occasionally the person had to be supported, even carried, to approach the boy. He did not shrink back from the horror of the disease, reaching out to touch the bloodied face as if there were nothing wrong. It was in these people that the change was most dramatic. They often sank to the ground, then managed to get to their knees and even stand. Someone would take a cloth and begin wiping away the blood. No new haemorrhaging was evident. I watched one woman for about ten minutes. She scarcely appeared conscious when the boy touched her, but gradually she gained strength and was able to stand. She smiled happily at everyone around her and whispered something in the direction of the boy, who had moved on to other people.

"Go, Madame Doctor," urged Denis. "Let him touch you. He has a magic."

I did as Denis instructed, and leaned forward towards the boy. He looked into my eyes and smiled slightly. The smile was on his lips, though, not in his eyes, which were full of some great sorrow. "Help me," I said quietly.

He reached out and put his fingers on my forehead. For an instant, the sadness went out of his eyes and he smiled at me again. I felt a rush of coolness flow through me, and a sense of peace such as I had never dreamed existed. Still today, more than a decade later, I experience the same thrill when I remember.

The boy moved on to the next person, and the next, lingering only for a few seconds with each. The crowd parted silently to let him reach each person, and despite the desperation many must have felt, there was very little pushing or crying out. As if by instinct, each of us moved back when we were able, so that others could reach the boy.

Denis was happy. "Madame Doctor. Look at your fingers." Indeed, the darkness under my nails was fading back to the normal color. I had never felt healthier. "Madame, I have watched for several days now. Those who are touched always recover, even if they are very ill. I think those who are not sick already will be protected against the infection, like a vaccine, but I can not be sure of that. " It was only then that I realized Denis had seen my fingernails, known I was infected, and yet had taken my hand.

"Denis," I said. "Can you take me to General Mbaye?" He nodded.

Once in the jeep, we were able to drive fairly quickly to the government offices at the Assemblée Nationale, just a couple of kilometres further up the avenue de l'Indépendence. We pulled up beside the yellow and red structure and Denis held the door of the jeep open for me. We were entering through a small door, not the imposing main entry, and once inside, Denis led me down a corridor past rows of offices. Furniture was piled in the corridor, as if the building was being renovated or at least given a thorough cleaning.

"Here is the general's office, Madame. I will wait for you here."

I pushed open the door and found the reception area deserted. "General Mbaye?"

He answered from the inner office. "Yes, Madame Doctor. I have been expecting you. Please come in."

I stepped into his office and extended my hand. "I am grateful, General Mbaye. Everything you told me was true. I am sorry for doubting you."

He laughed. "I know, Madame. It is difficult to believe, is it not? Even when one has seen with one's own eyes. I think the boy has touched you, has he not?"

I nodded. "General, there is something I must ask of you. In Brazzaville, the government and military are very concerned about the pandemic.

They will not believe me—or you, for that matter—if I tell them what I have found here. Do you have a plane I can take back to my city? I would like to bring my family here and invite the authorities in Brazzaville to send observers to verify the report I will give them. I am hoping the boy with the magic will continue to work, not just in the Central African Republic, but in other areas where the pandemic is causing so much suffering. I do not understand how he does what he does, but I have seen enough to believe he can work miracles."

"Do you think the Congolese authorities will accept your invitation? I am not sure I would have, had the situation been reversed."

"General, I would like to bring my family here mainly so they can be spared the disease. Your young driver tells me the touch of the boy may prevent infection as well as cure it. That is my selfish motive; there is another reason. If I am willing to risk my own children that may help to persuade the authorities that I am telling them the truth."

"Or convince them you have gone mad," suggested the general. "We do not have many aircraft in our armed forces. Central Africa is a poor country even now. I have ordered all of our planes to the outlying airfields, to collect as many people as they can and bring them to the boy."

"But the airport is deserted. There is no air traffic control."

"Not when you arrived, Madame. But there will be staff on duty now. The first of the planes will be arriving within minutes. Once the passengers have been attended to, I will spare one plane to take you to Brazzaville and bring you back with as many people as the plane will accommodate. That should be about twenty. The larger aircraft, the troop transports, I will retain on their missions within the republic."

"May I use your phone? My mobile does not work beyond Brazzaville."

"Of course."

I called Alain first, and told him I had exhibited the early signs of the disease, and that I had come to Bangui. He was shocked.

"This means that we are all probably infected," he said softly. "The twins, too." I said nothing for a few seconds.

"Alain, here in Bangui there is a cure. I cannot explain everything right away, but I am coming to pick you all up and bring you here. You must take the girls and my parents to the airport now. The plane is a Central African military short-range jet. I will meet you at the airport." Alain refused absolutely. He would not risk the twins' lives on such a dubious project.

We argued back and forth for about ten minutes, then Alain simply hung up on me. I felt a wave of despair.

Then I worked up the strength to make another difficult call. I dialed Colonel Obengu and explained that there was a cure for the fever available in Bangui and that I was coming back on a commuter jet to pick up any members of the Congolese administration who wished to make the trip to Bangui. "You are welcome to come yourself, Colonel, and to bring another dozen or so people with you. You may wish to contact the president and the health minister; perhaps the interior minister as well."

"Doctor Lissunga, what is this cure? Have you told WHO?"

"Not yet, Colonel. I will contact them from my office when I return. In the meanwhile, please give clearance for the plane to land in Brazzaville and make your way to the airport if you wish to come to Bangui."

"I will get the authorization for the plane. As for the rest of your request, I will have to consult with the minister, perhaps even the president. Please keep me informed."

Denis drove me back to the airport. The contrast with my earlier impression was striking; the terminal was alive with people, many of them obviously ill. Trucks, buses and a couple of ambulances were boarding the arrivals, ready to make the trip to the Palais des Sports. I made my way through the departures area to the check-in desk, where a single air force officer sat. As I approached, he stood and held out his hand.

"Doctor Lissunga? Your plane is ready to depart for Brazzaville. Please follow me." He led me out onto the tarmac to a small passenger jet with CAR military markings. The boarding ladder was in place, the doorway open.

On the flight back to Brazzaville, I wondered how I could explain the events of the day to Alain, and especially to Colonel Obengu. I was not at all certain that the Colonel would be at the airport. And then there was the question of informing Geneva. How would I ever convince them that I had been cured of the fever by the touch of a young boy? And that multitudes of people were being healed, even in the final stages of the disease?

As we landed in Brazzaville, my phone rang. All the time I had been out of the country I had left it on, even though there was no connection. A quick glance told me it was Alain. I picked it up.

"Corinne," he started. "I've changed my mind. We will come with you to Bangui." His voice sounded odd, as if he was speaking from a great depth, or was distracted by something that made him turn away from the phone. Before I could respond, he had closed off his phone. Despite not knowing why he had reversed himself, I was grateful for this new decision.

Alain was waiting in the airport terminal with the girls and my parents, all of them looking very anxious. Colonel Obengu was there as well, with the Minister of Health and another man I did not recognize. Colonel Obengu introduced the Health Minister and the other man, who turned out to be an official from the Interior Ministry. Alain hugged me and the girls came and took my hands. That was when I noticed with a jolt of horror that both the girls had deeply bloodshot eyes. I looked quickly at Alain. His eyes were filled, not with blood but with tears. The other two men appeared oblivious to this situation. I almost didn't hear the Minister speaking.

"Monsieur Mbiala will accompany you back to Bangui. He will consult with officials in the Central African Republic government and report back to the president himself. We have already made the arrangements. If you go to Bangui, you will not return to Brazzaville, Madame Doctor, unless you receive authorization from Monsieur Mbiala or me. This will apply as well to the members of your family. Do you accept these terms?"

I glanced quickly at Alain. "Yes," I said.

We passed the flight in almost complete silence, the girls snuggling in on either side of Alain, my mother smiling weakly at me from time to time. Monsieur Mbiala was reading through a sheaf of papers and glancing every so often at his phone. Halfway through the trip, Hélène looked directly at me, her eyes wide, and I was horrified to see blood starting to bead on her lower eyelids. I had to get my girls to the stadium.

When we landed in Bangui, the terminal was once again filled with people. An official of the foreign ministry came up and introduced himself to Monsieur Mbiala. "We have a car waiting to take you to the ministry, Monsieur. Please come with me. Madame Doctor, I believe there is a military car for you as well."

I was pleased to see that it was again Denis who had been assigned to drive. This time he had a small military bus. "We were not sure how many people to expect, Madame. If you have no objections, we will also board some of the people who have just arrived from the northern towns."

Soon we were once more heading to the Palais des Sports. I explained to Alain and my parents what had happened to me. They were incredulous. I could see that Alain was panicking, wondering how he could avoid exposing the twins to the crowds in the centre of the city. Having a very ill woman as a fellow-passenger on the bus was making matters far worse. The girls were fascinated with the blood on the woman's face, but I knew from the rigid expressions of Alain and my parents that they were in an agony of worry. I think that if he had been able, Alain would have ordered Denis to turn around and go back to the airport.

At the Palais des Sports, Denis stopped the bus and we walked through the crowds to the spot where I had met the boy. He was still there, still touching people, showing no sign of weariness or boredom. I took Hélène's hand and Alain's; Éloïse attached herself to her father's other hand. My mother and father followed behind us. The girls watched this boy touching people, watched the people stiffen and then relax, watched the smiles on the faces of those who had been touched. Suddenly he was in front of us. Hélène stepped forward and the boy touched her brow. I felt her hand tighten on mine. The boy passed me with a quick glance and the hint of a smile; Alain was leaning towards him to be touched. Again I felt a hand tighten on mine. Éloïse was next, then Alain stepped aside to let my parents through. No one spoke.

We made our way back to the bus, which Denis had loaded up with passengers returning to the airport. People were quiet but looked happy.

At the airport I found an official and asked to make a call to Brazzaville. Colonel Obengu had already heard from Monsieur Mbiala, and Monsieur Mbiala was on his way to the Palais des Sports to investigate the situation for himself.

"We hope to invite this boy to Brazzaville whenever he is finished in Bangui. This whole event needs much further study. The stories I have heard from Monsieur Mbiala are unbelievable. Why did you not tell me the nature of this 'cure' you had found?"

"Would you have believed me?"

"I would have had you detained for psychiatric evaluation, Madame Doctor. I may still have to do so for Monsieur Mbiala. We are sending a plane for you. As soon as Monsieur Mbiala returns to the Bangui airport, please fly back here. I have many questions, and so does the Health Minister. I am sure you will want to apprise Geneva of your findings as well."

It was difficult to tell whether Colonel Obengu was accepting the report from Monsieur Mbiala; obviously the Central African Republic officials had briefed him on what was happening. I had no doubt that Monsieur Mbiala himself, if he met the boy, would be convinced, but I wondered if we might all find ourselves in a ward of the Brazzaville Teaching Hospital.

This was unlikely; the hospital had too much work already with the fever patients.

Nonetheless, his words made me start planning how I was going to phrase my report to Geneva. Perhaps the best approach would be to have senior officials fly to Bangui and see for themselves; I didn't need to mention the boy until they were on the spot in front of him. Why had I not thought to video the healing process? I had my phone; the camera was functional.

When Monsieur Mbiala arrived about two and a half hours later, it was clear he had seen the boy. I did not have to ask; his eyes said everything. We found the Congolese plane waiting for us. Bangui airport was busier than ever, with passengers arriving and leaving. The difference in facial expression between the newcomers and the departing visitors was instructive.

Alain sat beside me on the return flight, and we each held one of the girls on our laps. I looked down at Hélène, snuggled against me; her fingernails had already returned to their normal color. The weakness was gone from my mother's smile; she was filled with a new light.

It was already dark when we reached Brazzaville. Colonel Obengu was waiting for us at the airport. Alain took the rest of the family home while I went with Monsieur Mbiala and the colonel to the health ministry to debrief. In the car, my phone sounded. I was momentarily startled; I had forgotten all about it.

"Yes. Corinne Lissunga here." I listened to the voice on the phone. "But that's impossible. I just saw him in Bangui. There must be more than one. Yes, thank you. Please keep me informed."

"Colonel, my office has just received a report of a boy in Jos, Nigeria. He has attracted a large crowd of people and the rumor is that he is curing the disease. We may have more than one of these miracle children at work."

"Let us hope someone from this miracle army arrives in Brazzaville also."

At the health ministry, Dr Mokosso, the head of the Co-operation Directorate, met us. He had coffee and refreshments prepared.

"You must be very tired, Madame Doctor, after such a long day. Not to mention four flights, one after another. Perhaps we can go over the most important information and fill in the details when you and Monsieur Mbiala are more rested."

Between Monsieur Mbiala and me, we reported the most vital information: that in Bangui a young boy had attracted large crowds of people and seemed to be curing the fever, or at least relieving the symptoms. The

Central African Republic administration was convinced of his abilities and had been transporting people to Bangui for three days. I myself had had the symptoms of the disease, and these had disappeared after the boy touched me. No one was asking for payment or any other favor. There was a report of another boy doing similar cures in Nigeria.

Dr Mokosso had news of his own. "The boy has left Bangui. No one saw him depart, which is astounding, given the hundreds of people who were still at the stadium. He does not seem to have anyone with him—no parents or other adults."

This was a puzzle. There was no possibility that he could have traveled to Nigeria after leaving Bangui. I myself had seen him less than three hours ago, and anyone flying out of Bangui would have had to go through the airport. Even by jet, he could not have reached Nigeria in such a short time, and there were no jets. There must have been two boys.

When I returned home, Alain had already put the twins to bed and prepared a meal of rice with mangos, lime and chillies for me.

"Thank you, Alain. You have no idea how much I appreciate your coming to Bangui. I have thought long about what you said, about duty being a god unworthy of my worship. Perhaps you are right. I am reminded of the story in the Bible about Abraham being ready to sacrifice his son Isaac in accordance with God's command. God sent a ram as an alternate and Isaac was spared. Maybe this boy in Bangui was my ram. I need to make some changes in my life."

"Corinne, I am grateful. I was afraid for the girls and for all of us. I still can't quite understand why you did what you did. I am sorry that I was so judgmental; you saved the twins' lives. I suppose you have loftier principles than I do, and I have to offer some respect for that. I don't have the same strength."

I wasn't sure quite how to interpret this, and I changed the subject. "How are Maman and Papa?'

"They have gone to bed. The flight has left them a little tired, although they both say they have never felt better—forty years younger, your father says." I smiled. That would make him about ten years old.

Explaining all these events to Geneva was not at all as difficult as I had expected. Bangui was not the first, it turned out. There were very well documented events in Canada, Finland and Korea, and a hundred or so less researched incidents in other places. One in Uruguay had resulted in the healing of injuries, and also in the remission of severe psychiatric diseases.

More than a thousand inmates at a prison were so changed that they were being considered for early parole.

Over the next weeks, the boy was reported in many places in equatorial Africa, often in major cities but also in tiny remote villages. As Colonel Obengu had hoped, he came to Brazzaville. The news was always the same; he was curing the fever. Soon, though, additional information was coming in. Not only the hemorrhagic fever, but many diseases—river blindness, encephalitis, even cancer—appeared to clear up. As in the Uruguay case, psychiatric conditions like schizophrenia receded with the boy's touch. A ceasefire was declared in the other Congo so people could travel to the boy. The ceasefire became permanent.

The boy—or the boys, if there truly were more than one—eventually began appearing farther from Central Africa. It was reported that in one ten-day period in Dakar, he had touched four hundred thousand people. This seemed impossible—it would mean the boy was touching someone new every two seconds, twenty-four hours a day, without pausing to eat or rest. Still, there were many impossibilities involved in these events.

Then Nairobi, Johannesburg, Luanda, Tripoli. The boy was in Somalia, Ethiopia, Madagascar. He was outside the WHO Africa Region—into the Middle East and Asia, eventually in cities, towns, villages all across the world. Last year, after more than ten years of appearances, he vanished as mysteriously as he had come.

Looking back over that decade to Bangui, I am conscious of many changes. My daughters are now sixteen years old, but showing no signs of puberty. They look and act like ten year olds. This is true for tens of thousands of other children across the world; what evolutionary advantage can be derived from this slowing of the maturation is still a mystery, but it is very prevalent, and not just in the children the boy is said to have touched. Now parents who were touched are giving birth to children who exhibit the same slow physical development. Childhood is lasting much longer than before. Those who have undergone the transformation seem to be free of disease and disability. There is evidence that the range of intellectual ability has shifted dramatically upward. Antisocial and criminal behavior among those with the genetic changes has dropped to almost zero.

The World Health Organization and innumerable other organisms are researching this phenomenon. Scientists generally feel that the appearance of the boy himself was a side effect of a massive genetic change, a sort of accelerated and purposeful evolution. When the chromosomes underwent their transformations, people hallucinated this boy.

I'm not so certain. When I look back to Bangui, the boy is as real to me as anything else that has ever occurred in my life. I have yet to find anyone who was touched by the boy who feels there was anything hallucinatory about him.

If the theories are correct and living organisms—people like me—have undergone an evolutionary shift after conception, then evolutionary biology will have to be reformulated in fundamental ways.

Perhaps those reformulations will be more fantastic even than the boy. As for me, I will always draw comfort from the memory of that day under the hot sun of Central Africa.

4.

CAIRNS

SO YOU THINK YOU know all about Cairns, do you? You will find that none of the rumors about us are true. We are not a cult, not a congregation of poor losers, not some radical crowd of apocalyptical hysterics. We have nothing to do with the survivalist bunch in eastern Siberia, the ones who insisted on going "back to the land" armed with semi-automatic weapons to avoid the coming disaster, but who still wanted every possible convenience to accompany them. They ended up almost killing each other before they decided to end their experiment. Here in our community you will find a few people who may seem eccentric, perhaps even a bit unbalanced, but that's to be expected in a population as large and diverse as ours.

When the Cairns Project was initiated, the agency chose Cairns for two reasons. The first, of course, is that the boy never appeared here. As a result, we already had a substantial base population who had never undergone the transformation of the genome. The second reason, obvious if you stop to think, is that Cairns offers so much to anyone. The climate, although at times unbearably hot in January, is for the most part very comfortable. There are plenty of employment opportunities here, and the city has always had a very low crime rate and very great appreciation of diversity. This has meant that Indonesians, Papuans, Filipinos have been welcomed here, along with the Australians who have migrated in from all over the continent. The environmental stresses that were beginning to build to catastrophic proportions have eased dramatically, and we have the glories of the Great Barrier Reef at our doorstep and the spectacle of the mountains out our back door. Most importantly, given our history, is that Cairns for the past two decades has had superb medical facilities. This has allowed the Project to concentrate the medical and psychiatric personnel in one area.

Okay, I exaggerated about the crime rate. We do have a problem when you line us up against other cities.

Of course, many people from Cairns did travel to Townsville or Brisbane or even further away when the boy made his appearances in Australia. Throughout the past years many more have intermarried with people who underwent the change, and now their children all bear the new genetic traits. The majority of these changed people elected to remain in Cairns.

We hold no prejudice against the changed people, the ones we call CPs (confusing at times, since "CP" is also used to refer to the Cairns Project itself), and they certainly accept us, although it's possible to read a certain amount of pity into their attitudes toward us. Cairns is now, thanks to the influx of unchanged citizens, split more or less evenly between those who have changed and those who haven't. New unchanged people, especially from Indonesia, join us every so often, even as some of us marry out to CPs. Our birth rate is edging upward just a fraction. The balance in Cairns is tilting slightly further towards the unchanged with each passing year. This makes us, and a handful of communities like ours on four other continents, somewhat unique. We grow slowly as the rest of the world's population declines.

We see ourselves as a modern-day Noah's ark.

The accusations and suspicions of cultism and hysteria come not from CPs, but from others like us. Sometimes they have bought into the self-hatred, the feeling that they have missed the boat, that they could have been so much better off if only they had managed to reach that boy, that so-called "El Niño". Why, by the way, do we persist, even in this corner of Australia, in calling this boy by some Spanish title? Or better off if they or their parent had somehow managed to snag a life partner who had undergone the shift.

Moreover, it doesn't help that some of us proclaimed so loudly that we needed to keep a strong contingent of non-CPs in reserve, a sort of back-up army of men and women who were capable of violence. Preaching that if there were ever to be an alien invasion, we would need soldiers, folk who were willing to kill another life form. It was a disturbingly comical echo of the old fears of apocalypse - environmental, social, even supernatural - that preoccupied certain thinkers (I use that term loosely) over the past century. Suggesting that we relinquish the chance to pass on the new genetic structures to our children, that we maintain our ancient predilection to violence, just so we could repel any invasion from Galaxy Whatever, did our cause no good. Changed people tried to accommodate these bizarre arguments, but most of the rest of us just found them embarrassing.

Once, when I was a little girl, my family went to Kuranda. There was a young Djabugay boy, about my age, dancing a traditional dance on the sidewalk outside a shop. He was very slim and had dark curly hair; he moved with a grace that even as an eight-year-old I recognized as balletic. He neither smiled nor frowned. His face showed a serenity that fascinated me. An older boy, maybe his brother, provided the music on a didgeridoo that was taller than either of the boys. Both of them were clad in short pants that protruded out from under the wrappings of bright red loincloths. Their upper bodies and feet were bare. Their chests and faces, their arms and legs, were decorated with traditional markings in white paste. I sat down nearby to watch, and when the two boys finally stopped for a break, I slipped over, pretending to look more closely at the didgeridoo. The older brother glanced at me and grinned, but the younger lad maintained that calm non-expression he had worn during the dance. I was just about to ask where they had learned their arts when my mother called to me and I had to pull myself away.

I never forgot that boy. That is my image of El Niño. That serene look on the young Aboriginal boy's face. I never saw the miracle boy who made such a wrenching change in all our lives, and inexplicably there are no photos of him. People can't seem to agree on any of the details of his appearance, but in my mind, he bears the same features as the dancer on the sidewalk in Kuranda.

I wasn't even in Cairns when the boy was in Queensland. He did show up in Brisbane, Townsville and a few other places, but I was never able to make a connection. I didn't even try. Having decided to take a year off from school, I was working that winter as a cook - a title that elevated what I was serving higher than it deserved - in a fast food establishment out on one of the islands in the National Park, feeding all kinds of questionable stuff to the tourists who came to scuba dive and sunbathe, escaping the rainy, chilly streets of Sydney and Melbourne. We had been hearing reports of this miracle boy, El Niño, for more than two years, and he had already reportedly been seen in Australia on two separate occasions.

But I was wrapped up in a winter romance, smitten by a boy who would eventually disappear from the Reef and from my life, strangely without leaving much trace of his impact on either. While my erstwhile boyfriend and I were strolling hand-in-hand down the beach on Green

Island, or grabbing a quick few fumbling moments together in the darkness behind the restaurant, this mysterious boy was wandering about the world, making radical changes in millions and millions of lives. Although I didn't realize it at the time, he was changing my life, too, in ways I could never have anticipated.

When I returned to Cairns, most people had not even ventured as far as Townsville in search of the boy, but there were some who had. They spoke in glowing terms of the profound effect he had had on them, how they had been cured of pains and illnesses, how he had made them feel comfortable in their own skins for the first time, how he had opened their eyes to the love that was all around them. As a cynical and self-styled worldly eighteen-year-old, I found these claims maudlin and pompous; my first instinct, and the one I acted on, was to wax sarcastic about these "born-again El Niñoites". So much of their story - and it was almost always the same story - struck me as too messianic, too contrived, too scripted. Along with my unchanged friends, I teased the kids who had undergone the change. They grew up very slowly, making them easy targets both physically and socially.

It wasn't until much later that the tide turned, and now our children are viewed with sympathy because they grow up "so fast". This became my *Eureka!* moment.

But here I'm getting ahead of myself. You probably have heard a little bit about the Cairns Project by now. How we are trying to preserve some semblance of genetic diversity in the population. A century ago, people grew concerned about lack of such diversity in other organisms: agricultural crops, endangered species, forests. Seed banks were established, zoos began to chart the genealogy of their collections, monoculture was discouraged. It wasn't too big a leap to imagine that human genetic diversity would be a good thing, too.

After my year working in the fast-food industry, I went into the Accounting and Business Management program at Central Queensland University. The program, which had been offered at the Cairns site, had been moved back to the North Rockhampton campus, so I ended up living in a small flat within walking distance - a long walking distance - of the university. Four years later, with my diploma in hand, I was able to come back to Cairns and obtain a position as assistant manager in the restaurant at the Pacific Hotel, down by the waterfront.

It was in Rockhampton that I first encountered large numbers of CPs. They were in my classes, they were at the club I frequented, they were on the tennis courts and at the beaches. Somehow, they were easy to recognize - or so I told myself. The aura of good health coupled with a certain confidence in the bearing seemed to me to be the telling signs. You will recognize, no doubt, that I was over-simplifying to an outrageous degree, but you will also have to allow that there is indeed a certain sameness to the changed.

At any rate, my guard was up whenever I interacted with changed people. To this day I am unsure why this would be so. No one has ever accused CPs of being violent, intimidating or even discourteous. They might mutter a bit behind their hands, but they avoid confrontation to an extraordinary degree.

It is this avoidance of confrontation that worries some. What if some foreign unchanged communities - like the one we have here in Cairns - grew in power and influence and decided, using the logic of our ancestors, that they should control and exploit whomever they could? We are not at all certain that CPs would be capable, emotionally as well as physically, of fighting off such control. It is true they have strength of numbers, but it's equally true that they seem totally unsuited to using that strength to their advantage. That is where we, as Australia's unchanged people, might have to step in. I'm not too sympathetic to this viewpoint, and it is not what the Cairns Project is about. The enemy we fear is not a human foe.

Certainly in Cairns there is no animosity between the two groups. We unchanged people have our mission - to maintain the diversity of the genome - and the changed people have theirs - to live life in peace and to help others to do the same.

The Cairns Project sees diversity as essential because of the possibility, however remote, that there might be some feature in the changed genome, one which would allow some new disease to insert itself into an apparently impregnable immune system. All the walls could collapse simultaneously. Given the genetic near-identity of the CP population anything that could exploit weakness in that genome could roar through the world's population like a bushfire through the eucalyptus. We have debated and discussed this ad nauseam, both among ourselves and with CPs, and even they recognize that there is some imperative that we maintain our genetic Plan B. They are just very reluctant to put us in the position of denying our own children and grandchildren the benefits that the change has brought to them.

I have two children. Julia is eight and Hiro is five. They are both unchanged, and I guess that's the point. We want genetic diversity and my children are in a sense being sacrificed for that goal. I know that at any time some virus, some cancerous growth, some auto-immune condition might carry off my daughter or her brother. They didn't make this choice. I made it for them. I can tell myself that I also made it for the sake of humanity, a sort of insurance policy on the species, but there is a huge dollop of self-congratulation if I take that route, and precious little payback at present for my children.

And for the succeeding generation more of the same awaits. The fact that we live in a community increasingly populated by unchanged people means our children are more likely to find their life partners are also unchanged.

These are the doubts we live with.

Cairns has a certain magnetism. As I said before, the city has much to offer. The location is spectacular, for one thing. We have the ocean, the reef, the mountains, the forests. As a tourist centre, we have a variety of employment in addition to the agriculture that still sustains our economy. That's not what draws most of us, though. We pull in newcomers from all over southeast Asia and the southwestern Pacific. Newcomers who are unchanged, and want to be part of our planet's insurance.

To some extent, our children are in less danger of disease because of the changed people. We do benefit a great deal from what they once called "herd immunity". With fewer people susceptible to disease, there are fewer carriers to infect others. In centuries past, it was vaccination that provided the herd effect. Now it's the enhanced immune systems of the CPs. They don't contract diseases, and they don't carry diseases. We all win. Even though the population of Cairns is half composed of unchanged people, we have a large enough reservoir of CPs to dilute the threat of infection.

That still leaves non-infectious disease. It leaves mental illnesses. It leaves crime. Big-city Sydney, formerly a place where you kept an eye on your belongings, is now virtually crime-free, thanks to the overwhelming genetic restructuring of its residents. Here we suffer from crimes both petty and major, to a degree that makes other Australians nervous about us. It doesn't prevent them from coming, but they are always a little more guarded than when they are in their home regions.

Skin cancer. Once we had a team of scientists working on ways of treating the disease that affected Queenslanders more than any other people on earth. With the change, most of that research has slowed, although we unchanged people are still just as likely to be stricken. A few people are still casting about at the Cairns Medical Research Centre, part of our extensive hospital complex, but the urgency isn't there to the degree it once was. The irony of maintaining the old gene bank as insurance for a population that doesn't see us as a priority hasn't gone unremarked, as you may already know. We harbor some resentment, but of course the CPs don't recognize an emotion they don't really get to feel themselves.

I've been to Sydney many times. Of course, it's now a much smaller city than it once was, with birth rates among the CPs being what they are, but it still dwarfs Cairns a couple of dozen times over. People there are always polite, always helpful, and always the same. In Cairns you can still see a drunk staggering along the sidewalk late at night. You can hear a couple arguing in their back garden. Not in Sydney. In Sydney, everyone is proper.

You think I am being snide, and you're probably right. You think my attitude stems from jealousy, and again you're probably on to something. If I wanted to continue being snide, I'd put my nastiness down to my genetics, which impel me to be the way I am. Still, I have the freedom to be naughty or nice.

I wonder why we have found no other species that have undergone this transformation. Only in humans does there seem to be any evidence of this massive change. Perhaps other creatures are also experiencing such a renewal, but if so, they are more obscure, perhaps some little mollusc on the ocean floor, or an insect in the rainforest. Certainly there is no evidence in the plants and animals closest to us.

I've read somewhere that the average lifetime of a species is one million years. In other words, a species evolves as a distinct species, survives for a million or so years, then either vanishes or evolves into something different. The genetic changes we've seen since El Niño haven't run their course for a half a century yet, let alone a million years, but the question arises: can we remain as a population separate from the CPs without becoming a different species? Perhaps the proper question would be to ask whether the CPs are already a separate species. I sometimes wonder what it must have been like for early humans, to have several other hominid species living alongside them. Did those ancient groups see each other as rivals or allies? I think we know the answer to that question. Homo sapiens and Homo neanderthalensis must at some point have gotten together long enough to insert Neanderthal DNA into our genome.

Not that that could happen today. If we marry (you might be more blunt and say "mate") with a changed person, any resulting children will have the new genome. We become extinct.

I am chairwoman of the Neanderthals. As mayor of Cairns, chosen by lot to the governing council and then by lot to the executive position, it is my task to ensure that everyone in the community is happy, while at the same time shepherding the Cairns Project. With the high concentration of unchanged people in the area, this is not always an easy task. Our rates of crime, illness and addiction are the highest in Australia. We have to spend money on things other municipalities have long since abandoned: policing and health care. It's true that Canberra subsidizes almost all of these costs through the arrangements for the Cairns Project, but this does not mean we feel less anxious about crime or illness. We lack the security and confidence of other places similar in size to Cairns.

And then there's the disconnect between the rates of maturing among our children. Our kids - I mean the children of unchanged people - grow up so fast by comparison. While changed children are still playing with their toys and watching animated shorts, our children have started on thinking about employment and taken a consuming interest in finding a life partner. Two separate worlds becoming increasingly distant from each other.

I am not a good administrator, even at the hotel. Everything I do seems to be done on the fly, at the last minute. My attention span needs attention. There's the trouble with the lot system of choosing a leader. The short straw doesn't usually go to the most appropriate candidate. When I argue this point, I am always told that the old system of elections didn't usually elevate the most worthy candidate, either.

So here I am, sort of managing to stay afloat in the political ocean. I have the advantage of a council that is focussed on doing the best for our community, CP and unchanged people alike. The people who work for us are capable and dedicated. The director of the Cairns Project knows what he's doing and offers me useful advice.

Yet things are not completely right in this little Eden. Our biggest challenge comes in the secondary school system, accommodating both groups of students - the intellectually able but socially and physically late-blooming CP kids and the rest of the students - our own unchanged kids, a mixed bag of learning abilities, and also often struggling with adolescence while their peers are still children. There are pressures from a number of articulate unchanged parents to have two streams in the system, one for each group, while teachers and CP parents are urging integration. My own two youngsters are not yet of an age where I have to concern myself with their personal situations, but they are going to reach the same point as other unchanged teenagers in fewer years than I like to think.

I'm still working at my restaurant three evenings a week. With the new full-employment regimen enacted by Canberra, my hours have been cut back a little, giving me more time to deal with the political side of my life. To tell you the truth, I will be glad to see the end of my term and hand the responsibility over to someone else. Though with my luck, my name will be drawn for the state parliament as soon as I'm finished here.

The school question is complicated a little further by the declining birth rate of CPs. The more they increase as a percentage of the population, the fewer children they seem to produce. At the moment, CPs comprise almost fifty percent of the population in Cairns, but only thirty percent of the students in our schools. Language classes for new arrivals in Australia are almost one hundred percent populated by unchanged kids.

My own Julia has no friends who are CP, although I believe she would be accepting of anyone. It's just that she has little contact with them. I know there are a half-dozen or so in her class at school, but none of these live near us, and she has already established quite firm friendships with three other girls who are unchanged. There was a campaign several years ago to prevent schools from disclosing which students were CP and which were not, but the attempt was unsuccessful, largely because everyone already knew who was who, and because no particular problem would be solved by suppressing the information.

Then there is the question of health care. We unchanged people obviously consume a great deal more, susceptible as we are to infection and other diseases. Our CP neighbours do call on medical assistance from time to time, of course; accidents happen. One of the desk clerks at my hotel, for instance, rammed into a rock while he was surfing a few months ago. Fractured ribs and a lot of torn flesh. Still, even when the injuries seem severe, CPs recover very quickly and therefore use up fewer resources. In a sense, they subsidize the rest of us when it comes to health care.

This is the blade on which we are balanced at the moment. How much longer can we continue in this way, with two groups whose needs are so different?

This is the burden that El Niño has bequeathed me. My first job is to protect the Cairns Project, but I must also answer to the CP population.

As mayor, I must spend my time navigating the regions between our two constituencies, both on council and in the wider world. It's a responsibility I take seriously, but nothing has really prepared me to face the questions with any confidence. There is no guide book to this task, and I know my weaknesses in managing big assignments.

But it is what it is. In the larger sense, the political and administrative background for the Cairns Project is not as important as the fact the project is underway. Some days I feel like we are specimens in a museum, the world strolling past the display case that houses us, staring intently or glancing distractedly at these relics of a history fading slowly from consciousness. Then I think about Hiro and Julia, and all the others like them, growing up in a world where they represent both loss and hope, and I wonder where we will finally arrive.

5.

MIAN YANG

MY FATHER SAYS AT least once a day that he is an unlucky man. "But Baba," I always answer. "You have a beautiful wife. And you have me."

"Yes, yes, Mei Xing, you are a fine daughter," he responds. "There is some good luck, it is true. Most of the fortune, though, is bad."

Of course, he is telling the truth. Life has not been easy for him. His parents came from Weifang, in Shandong Province, part of the resettlement to Tibet and Sichuan that was the government's attempt to make the ethnic areas more Chinese. Tibet was still sullenly resisting the national authorities, and sometimes violence broke out in the monasteries or even in the city streets. I thought monks were always peaceful people. In the end, his mother and father came to live in Beichuan, a holiday town in Sichuan Province. My grandfather worked in the China Post banking office and my grandmother was a bus driver. Because both my grandparents had no brothers or sisters, they were allowed to have more than one child themselves, and my father had an older sister.

On the day of the great earthquake, his parents were at work, his sister in her primary classroom and he in the bus company day nursery. Just before the earth shook and the mountainside swallowed up part of the town, my father's *bao mu* had taken her group of children out to the play area. When their day nursery building collapsed, they were spared, although several of them suffered injuries from flying glass fragments.

Baba's sister was killed in her classroom, and his father at his desk in the post office bank. His mother was crushed when a building toppled into the roadway and struck the bus she was driving. In less than five minutes, Baba lost all his family. I have been several times to visit the old town of Beichuan. The roadways have been cleared of rubble, but most of the rest has been left as it was after the earthquake, as a sort of memorial to those who died on that terrible day.

I get off the bus at the checkpoint, no longer guarded by soldiers, and walk down the long road into the town, passing small groups of people returning from the ruins. I bring a white carnation to tie to one of the fences in memory of Baba's parents and sister. In the town, other visitors speak softly and wander along the streets, stopping occasionally before the small photographs of the people who died in the earthquake. I fasten the carnation gently to the chain link barrier that prevents visitors from going right in to the ruins of the primary school, bow three times and continue to the ruins of the post office bank. I repeat the bows and ask the spirit of my grandfather to find peace. I think my grandmother is buried in the communal grave in the centre of town, but we have no record of that. I bow and whisper to her spirit as well.

At the old hotel, still standing but with the glass missing from all its windows, the wind is moving a loose piece of painted metal siding, making a sound like someone moaning in deep pain. It is an eerie reminder. The river spills out of the old road tunnel and across part of the collapsed bridge, flowing over it instead of under. A curtain waves in the glassless window of a ruined apartment, the fabric faded and ragged. As the sun sinks lower, the hills to the west cast a heavy shadow over everything, and the air grows cool. I begin the long walk back up the road to the bus stop and the ride back to Mian Yang.

To say that Baba was lucky to escape death that day is not completely true. He escaped death to become an orphan, eventually to forget what his mother's face looked like, to forget the shoulder rides his father perhaps had given him, to grow up without his sister to guide his path.

The calamity was eased by his *bao mu*. She and her husband had been unable to have any children, not even one, and Baba was a healthy three year old boy with no family. Her husband, who was a town functionary and party member, made arrangements to adopt Baba, giving him a new family name, Zhou, instead of Ma. His *bao mu* became Nainai, my grandmother. They moved to Chengdu, the provincial capital, where his new father was appointed to the party commission overseeing the rebuilding of the villages and towns damaged by the earthquake.

Most of the suffering was borne by the Qiang people, an ethnic group who have lived in this part of Sichuan Province since the beginning. Thousands died; the middle and primary schools in Beichuan crumbled just as afternoon classes were beginning. Few children escaped. The investigation afterward found that corrupt officials in the government and the construction companies had failed in their duty to the people, especially in school buildings. Schools a hundred kilometres away were destroyed, when buildings around them were spared. The people were enraged in their sorrow; the Party was forced to act and many officials were punished severely.

The Party decreed that a new town would be built, south of the old town, to house the survivors and become the new administrative centre of the county. New Beichuan would have the most capable engineers; money was coming in from Hong Kong, Taiwan and the overseas Chinese. Japan, Korea and other countries offered aid and technological advice. Soon Baba's father was traveling every week to the new town; eventually, once the first apartment buildings were ready, he moved his wife and Baba to the town.

The river in Old Beichuan is a wild, clear stream, rushing noisily over the gravel. The new town has its own stream, but it is sluggish, brownish-green and covered in scum. Nonetheless, the parkland is beautiful, with many trees and shrubs. Azaleas bloom in abundance in the spring. Plum trees perfume the air. There is an astonishing pavilion decorated in traditional style in blue and gold; I go there sometimes just to sit and reflect.

This new town became Baba's home. He and his friends would play in the parks, watch outdoor movies in the Memorial Square. He attended the primary school in the centre of town. When it came time to go to high school, he was enrolled in Beichuan High School, a school famous throughout Sichuan for the excellence of its program, especially the quality of its English language classes.

In high school, though, Baba was always an outsider. "The Qiang boys and girls were always kind to me," he says, "but I wasn't one of them. I learned the Qiang dances in kindergarten; I knew the songs and many of the stories, but I wasn't Qiang. Like most of my teachers, I was Han, the adopted son of Han parents. We were the majority in China; we still are. Even the friends I had in primary school knew I was different. I was never invited to their homes, and they never came to mine. We played together, studied together, did our school chores together, but there was always a distance between us. I don't know why. It was my bad fortune."

Baba went back to Chengdu to study chemical engineering at Sichuan University. As the son of a Party official, he got preferential treatment, but really didn't need it. He had done well in Beichuan, especially in mathematics and chemistry. "Mei Xing," he sometimes tells me, "I was a good student.

I studied hard, but everyone thought my success was because of my father's position. This troubled me often."

He was hoping to find a position in an export company after he graduated; instead, he was recruited by the army to work in the new Military Institute of Chemistry here in Mian Yang. This came as a surprise, because Baba had not done any military service. The laws on military service had never been changed, but no one seemed to think it was compulsory any more.

"They put me to work on explosives," says Baba. "I spent every minute in that laboratory thinking I might be blown to pieces at any time. Then I was supposed to develop more efficient gas masks; experimenting with toxic gases did not feel any safer. Now that the Institute studies ways to clean up China's pollution, I feel better, but there are still some very dangerous parts to the job."

My grandmother, Nainai, had progressed from working in a day nursery to becoming the director and then at last being appointed inspector of day nurseries throughout all of Mian Yang municipality, and on one of her visits to a day nursery in Anxian she met a young woman who was not at the nursery the last time she had come to inspect. She had arrived only three weeks earlier from Yichang, much further down the Yangtze River.

"The first thing your grandmother noticed was how beautiful this girl was. Then she saw how the children flocked to her. She was firm but gentle, teaching the boys and girls how to behave in correct ways. She did not punish them; she had a skill of making them want to be good children. When your grandmother talked with her afterward, it was clear this young woman was clever and modest as well."

"That sounds like Mama," I always answer. Baba smiles and nods. If Mama is around to hear us, she clucks at us, but smiles anyway.

"Yes, Mei Xing. Your grandmother had an eye for perfection. Remember that at the time there were many young men and fewer young women. It was not easy to find a wife; we were paying the price for always wanting boy children—somehow we always thought someone else could bear the girl children for our sons to grow up and marry. How foolish we were."

"When Nainai had finished the inspection of the nursery, she stayed to talk with this young woman. Nainai was very bold—she asked her about her family, about her schooling; whether she had a young man in her life already. Only your grandmother would have had the daring to ask such things. That evening she came to tell me about her meeting and to ask my opinion."

This is the point where I am supposed to ask what happened next. Baba waits patiently for me to prod him, then continues.

"Ah, Mei Xing. I had been so busy with my education, then with my work, that I hadn't given much thought to marriage, but I certainly agreed to meet this young woman. We went two days later to Anxian. Your grandmother had already called the nursery, spoken to the young woman and the director, and arranged for us to have our midday meal at a small restaurant nearby—with the young woman, me, your grandmother and the director of the day nursery all seated around the table. Nainai introduced us and made a little speech of welcome. As host of the luncheon, she was expected to deal with the formalities. I was so nervous I could hardly hold the chopsticks. I was afraid I would drop noodles onto the table, or worse. The young woman seemed calm and slightly amused; she did not look directly at me, but it was clear why we were all at the table."

This is my signal. I am to ask if they spoke with each other.

"We did not say a single word to each other. We spoke only to answer the questions Nainai or the director posed to us. Nainai scolded me afterward for being too shy. 'How is the girl to know if you will make a good husband?' I was just grateful the noodles had stayed off the tablecloth."

I know my role perfectly. "Did you see the girl again, Baba?"

"Ah, yes. A week later we went back to the same restaurant, but this time without our elders. I was not as nervous and she was not as silent. She looked at me and smiled several times. I think we had both decided."

"What was her name, Baba?"

"Ah, patience, Mei Xing. She was so beautiful, so graceful, so gentle, so wise. There were many names that would have suited her. After we met for the third time, at another small restaurant near her apartment, I asked Nainai to contact her parents and make arrangements for the families to meet and discuss marriage. At this time, your grandfather was an important official, but I did not want that to frighten the girl's family, so I asked Nainai not to mention it until we had met."

"We traveled to Yichang to meet her family. She, of course, stayed in Mian Yang, but her father and mother knew her feelings. I was worried they would not approve; after all, I was not handsome or strong or rich. I had been a good student, and my father and mother were both important party officials, but I didn't want the girl's parents to consent out of fear."

"That is very wise, Baba. A marriage should be based on true feelings." I smile at the game we are playing.

"I did not need to worry. The girl had told her parents how she felt about me. It is the only lucky thing that has ever happened to me. I married An Ming later that year."

"She has the same name as Mama!" As a small child, I said this in surprise. Now it is part of the ritual Baba and I share. I continue with the game. "Wasn't having me a lucky thing for you, too, Baba?" I already know the answer.

"Of course. But you should have had a brother, to carry on the family name." When I was small, I just accepted this idea as given, but later I grew to question it. Which family name? His birth name or his adopted name? And what of his claim that our old preference for boys was foolish? I never spoke these questions aloud; it would be disrespectful.

"You are lucky, Mei Xing. You have your mother's beauty and wisdom, and her good fortune. You will do well."

This conversation was repeated many times. It once ended with me climbing onto Baba's lap and getting a hug. Now we just smile at each other.

Mama has a slightly different story. In her telling, Baba is a kind boy who shows interest in her when she is far from home and beginning a new career. She says it is lucky I am a girl, because it would have been difficult to find a wife for me if I had been a boy. She says I have Baba's strong brain and his willingness to work hard.

Mama has another story, one that Baba does not tell me. Even Mama waits until I am already finished high school to tell me.

"Mei Xing, you have never asked about Baba's father. In all the stories you have heard about him, he is an important person. Does it not seem strange that you know Nainai, but have never met her husband?" I am suddenly flooded with shame. How could I not have wondered about him? My self-centered thinking shows disrespect. I turn red and look at the floor.

"I am sorry, Mama. I have not been a good granddaughter."

"No. You have been very polite. Baba does not talk about his father because he feels shame."

This shocks me. Baba is ashamed of his father?

"Your grandfather lives in Chengdu, Mei Xing. He has a sickness of the mind. This began to show openly the year before you were born, and he has never recovered. He is in a secure hospital in the city, where he cannot harm himself or others. Baba visits him, but the visiting does not go well.

Nainai also goes to see him, but your grandfather grows very angry when he sees her and she does not go often."

I am silent. How can I have failed to notice all of this?

"There is much more to tell. I think you should know the whole story, Mei Xing. You are old enough now to understand. Your father blames himself, but this is not fair. The times were not simple, and there were many things to be considered."

"You know that many of your school mates have not grown up as quickly as you. They are *Xin de jian kang*." This much I already know. I also know that no one in my family is *Xin de jian kang*. We talk about *Jian kang*, the healthy people, with just a touch of envy. They grow up more slowly, it is true, but they are never sick, never quarrel, are always polite to everyone, and study very well in school. More than half the students in my high school are *Jian kang*, and there are more every year.

"Do you know why they are *Jian kang*?" I nod.

"They have rapid evolution. Some say it is because of a boy."

"The year before you were born, the same year your grandfather grew ill, something very strange happened. Beijing television was reporting unusual events in Africa. People claimed that there was a boy there who could cure diseases."

I had heard this story. I also had heard that the boy came to China; in fact, he had been here in Mian Yang, as well as in Deyang, Chengdu and some of the mountain towns.

"The boy was here. I had gone to Yichang to see my mother, who was sick at that time. Baba stayed here, partly because of his work and partly because Nainai was growing more worried about your grandfather. You see, Mei Xing, his sickness made him think someone was trying to hurt him, maybe even kill him. He didn't know who, and this made him suspicious of everyone, even Nainai and Baba. The people who worked with him in the Party office found it more and more difficult to bear his accusations. Soon the Party Secretary in Chengdu was called in, and your grandfather was given a medical leave and ordered to seek treatment.

"Still, he did not trust the doctors at all, and even after several weeks of medication, his condition did not improve. He began to speak about killing his enemies, and Baba grew very alarmed. He was afraid his father would try to act on his threats.

"Just as your grandfather reached the worst point Baba had ever seen, that boy, the one they said could cure diseases, appeared here in Mian Yang.

We knew what to expect, because he had already healed so many thousands of people in other places. He had come already to three small villages in the Tibet border area, and when word of his being in Mian Yang spread, people hurried to see him. He was in the large park in Puming Area at the time, you see.

"Baba heard the news and immediately thought to bring his father to the boy. Your grandfather was very displeased at this idea, but with Nainai's help, Baba persuaded him to come, just to have a walk in Puming. Baba did not know that his father had a kitchen knife—one of the curved fish knives—inside his jacket. We never learned how he had come to possess such a weapon, although the utensil was perhaps common enough in those days. The buses seemed to be running at odd times, and all were going towards or away from Puming. Baba and his mother and father got on a bus heading for Puming. Your grandfather was quite agitated, and it was all Baba and Nainai could do to keep him in his seat.

"Suddenly they were slowing down, with army vehicles on either side of the bus. There were many soldiers, and your grandfather cried out that it was a trap. He pulled out the knife from his jacket and swung it at Baba.

"Baba was caught by surprise, but managed to jump away in time to avoid injury. The driver opened both doors of the bus and people began to run out. Your grandfather dropped the knife and ran after them, then turned and headed away from Puming. Baba followed, calling out that there was no danger, but your grandfather would not stop, or even listen. More army trucks passed, and one of them stopped. Soldiers clambered out of the back, some surrounding Baba and others running after your grandfather. Soon they caught up with him, but this only made him more upset. He dodged away and ran again, faster than before. He was very strong and could move so quickly. Baba explained what he was trying to do, but by this time your grandfather was already into the narrow streets south of the highway, and within minutes the soldiers had lost track of him.

"Baba sent Nainai on to Puming on another bus, and ran into the neighborhood where your grandfather had gone. He spent four hours searching, but had no luck. Later, after it was dark, some citizens found your grandfather lying unconscious near the river. They sent him by ambulance to Meikang Hospital, where he was examined in the admitting area and then assigned to a ward.

"Baba went to the police to report his father's disappearance, and then began to check the hospitals. By luck, Meikang was the first one he went to, and there he found his father, still unconscious. He wanted to take him to Puming, but it was now dark, and he was not sure that the boy was still there, so he called Nainai's mobile. She did not answer.

"You must understand, Mei Xing, he faced a very difficult decision. He could try and take his father to Puming, but the trip might be in vain and his father might come to new harm on the way. If he left his father at Meikang, the boy might be gone before he had another chance to take your grandfather there. We knew the boy did not stay long in one place, but he had been in Xi'an, it was said, for almost a week. Of course, Xi'an is a much larger city than Mian Yang.

"In the end, Baba chose to stay at the hospital with his father, and by the next day, when your grandfather was again awake, the boy was gone. Baba found out later that the boy had stayed at Puming well into the night, and that people were still crowding to him while Baba sat for hours beside your grandfather's bed in Meikang. Baba has not forgiven himself for this. He is sure that he made the wrong decision, and no matter how many times Nainai or I try to reassure him, he always comes back to blaming himself."

"What about Nainai, Mama? Did she go to Puming? Did she see the boy?"

"No. She was worried about her husband, and even more worried about Baba. She did not know whether your grandfather had yet another knife or other weapon besides the one he dropped at the bus. She went to the police, and somewhere along the way she also lost her mobile. She never found it. The police had no information at that time, and in fact they were very busy with the crowd at Puming, and Nainai went home to see if Baba or your grandfather would be there. Of course, they were not. She used the extra mobile to call Baba, but he had accidentally turned his own mobile off. She left a message and spent a long night waiting for him to call.

"In the end, none of us—not Baba, not his parents, not me—met the boy. By the time he reappeared in Deyang and then Chengdu, it was impossible to move your grandfather without some sort of sedation, and the highways were a confusion of traffic; ambulances and police, even soldiers, were being called in to help sort things out. I came back from Yichang to find Baba in despair, trying to persuade Nainai to go to Chengdu without him, and Nainai refusing to leave her son and husband. I tried to persuade Baba and his mother to go with me to Chengdu, saying that your grandfather would be well cared-for in the hospital, but they would not hear of it. Now Baba also blames himself for refusing to follow my advice, leaving

Nainai and me without the protection the boy was offering. And of course, when you were born, that was one more. We learned later that the children of *Jian kang* also become *Jian kang*, even if one of their parents is not. His decision—and I must say our decision, because I too gave up when I should have persevered—meant that you lost your chance to be *Jian kang*."

"It is all right, Mama. I do not care. You and Baba honored your duty to Grandfather. No one will blame you."

"We blame ourselves, Mei Xing. We cannot escape the accusations we throw in our own faces."

This is my introduction to the world of adults. There are secret stories we hold back from our children, to protect them or perhaps to protect the stories. In the end, perhaps some stories die with their keepers, but many seem to find a way out of the darkness. I am happy that my mother trusts me with our family secret; still, I have not told my own children. My children, however, are far in the future when the secret reaches me. I have many years to make peace with it.

In high school, I do well in sciences, especially biology, and for a while I think perhaps I will study medicine. After the boy's visit, though, it slowly becomes clear that medicine is a dying profession. *Jian kang* do not need doctors unless they are severely injured; either they heal quickly or they die quickly. They do not contract diseases like the rest of us still do, and even we are healthier because fewer people carry harmful viruses and bacteria. Veterinary medicine is a possibility, but the nature of farming is also changing because of the *Jian kang*, who do not eat meat. In the end I abandon biology and go to Chengdu to study engineering like Baba did. He is a chemical engineer, and I study industrial engineering. Technology is transforming as well, especially in the production of energy.

At university, I meet many students who are *Jian kang*, and many who are not. We are all friends. *Jian kang* are polite and honest; the rest of us are just as polite but perhaps not as honest. I do not believe any *Jian kang* would cheat on an examination or plagiarize work for a paper, but I know of some others who have done so. This makes me ashamed, but my *Jian kang* friends do not seem to judge the dishonest ones.

Some of us, however, judge the *Jian kang*. "They do not have to work hard like us. They are lucky—they learn so easily. They are born with intelligence and good memory. It is not fair to the rest of us." I do not like to hear such talk.

The other difference, of course, is that *Jian kang* students seem so much younger than we do. The boys do not shave, and the girls sometimes have not even begun their monthly periods. They do not think about man and woman matters; they are concerned with doing well in their studies and bringing honor to their families, but not about finding a husband. Often I wish I could be more like them. I am finding the boys, sometimes even the *Jian kang* boys, more interesting than my studies.

Still, I graduate with excellent reports. Baba is proud of me. He, Mama and Nainai are all at my graduation ceremony. Afterward we go to a small restaurant to celebrate. Baba orders all my favorite foods: duck, pork and fish. There is tea and durian pudding to finish off.

It is not until we return to Mian Yang that Baba tells me the news. Nainai has stomach cancer and will not live much longer. I realize then that even during the meal at the restaurant she had seemed pale and tired, and I am shamed by my failure to see sooner.

"This is my fault," Baba says, with tears in his eyes. "If I had taken her to the boy, she would not become sick. She would be strong and live for many more years. I have failed in my duty."

I can think of nothing to say that will comfort him. I reach out and touch his hand. He does not withdraw from me; he looks into my eyes with such intensity that I am forced to turn away. I know he is thinking that he has failed to protect me as well. I should tell him that no, he has not failed in his duty. He has brought honor to his family and done all anyone could ask. My head aches from the sorrow of losing Nainai and I can find no words.

I could also tell him that at the university, some people are saying that the boy did not exist, that the changes in *Jian kang* are simply evolution at work, and would happen whether the boy were there or not. Again I keep silent, although I do not know why.

As Nainai grows weaker, I find employment with the People's Liberation Army. The factories in Mian Yang supply much of the equipment the army uses, and I am assigned to the research laboratory that works on battery development. As we try to eliminate gasoline and diesel fuels, we must find ways of storing large amounts of electricity to operate vehicles for many hours a day, and develop processes to recharge the cells quickly and completely. Much of this research has been started by teams in North America, and we are partnered with engineers in Vancouver and Seattle; such sharing would have been unthinkable even two decades ago, but it is becoming almost routine now.

As I begin my new duties, Baba spends more and more time caring for Nainai. It is Baba who takes her to her hospital treatments. She protests that it is a waste of his time; the doctors have already told her there is no real chance of a cure, but Baba insists on trying. While I have been away at university, Nainai has moved into my old room in the apartment. Baba and Mama say I can have their room, but I am just as comfortable sleeping on a quilt on the floor in the front room. There is not much privacy, of course, but I have not had privacy at university and do not much miss it.

We have worked for two years now without making the breakthrough we had hoped for in the battery design, but now there is good news about Nainai. In spite of all the predictions the doctors made, she has survived for these two years, although she is very frail. Baba is still hopeful she will recover and searches the markets every day for foods he thinks will help restore her strength.

I have met a young man at the laboratory. He is *Jian kang*; his name is Zhou Bao Jia. I think he may be interested in me, because he is more attentive than he needs to be and asks questions when I think he already knows the answers. I am not sure if he knows I am not *Jian kang*. When I tell Baba about him, though, Baba is alarmed.

"Mei Xing, he has the same family name as you. It is bad luck to marry someone with the same family name."

"But Baba, no one is getting married. And even if we do, isn't our real family Ma?"

"No. Our real family is the family of Nainai, the family Zhou."

"That is grandfather's family name. Nainai's family name is Wang." Baba catches his breath; he looks stunned. I am ashamed to make him lose face. I should not argue with him.

"You are right, Mei Xing," he sighs. "Do you like this Zhou Bao Jia?"

"I do," I reply, "But there is much still to learn about him. I will listen more at work and see what he tells me. I need to let him know more about myself, too. Perhaps he will not see me as suitable if I am not *Jian kang*." By now, to be *Jian kang* is an advantage to bring to marriage, because children will also be strong and healthy.

"Many *Jian kang* have married wives or husbands who are not *Jian kang*. You are beautiful and clever, Mei Xing, and you work hard. You are kind and polite. No one could ask for more." I am embarrassed by Baba's praise, and I look away so he cannot see me smile.

During the next few weeks Zhou Bao Jia and I work together on a rare-earth battery. Most days he speaks only of the research we are doing, but occasionally he gives me some small piece of information about himself. He was born in Chongqing; studied, like me, at Sichuan University School of Engineering. He is the same age as me, but I did not share any classes with him in university. He was in chemical engineering, like Baba. His parents are *Jian kang*, too. He has no brothers or sisters, so it is good his parents will not need care when they age.

"What of you, Mei Xing? Have you a brother or sister? Have you always lived in Mian Yang?" No one has asked me such questions since I was in the residence at university—and no boy asked then. I have trouble answering him without shaking. He does not ask if I am *Jian kang*.

One of our colleagues, Miss Wu, is leaving to take up a position in Beijing with the Central Military Commission. There will be a formal dinner to honor her, but we in the laboratory also plan a small dinner to say goodbye and wish her success. At the table I notice Bao Jia is seated only one space away from me. I wonder if this is accidental, or whether someone has arranged to place us close enough to talk. During the conversation, Bao Jia offers to go with her to the airport, to help carry the luggage. He suggests that I and another colleague also go along to see her off. Before I can answer, she thanks him warmly and says how moved she is by our kindness. I can not refuse now.

On Saturday, Bao Jia calls at my house with the laboratory's van. One of our male colleagues, Mr Zhang, is already with him. Bao Jia gets out of the driver's seat and speaks politely with Baba; I climb into the van, afraid someone will notice my blushing. Within ten minutes we have called at Miss Wu's apartment, helped her load her luggage into the van, and turned south toward Nanjiao Airport. Miss Wu is very excited about her new position, and talks almost without stopping, all the way to the airport. I am grateful for her chatter.

Bao Jia and Mr Zhang unload the luggage and place it on an airport cart, then we all push into the departures area where Miss Wu checks in with Air China. There is no reason to linger, but we do. Miss Wu's flight departs in an hour and twenty minutes, and we find ourselves in a corner of the airport where a small café sells tea and cakes. Bao Jia buys refreshments for all four of us and we sit at a small table to share. Miss Wu speaks of the responsibilities she will have in Beijing, but I am not really listening. Twice I see Bao Jia's eyes on me. I know.

Bao Jia takes Mr Zhang back to his apartment before driving me home. On the way to my apartment, he asks if I have ever been to the Sanxingdui Museum in Guanghan. I have not.

"Will you go with me next weekend? I have only been there once myself, and there is so much to see." I agree to accompany him to Guanghan on Saturday.

When the day arrives, I find myself paying close attention to the way I dress. I shower and shampoo more thoroughly, put on a tiny bit of eau de cologne. I choose my royal blue skirt, a white blouse and a blue cardigan. I pin up my hair and apply a hint of makeup. This is not a wedding, I tell myself. But it is not a regular working day, either.

Bao Jia has borrowed the laboratory van again. We head down the G5 highway. It will take almost an hour to reach Guanghan and find the museum, but the road is not busy. Bao Jia seems relaxed and happy. He talks about the museum and about the Shu people, the mysterious ancient culture that once lived and ruled here in this part of Sichuan. He tells how they were lost to our history until a farmer unearthed a large jade wheel more than a century ago.

The museum is set in beautiful tree-covered grounds, with lovely pathways winding around great earth mounds that represent the structures of the Shu people. Over three thousand years have passed since this site was the centre of the Shu civilization, and as I walk silently beside Bao Jia I can almost sense the souls of the people who lived and died here so very long ago.

Inside the museum are breath-taking treasures of gold, silver, bronze and jade. Strange masks of all sizes stare out at us from their glass cases, the eyes stylized and inset with jade, contrasting with the gold or bronze. Jade discs, gold knives, sceptres in precious metals—there are so many treasures one can only wander in a daze from one room to another. The most amazing objects are the gigantic masks and the gold and bronze "Trees of Life", which stretch upwards to the ceiling, their metallic leaves glittering in the light. It is difficult to imagine that these beautiful objects are three thousand years old. Life must have been good for people to be able to make such things.

By the time we leave the second gallery, Bao Jia has his arm around my waist. I am not comfortable with such a public display, but I do not want him to feel rejected. When we reach one of the reconstructed temple pyramids on the museum grounds, he clambers to the top. I remain at the base.

Climbing a pyramid in a skirt is not prudent. I use my phone to capture a photo of Bao Jia at the top. He is smiling down at me.

We find a small noodle house on a narrow side street in Guanghan. Across the road I can see a market stall selling the most beautiful oranges and watermelons I have ever seen. Bao Jia orders for us and we sit looking at each other. I am unsure what to say, and Bao Jia rescues me from my silence by chatting about the museum and the life of the Shu people.

Then he turns serious. "Mei Xing," he says, then stops. I look at him and nod, prompting him to continue.

"Mei Xing, I have been thinking a great deal these days. It has been almost a year since we have begun working together. I enjoy being in your company. I hope you find me acceptable too." He looks at me intently. I smile and nod.

"I think we are good for each other." He is interrupted by the arrival of the noodles, and I find myself disappointed as he busies himself with arranging the bowls, the extra rice, the pickles, the chopsticks.

"I hope you like the food," he says. I begin to eat, and the noodles are done perfectly.

"It is very good," I say. He does not pick up the thread of his talk; he just smiles and eats.

On the drive back to Mian Yang, he asks if I would like to go to Chengdu to revisit our university grounds and perhaps see the panda centre again before it is closed down. I agree and we arrange to make the trip the following week.

It is a trip we do not make. On Wednesday, one of the battery prototypes we have been working on overheats and explodes, wrecking part of the laboratory and spraying Bao Jia with caustic chemicals. I run to help him up. A piece of metal has become embedded in his neck, but does not seem to have struck a major blood vessel. I know not to remove the metal, and as others rush into the laboratory, I ask someone to call for medical help; I take a towel and begin wiping the chemicals from Bao Jia's skin. By the time the paramedics arrive, I have cleared most of the liquid from his face, which shows deep red patches of burn.

I am not allowed in the ambulance, but I learn that he is being taken to Central Hospital. I leave the others to secure the explosion site and call in the investigators, and take the bus to Central Hospital. I know that Bao Jia has no family in Mian Yang, and it will be a day or so before his parents can arrive from Chongqing. I decide to stay with him until someone else comes.

By the time I find him in the hospital, though, he is already sitting up, a white bandage on his neck. His skin looks as if it has been briskly scrubbed with a brush; it is the burn from the chemicals. His eyes, luckily, have been spared.

"Hello, Mei Xing. Are you all right? Did any of the chemical touch you?" I shake my head no, and ask how he is.

"A little sore from the burn and the cut in my neck, but not bad. I can come back to work tomorrow. It is lucky I heal quickly."

This is the time I must tell him. "Bao Jia," I say. "I am a little jealous. If it had been I who was burned, it would take weeks to recover. I am not *Jian kang*."

"I know," he replies. "That is why it is good I was burned, not you."

"You know? But how? I have never spoken of it."

"A mosquito bite. When we were taking Miss Wu to the airport, you had a mosquito bite on your arm. You must have been scratching at it; there was a red bump. *Jian kang* do not react to the mosquito like that."

"But if you knew, why did you not say anything?"

"It was not important. We are not defined by *Jian kang* or not *Jian kang*. We are who we are. Mei Xing, let us marry."

This catches me off guard. Bao Jia speaks in a matter-of-fact manner, but he is smiling widely. Is he teasing me?

"Are you serious?" is all I can manage to stammer out.

"Yes," he says. The smile remains.

"Then yes, from me also."

"I must call my parents and ask them to begin the arrangements. When shall we hold the wedding?"

"Bao Jia, you are still in hospital. We can make plans when you are well again. We do not need to hurry."

"I am well enough now, but you are right. There is no need to hurry. I will ask your parents for permission as soon as my mother and father can get here from Chongqing."

Thus I find myself betrothed; Bao Jia's parents arrive soon after with the gifts for my family, and the engagement is blessed. Nainai is very pleased. She will live to see me married.

I have not told Bao Jia about my grandfather; when I do, he is sympathetic. He says this saddens him, but it is not something we can change; worrying about it will not help.

There is no reason to delay the marriage. We arrange for our work supervisor, Mrs Li, to preside. Bao Jia will decorate his apartment and set up the wedding canopy; we will live there, not with his parents. We go together to the city offices to complete the documents, then I return home to my mother and father. Baba is very pleased with this marriage. "Mei Xing, your children will be *Jian kang*. They will have the protection from their father that I failed to give you."

I think of repeating Bao Jia's comment about *Jian kang* and not *Jian kang*, but decide to keep silent on the matter. Baba is happy and I am happy with him. There is much to do. Our parents arrange a restaurant for the wedding feast, Mrs Li is contacted again, the dowry is prepared. We must wait four weeks for the day, but I wonder if there will be time for everything. Bao Jia says I need not worry.

When the day arrives, I go by car to Bao Jia's apartment building. It is a beautiful warm day, with no sign of the rain we have feared. There are few guests, mostly colleagues from the laboratory and some of our parents' friends. We have no brothers or sisters, and friends fill in for them at the ceremony. Someone lights the firecrackers and everyone throws the ribbons over me as I step from the car. Bao Jia has a speaker playing traditional music. Neighbors gather around to watch; even some passers-by stop and join the audience.

Mrs Li has the authority to conduct the ceremony, and she does not take long to begin. There are speeches in praise of Bao Jia's hard work, his ability to care for a family, his politeness and his good looks, and other speeches about my wisdom, my appearance, my gentle manner. Blessings are said so we will have healthy children. There are no children in the gathering to climb up onto the marriage bed, but that does not trouble us. Our wedding is only partly traditional, after all.

The wedding feast brings me knowledge that I should have already found: Bao Jia and his parents do not eat meat or fish. There is a brief period of embarrassment on both sides, and Bao Jia whispers to me that for *Jian kang* meat is difficult to digest and therefore unattractive. I look at the platters of duck, chicken, pork and fish, and Bao Jia tells me not to worry. There is plenty of food without meat. He has ensured there will be something for everyone at the feast. It is true; there are noodle dishes and rice and all manner of vegetables. No one goes hungry and Baba does not lose face in front of the guests.

If the wedding had been more traditional, the young men—our brothers, if we had any—would have accompanied us to the bridal chamber, making jokes about the married life we were beginning. It is a relief just to say good night to everyone and return to Bao Jia's—our—apartment for the evening. I am not shy, but I worry that I will not be everything Bao Jia is hoping for. Luckily, he does not seem displeased. We help each other undress and then we slip under the cool, smooth covers.

We have three days off work, and we finally make the trip to Chengdu, but we do not visit either the university or the panda centre. Bao Jia has booked a room at the Crowne Plaza Hotel, the most luxurious hotel in the city. The lobby is as vast and open as the airport arrivals area in Mian Yang. The hotel has large, western-style rooms with views of the city that are astonishing. The bathroom has a whirlpool tub and even a western-style toilet. I feel as elegant as a princess.

The restaurants all have floor to ceiling windows, and at night the lights of the city transform Chengdu into a magic place. I wonder how I can return to Mian Yang and the laboratory.

When we do return, we find things have changed. Australian researchers have announced major advances in the same type of battery technology we have been working on; including neodymium in the battery itself as well as in the motor makes it last longer. The Australians are allowing other scientists to study the reasons for this, giving access to all their data. The important news is that the new batteries will allow a long haul train to travel from Melbourne to Sydney, a distance of almost a thousand kilometres. This is much farther than a battery-powered train has been able to travel without recharging. The train will have only two wagons at first, but Australia plans to expand this as the technology permits.

The Party asks us to start work immediately on this new battery and motor combination; the Ministry of Transport has two rail projects they want to convert to battery power: Beijing to Tianjin and Hong Kong to Guangzhou. Both these lines are already high-speed corridors, but much shorter than the planned line in Australia.

"This is a good reason to leave off the military work," says Bao Jia. "The government will not say it out loud yet, but the army is growing less important every year. Most units are now being trained in disaster relief, even more than in warfare."

"How do you know this?" I ask, a little alarmed that Bao Jia might be risking security offenses.

"It was on television," he says, smiling. His information must be correct; we have never been asked to resume our work for the military.

Exactly six months after our wedding, Nainai dies of her cancer. At the end she is given many drugs that dull the pain but also make her sleep. When I go to visit her in the care centre, she is not conscious. Baba sits with her many hours each day until one day her heart simply stops and she is gone.

"Nainai is now at peace; she is with the ancestors, and she has had a good life," says Baba, but I can see he is very sad. He no longer speaks of the boy who came to Mian Yang almost thirty years ago, but I think he still blames himself for not taking his parents to Puming that day. My grandfather, too, is in poor health; his mental sickness has been worsened by a stroke. He has only partly recovered the use of his right arm. He also finds it difficult to walk, and this makes him even angrier than he was before. He does not come to Nainai's funeral.

We begin to manufacture the battery and motor combinations that the Australians have developed. Our partners in Canada and America have also begun to change the rail systems, with battery-powered trains planned for the Edmonton to Calgary and New York to Washington routes.

It is another two years, though, before the first train makes its trip completely on battery power. Our Beijing to Tianjin run is ready before the Australian project, and we are able to reach a speed of almost three hundred kilometres an hour on the short distance; it takes less than twenty minutes. The Australians, we learn, have been developing solar powered recharging stations as well, and again they share the technology with others. China has been supplying most of the world's neodymium, but new mines have been opened in Australia and Russia as well.

It is a surprise to discover I am pregnant. Bao Jia wants to tell everyone right away, but I insist we wait until we are sure the baby is growing well. Bao Jia does not understand what could possibly go wrong, but I am uneasy.

Eventually, though, we tell his parents and mine. Mama and Baba are very excited, and Mama begins looking for baby clothes and blankets. I tell her we do not even know if the baby will be a boy or a girl, but she continues her search. Baba is quietly happy. I find him smiling at me when he does not think I am looking, and he is a little embarrassed when I turn and smile back.

The baby is a boy, healthy and content. We name him An, because he brings us peace. The blood sample shows that An is *Jian kang*, like his father. We are reminded that the stages of development will come much later than they did for me, and that I should not worry about this. An is so wonderful that I am ready to spend my lifetime raising him if need be.

Big changes are beginning to come in the Chinese economy, changes that make life easier for us. The old corruption of officials seems to have ended, and the public service really serves the people. The government is now spending much less on the military, on health care, on policing, and many who were employed in these fields are being retrained for new positions. To make sure everyone can work, many positions are now four days a week instead of five or six; some people are working only three days. Salaries have been maintained, though, so no one is going hungry. Bao Jia and I are both on four day weeks, as is Baba, but Mama is working three days. An stays with her when Bao Jia and I are both at work.

Baba has been transferred to the Ministry of Environmental Protection, where he works on the problem of China's polluted water, air and soil. With our population stable and even declining slightly, we have plenty of farmland for growing crops. There are fewer and fewer farms that have animals, and the runoff from fertilizer is less than it has been in a century. Still, there is enough toxic waste in our country to keep Baba and his fellow engineers busy for many years.

He likes the work, but he still complains. "Mei Xing, I am unfortunate. I must travel all over Sichuan for my work, and sometime I have to go to Chongqing or even Beijing. I can not spend as much time with you and with An as I would like." I know he really means time with An; he clearly adores his grandson. Unless he is attending a meeting in Beijing, he is always home for the weekend, so he does see An at least three days of every week.

When An is three years old, I am pregnant again. This we have hoped for, but many *Jian kang* parents have only one child and are unable to have a second. Again the baby is healthy and peaceful, again it is a boy. We name him Cai, because we are fortunate to have two children. Cai is also *Jian kang*. An is still in diapers and still feeding from the breast, but now Bao Jia and I are both on three day weeks like Mama, so there is plenty of time to care for the babies.

Like most children now, An does not start kindergarten until he is six. He looks so small; I am reluctant to let him go when we reach the school gates each morning, but he loves school and does well. He has been talking since he was eighteen months old, and can read and write. Baba or Mama comes with me in the afternoon to bring him home, and stays to play with the boys until dinner is ready. Baba has also changed to three day weeks, so the boys spend lots of time with him now. He is wonderfully patient with his grandsons, and does not mind looking foolish when he joins their games. Sometimes he will lie down flat upon the floor, letting An and Cai climb over him. An balances on one foot on Baba's chest, squealing with delight until he loses his balance and topples onto his grandfather. When the boys are exhausted, all three lie on the floor and look up at the ceiling for many minutes.

Terrible snowstorms come to Sichuan the winter that An is nine and Cai is six. Even in Mian Yang, where the temperature rarely goes below freezing, we have over a metre on the ground in January, and the winds make piles of snow as high as a house in some places. No one can remember anything like this. The snow is gone from most of the province within a week, but it stays drifted high in the mountains. Some villages have food airlifted in, because the roads are blocked with snow. Then in March it begins to rain. The snow melting in the mountains and the rain falling in the wide bowl of Sichuan fill the four great rivers that give Sichuan its name. Even the little Anchang River thunders into the Fujiang with such force that spray covers everything, and soon the streets are flooded in much of the city. Schools and factories are closed. Our building is on higher ground, but Mama and Baba are not so fortunate. They are on the second floor, but the river reaches the entrance of their apartment building and they come to stay with us until they can return home. An and Cai are delighted. Each morning they clamber into the bed with their Gonggong and Laolao and chatter away like magpies.

Bao Jia joins the volunteers filling sandbags and building levees. The water levels keep rising. We start to hear reports of people being swept away in Chengdu and further downriver, and the army is busy with rescue and flood control. In Mian Yang, two of the bridges break loose from their foundations and fall into the stream. The other bridges survive, but water flows over them as well as under.

Baba agrees to take the boys to see their father working on the levees, and they excitedly get their raincoats and boots. Bao Jia has told us he is helping to protect Torch Number 2 Elementary School, and Baba heads in that direction. The walk is about two kilometres.

All three return home completely wet despite their rain gear. Baba is limping badly. "We saw many army trucks," An tells me. "Gonggong was holding our hands in case we ran into the road. I said I was too old for that, but he would not listen."

Cai adds to the story. "It was raining a lot, Mama. Sometimes the water went into my boots. Gonggong wanted to come home, but we wanted to see Baba working on the flood."

"The road was covered with water, too, Mama. A big truck with soldiers came by. It ran off the side of the road and it was going to tip over, right on top of us. Gonggong pulled us back, and we all fell into a ditch full of water. It was so deep. I could not stand up in it. Gonggong held us both. That's why we are so wet."

"The truck did not tip over, but it slid sideways into the ditch. The soldiers all jumped out and made a lot of splashes. It was fun."

Baba is not happy. "It was not as much fun as they say," he grunts, sitting wrapped in blankets with the boys on either side of him. "Luck was against us. I was afraid the truck would fall on us. If it had been a metre or two closer, the boys could have been hurt. We did not go to the school and we did not see Bao Jia. "

"We can go again tomorrow," says Cai cheerfully. Baba does not look eager, but he does not refuse. I do not think he would refuse the boys anything. It is fortunate that Bao Jia has a rest break the following day and Baba does not have to guide the boys to see him at work. Instead, he hobbles to the clinic to see about his injured foot. It is badly bruised but not broken.

Later I learn the whole frightening story. The boys and Baba have to move right to the very edge of the roadway to allow the army truck to pass. The embankment gives way beneath the boys, and Baba is so startled he cannot hold their hands. An and Cai slide into the icy water that rushes down the ditch, just as the truck begins to tip sideways. They have not yet learned how to swim, and Baba immediately jumps in to stop them from being pulled under by the current. The front end of the truck catches his leg, and he feels his foot being crushed. He succeeds in pulling himself free and lifts An and Cai to safety before crawling up the embankment himself. He can hardly bear the pain in his foot, but he walks home, holding An's hand and carrying an exhausted Cai.

The floods ease by the end of the month and April is warm and dry. The plum trees and azaleas bloom and we all return to our usual routines.

Baba reaches the age of retirement for those who are not *Jian kang*, and he fears being bored. He surprises us all by deciding to study Chinese calligraphy, and soon he is working on beautiful scrolls of poetry by

Li Bai, the Tang Dynasty poet born in Mian Yang. Every school in the city wants "Quiet Night Thought" on one of Baba's scrolls. Now his scrolls hang on walls from New Beichuan to Chengdu, from Ya'an to Bao Jia's parents' apartment in Chongqing. It appears that the engineer's mind held an artist's soul.

An graduates from high school and is chosen for a scholarship to the University of Hong Kong to study materials engineering. Cai is right behind him, doing excellent work in physics and chemistry. He hopes to earn a scholarship like his brother.

When Baba is visiting one evening, he says, "I miss An. I wish he had gone to school in Chengdu so we could see him more often. Maybe earning the Hong Kong scholarship was not as fortunate as I thought." He turns to Cai. "Grandson, do you also plan to leave Sichuan when you finish high school?"

Cai has not thought about this. "Gonggong, I still have two more years to finish. I have not decided. Maybe I will go to Chengdu like Baba." Baba smiles at this and pats Cai's hand.

"Why do you not go to Hong Kong and visit An?" I ask. The new high-speed railway with its superefficient electric motors makes the trip in less than a day; there are hostels in the city that serve older people.

Baba's eyes light up. "I will take him a scroll," he says. "I know the line of Li Bai that I will paint: *And meet at last on the Cloudy River of the sky*."

Baba does not make the trip to Hong Kong. His father, who has slowly been wasting away in the Chengdu Psychiatric Hospital, has another stroke and dies.

Baba and Mama come to our apartment to tell us. I can see by Baba's face that he has bad news.

"What is it, Baba? What has happened? Come, sit down. You too, Mama. What's wrong?" I put water on to boil for tea.

Baba finds it difficult to speak. "It is your grandfather. He died this morning at the hospital. Another stroke. I should have been there to say goodbye."

"Baba, how could you have known?"

"I should have been more attentive. I have failed in my duty to my father. It is wrong that he should die without family to ease his passing."

Mama puts her hand on his arm but says nothing.

"All my life I have had bad fortune. I could have saved NaiNai and you; I could have saved your grandfather. Instead, I failed in my duty to protect my family."

I glance past Baba and see Cai standing in the doorway. He has a strange look in his eyes, as though he is filled with sorrow. Without a word, he comes and stands directly in front of Baba. He is so small; I have to remind myself that he will finish high school in two years.

Baba's eyes fill and tears run down his cheeks. Cai reaches out and wipes the tears away with his fingers. He takes one of Baba's hands and holds it against his chest.

"Gonggong," he whispers, so softly I can hardly hear the words. "You have not failed. You have given us Mama. You have given us Laolao and yourself. Do you remember that day when we almost drowned in the flood? It was you who pulled An and me away from the truck. It was you who held us up in the deep water. Without you, we would have both died. Gonggong, you have worked for many years cleaning the land and the water of the poisons. Being *Jian kang* does not save people from poisons. You do. It was you who walked to and from school with us all those years. It was you and Laolao who looked after us when Mama and Baba were working. You read us stories, you laughed at our jokes. Gonggong, we love you." Cai puts his arms around Baba's neck and hugs him tightly.

Baba's face is wet with tears, but he is smiling. When Cai releases him from the hug, they look at each other for long seconds, then Cai reaches up and gently pushes Baba's hair back from his forehead. Baba looks startled for a moment, then relaxes and smiles again.

"I love you, too, Cai," he says. "You mean everything to me. Thank you for helping me see that. I am a fortunate man." He turns to Mama and me. "When was the last time I told you how much I love you? I am grateful to Cai for reminding me of my duty. I love you, An Ming, and I love you Mei Xing. I always have, and I always will."

I lean over and hug him to me. "I know, Baba. I have always known. I love you."

6.

JAFFNA

THE WAR CAME TO me when I was seven. The Second Eelam Uprising, they call it now, and we wonder why no one learned anything from the first. Jaffna was a zone of conflict, with young Sri Lanka Army soldiers on almost every corner, cradling a rifle and looking frightened.

I was on my way to school, walking down Main Street in Chundikuli, scuffing the dust with my new shoes. I wasn't thinking, of course; my mother would be angry with me for spoiling the shoes, and I would be scolded. My school bag was slung over my back. My uniform, the blue shorts and white shirt, was clean, but my socks were covered in road dust.

At the new market near the corner of Temple Road, I smelled curry and other spices. I had not had anything for breakfast except a bowl of red rice with no curry, and I was hungry. I had a little tiffin box stuck in my bag for later, but my stomach was rumbling now. At a roadside kitchen, a man was steaming string hoppers, and I wandered over to have a look.

The man smiled hopefully at me, but I had no money. I shook my head and he went back to mixing the batter for another batch of hoppers. I felt a hand on my shoulder, and a strange man asked me in Tamil if I was hungry. "No, Uncle. I have lunch with me." I was going to thank him for asking, but suddenly everything went very wrong.

The strange man turned and dashed away between the stalls, heading south towards the church, and disappeared among the houses and trees. A couple of soldiers ran after him, shouting in Singhalese. Another soldier pointed at me and yelled in Tamil.

"You, boy! Don't move!" He had a gun aimed in my direction and looked very angry. I froze, but couldn't stop from shaking.

"Slowly. Carefully. Take off your bag and put it on the ground!" I did as he ordered.

"Now take off your shoes, boy. Go slowly. Don't touch your bag." I untied the laces and pulled off one shoe, then the other. That was when I noticed how dusty they were and thought about my mother's annoyance when she saw them.

"Good," said the soldier. He sounded a little less angry. "Now take off your shirt and shorts and put them beside the shoes. Don't touch the bag." I looked around and realized the market was empty. The merchants and farmers had all left their stalls and vanished. I was alone with this soldier. Slowly, with the tears starting to well up in my eyes, I did as he said. I was standing on the road in my socks and underpants, and there was no one to help me. My shirt was in the dirt, and I would be late for school.

"Come here, boy!" I didn't move.

"Come here, I said! Move, now!" I was very frightened, but I obeyed.

"What is in your bag?" he asked. I was too afraid to speak, and he repeated the question in English. My English was not very fluent, and I didn't understand. The other two soldiers, the ones who had chased after the strange man, came back and started speaking in Singhalese. I did not know what they were saying, but they kept looking at me, and then at my bag.

The soldier who had made me drop my bag grabbed me by the elbow and pulled me further along the road. An army lorry came up and stopped beside us. Three more soldiers got out, and one of them went over to my bag and put a little red box down beside it. He had a spool of wire; he attached one end to the box beside my bag and walked toward us, unrolling wire as he came. The first soldier kept a tight grip on my arm and pulled me further and further down the road until we were almost opposite the school where Appa worked as a groundskeeper. I desperately hoped my father would see me and come to help, but everyone seemed to have fled from the street.

"Now," the soldier said to me, this time in Tamil, "we're going to duck down into the trench, there. There will be a bang—maybe a big one if there is anything dangerous in your bag. Keep your head down so you don't get hurt."

I was already frightened and I had to pee. There was an explosion, like a big firecracker going off, and the soldiers looked up out of the ditch. I kept my head down as ordered.

"It's all right, boy," the soldier who spoke Tamil said to me.

My mother was running up the street towards me, calling out my name. "Ganesh! Are you all right?" Someone must have gone to the girls' school where she worked to tell her I was in trouble.

"Ganesh," she repeated, panting from the run. "Where are your clothes? What's happening?" Her eyes were wide. Instead of answering, I started to cry, big gasping sobs. Amma put her arms around me and held me tight. She didn't seem to care that my nose was running onto her sari.

The soldiers were going through the wreckage of my bag and uniform. The explosion had also damaged the string hopper stand, but the oil and propane tanks had not caught fire. I saw my tiffin box lying open in the gravel, dal spilled everywhere. The bag was ruined, and my uniform was covered in dirt. It looked like it had been partly burned.

Amma and I stood watching. The soldiers searched around the collapsed stall but did not seem to find anything.

Amma relaxed her embrace and took my hand. She began to walk down the road toward our house. We passed what was left of my bag without stopping and left my uniform on the roadside. We didn't even get as far as Saint Patrick Road.

"Wait, Miss!" Amma froze when the soldier called to her in Tamil. She turned to face him. "Where are you taking the boy?"

"I am taking him home. He is afraid, and his school uniform is ruined. He cannot go to class today."

"We will need to question him. He was seen talking with a man who is known to be connected to the rebellion."

"He does not know any such person," said Amma, but her voice shook and her grip tightened on my hand. "He is only seven years old."

"Yes, and the rebel criminals use little children to place their explosives in crowded places like markets and temples. Even schools. Our charge did not cause a larger blast, so we know that this boy did not have any explosives, but we must learn what connection he has to the rebellion."

"None," insisted Amma. "We are a poor family. His father and I work hard to feed our family and to send our son to school. We have nothing to do with rebellion."

The soldier ignored her and spoke directly to me. His Tamil words were hard to understand and my mother's fear made my own worse.

"Boy, what were you doing in the market today?"

I looked down at the dirt. "Nothing."

"Then why were you here?"

"It is on my way to school." I could hardly get the words out. I did not dare to look at him. I knew my nose was running and my face was wet with tears. I just wanted to go home.

"Why would that man speak to you? Why would he put his hand on you if he did not know you?"

"I don't know. He asked if I was hungry. I do not know why."

"Were you hungry? Did you say anything to him?"

"Not until he asked me. I told him no, I wasn't hungry, but I really was. That's why I was at the string hopper man's stand." Amma squeezed my hand. I thought maybe she wanted me to stop talking, so I did.

"We'll need to make a report," said the soldier. "Name, age, address, school, you know." I didn't know, but Amma answered his questions and he wrote the information in a small notebook he was carrying.

"Where do you and your husband work?"

"My husband is a groundskeeper at the boys' school down the road there. I work in the kitchen at the girls' college. It's just across the way from my husband's school."

The soldier spoke to his little group in Singhalese and then took out a mobile phone and called someone. Again he spoke in Singhalese. Amma understands a little of the language, but I knew none of what was being said. Finally the soldier turned back to us. "You can go home now. We might have more questions for you later."

The army lorry drove up and the soldiers got into the back, then they drove off down the road toward Columbuthurai.

Amma picked me up and wrapped the end of her sari around me. We headed back to our house. I was glad that people would not see me in my underpants, but even happier that Amma was not angry with me for losing my bag and school uniform.

"Don't be afraid, Ganesh," Amma said. "You're shaking. Everything will be all right. You will see." I wanted to believe her, but I could hear the fear in her voice. With her arms wrapped around me, I could tell that she was shaking even more violently than I was.

When we reached home, Amma told me to put on my gray shorts and a shirt. I would not be going to school today. As I dressed, she took some brown rice from the pot on the cooker, poured curry sauce over it and set it on the table.

"Here, Ganesh. You can eat this for lunch." I felt ashamed for having told the soldier that I was hungry. It made us look poor. Of course, we were poor, but Appa and Amma worked hard so I could have enough to eat and so I could go to school.

Amma brushed off her sari and straightened the folds. "I am going back to work, Ganesh. Stay in the house. Do not go to the door if someone calls, even if it is someone you know." I nodded.

When Amma left, the house seemed emptier and lonelier than it had ever been. I wandered around the room, touching things. For a few seconds, I stared at the picture of Sri Ganesha above the sideboard. His soft elephant eyes looked back at me; Overcomer of Obstacles, Sri Ganesha was supposed to help me with my studies. I prayed silently to Lord Ganesha, "Help me get a new uniform and bag. I will need shoes, too." This thought brought me a moment of hope. If we went to Stanley Road to get shoes, Amma would also stop at one of the many sari shops. Jaffna's shops seemed to sell only three things—saris, shoes and electronics, and I loved the sari shops with their multicolored bolts of silk and other fabrics.

The thought of buying shoes reminded me that we never had enough money. Appa always told me that I must study hard and graduate from school so I could gain a position with the government or a bank, and never have to worry about feeding my children. How could we pay for a new uniform, new shoes, new school supplies? I still did not understand why the soldiers had destroyed my things.

The neighborhood beggar woman was passing by outside. I could hear her before I saw her; her wheezing breath could not be mistaken for anything else. She had been badly burned in an attack on a city bus, and the fire had scarred her face terribly and left her unable to speak or to breathe properly. If Amma had been home, she would have opened the door and offered the beggar woman some food, maybe even a coin or two. I wanted to share my rice with her, but Amma had told me not to go to the door, even if I knew the caller. The beggar woman was not a caller; she shuffled on past, heading down toward Kandy Road.

Crows called from the mango tree and the little brown squirrels raced up and down the coconut trunks. A large lizard perched on the window sill, soaking up the midday heat. He didn't even stir when a handsome brown cockroach, looking like it was made of polished wood, scurried across the ledge in front of him. The silence in the neighborhood poured in through the windows and settled everywhere in the room. I was not used to being home alone during the daytime. I wished I had gone straight to school and not stopped at the string hopper man's stand.

Amma was home and I was lying on the floor. I must have fallen asleep. I hadn't touched the rice, and Amma had taken the bowl to the sideboard.

"*Alo*, Amma," I said. "I am happy that you are home." She smiled at me.

"Are you hungry yet, Ganesh? You didn't eat the rice. You can have it now."

I ate the rice quickly, then washed my hands in the bucket. Amma was getting supper ready for Appa, who would be home from work soon.

"I went to your school and told the principal what happened this morning. The principal is such a kind man. He agreed to meet me right away, and he was very disturbed about what happened to you. He knows we do not have a lot of money. He called Appa in and told us he will get you a new uniform. He says you are a hard-working pupil, and he doesn't want you to miss any more classes. Appa and I are proud of you, Ganesh. We will get you some new shoes, but I think it will take a little longer to get a bag and tiffin box for you."

I didn't know what to say. I was happy that I could go back to school, and that I wouldn't have to go barefoot. I wasn't sure how I could take my lunch to school, though, or carry my school work.

"I will sew you a bag for your books, Ganesh. That will have to do until we can buy a school bag. I have a plastic box you can use for your dal." Amma thought of everything.

When Appa came in, he was carrying a new uniform—at least, it was new for me. It was one of those the school had for boys from the displacement camps, and it was a little bit too big. Amma set to work with her needle, making it fit me.

Appa was clearly very worried. "It is not lucky to attract the attention of the army," he said. "This is not your fault, Ganesh. I wish that man in the market had never come near you." I felt ashamed, because if I had not gone to the string hopper stand, none of this would have happened.

After Appa had eaten and the electric bulb was turned on, I sat on my father's lap while he rocked back and forth, holding me close. I felt safe for the first time since that morning. Amma unrolled my sleeping mat on the floor and spread the mosquito net, and Appa carried me over and set me down. He squatted on the floor beside me, passing his hand gently over my shoulders. "Go to sleep now, Ganesh," he urged. "You have classes in the morning." I made myself a silent promise that I would not go near the string hopper stand—then remembered that the stand had been blown apart. I felt myself drowsing, soothed by Appa's hand softly rubbing my shoulders.

Suddenly the door was flung open and three soldiers pushed into the room. Amma gasped and Appa stood up quickly. I was wide awake. One of the soldiers pointed his gun at Appa.

"Sit down!" he barked in Tamil. Appa obeyed. His eyes told me to stay quiet.

A second soldier spoke to Appa in Tamil. "Mr Sugananthan, we have a few questions for you." He turned to me. "The boy will go outside for a short while." He gestured to the third soldier, who came over to my mat and opened the mosquito net. He took my arm and pulled me up beside him.

The second soldier said something in Singhalese and the soldier who held my arm—he was more a boy than a man I saw now—nodded.

"We're going for a walk, child," he said to me. "This will not take long." His Tamil was hard to understand, but I did not resist as he led me to the door and out into the dark. Amma's eyes were full of fear as we left.

"Please," she said, but the soldier held up his hand.

The boy soldier and I walked down to Kandy Road and along past Holy Family Convent in darkness. There would have been a full moon, but the sky was covered with cloud and the night wrapped around us on all sides. I could not see anything in the blackness; a few faint lights glowed off to each side like fireflies, but the road itself was hidden. I stumbled a few times, but the soldier held me back from falling each time. He said nothing and I too remained silent. His hand never let go of my arm, but his grip was not too tight. It was not yet time for curfew, but the road was deserted, with only an occasional three-wheel tuk-tuk, which we called tri-shaws in those days, driving by in a cloud of exhaust.

When we reached Bazaar Street, the soldier got a call on his mobile phone. He answered and listened for a minute, then spoke briefly in Singhalese. He signed off and turned to me. "We are going back to your house now, child." He let go of my arm and we walked side by side back down Kandy Road and into my neighborhood. The light was still on in my house.

He left me at the door and walked back toward the road. When I went in, I found my mother sitting on the floor and my father gone. Amma's hair was undone, and her sari was partly unwound. She was crying.

"Amma! What happened? Where is Appa?" She just looked at me without replying. The tears kept washing down her cheeks.

I threw my arms around her neck and held her close. She groaned in pain, but I did not let go. I started crying too.

"Amma, where is Appa? What happened to him?"

At last she reached her arms around me and spoke. "The soldiers took him. They think he is part of the rebellion. We tried to explain that we were just ordinary workers, but they wouldn't listen."

I noticed the dark liquid on the floor. "What is that?" I already knew it was blood—my father's blood. "Is Appa hurt? Did they hurt him?" Amma only cried more and held me tightly.

At last her crying grew quiet and she began to breathe more calmly. "Ganesh," she said, "you'd better go to sleep now. You have class in the morning." I couldn't believe that she would be thinking about school when Appa had been hurt by the soldiers and taken away. As if she could see my thoughts, she continued, "Appa would want you to go to class. He is very proud of your success in school. Do it for him, Ganesh."

Reluctantly I crawled back into the mosquito net and lay down on my mat. To my surprise, Amma crept in with me and lay down beside me. There wasn't much room on the mat, but I was relieved to have her close. She draped one arm over me like a shield and I snuggled in close. I didn't intend to fall asleep, but even with my long afternoon nap I was exhausted.

In the morning I put on the uniform and Amma packed me a plastic box of dal for lunch. She had not had time to sew the bag, but I didn't have any books to carry anyway. In the daylight I could see there was a large bruise on the side of her face. In the night it had looked like a shadow, but now it was unmistakeable.

"I will walk with you to school," she said. "I am sorry we didn't have time to get you new shoes, but I am sure the principal will allow you to wear your sandals today." I immediately began to fear that the other boys would tease me for my footwear, but then felt ashamed for worrying about such a small thing.

"I will have to tell the principal that Appa will not be at work today. Maybe he will be home tonight." Amma sounded very tired, and I was afraid she would start to cry again. If only there were some way I could make her feel better; I knew the only thing that would do that would be to have Appa home again.

We walked in silence to school, and Amma led me to the primary playground. The dusty area was crowded with my classmates and the other younger pupils, all running and calling out to each other. Amma held my arm for a moment. "Ganesh, go straight home after class. Stay inside. Do not open the door for anyone. I will come home as quickly as I can today." Then she was gone, heading to the main office building to see the principal. In spite of the flow of children all around me, I had never felt so alone.

It was a strange day. I felt as if everyone was watching me, but of course they did not know what had happened. No one said anything about my sandals. I wanted to be part of the games when we were sent outside, but I also wanted to be left alone. My teacher, Miss Navaratnam, did not seem to pay any more attention to me than usual. Perhaps she did not know why I had been absent yesterday. I took my turn reading aloud; I answered the question I was asked in the maths class. Time went slowly, and yet the day ended quickly. It was very confusing.

I hurried home and let myself into the house. In our neighborhood no one had a lock on their door, and of course we had no servants to watch over the house while we were gone, but I do not remember anyone ever being robbed. We were too poor for anyone to bother with.

I waited for Amma to come home. It would have been a good idea to pick a few bananas to eat, but I could not go out into the garden now. Amma had told me not to leave the house. Two of the neighbor girls were passing on the road, chattering away about a cricket match they were going to watch.

At last Amma came home, bringing some small pieces of cooked chicken she had been given at her school. She seemed as relieved to see me as I was to see her. She smiled sadly at me and set about chopping up the chicken and some peppers to put in the curry for the rice.

"Tomorrow is a poya day," she said as we ate the rice. "We will go for a walk. Most of the shops will be closed, but I think there is one small shop off Stanley Road where we can get you some new shoes. I know the wife of the owner, and he will let us pay a little each week without charging extra for interest."

Amma again slept beside me on my mat, her arm resting lightly across my shoulders. It was a comfort to feel her close, but I could tell she was worried about Appa, and I worried with her. It took a long time to fall asleep.

When we went the next day to Stanley Road, we found the shop open as Amma had hoped. I was not as interested in new shoes as I would have been before Appa's disappearance, and eventually Amma decided for me. The shopkeeper took the rupees Amma had with her and put the shoes into a plastic bag. We left, Amma promising the shopkeeper she would come back the following week with more money.

Stanley Road was almost deserted. None of the sari shops were open, but I would not have wanted to spend time in them anyway. Amma offered to buy me a Coca Cola, but I wasn't thirsty. We trudged home in silence. It wasn't until we reached our door that I remembered to thank Amma for the shoes.

"*Nandri*, Amma. I will be careful with the new shoes. I promise."

"I know, Ganesh." She put her arms around me. "You are a good boy."

For two weeks we heard nothing about Appa. Then one day, Amma was waiting for me after school, standing in the shade of a tree by the gates. I hurried over to her and she hugged me.

"Ganesh, I have news. Appa is alive. He is in the detention camp at Killinochchi. They still think he has something to do with the uprising."

I was shocked. I had never considered the possibility that Appa would not be alive. I realized that Amma must have been thinking the worst all these days since Appa was taken away. She was so brave to keep up the regular routines; no wonder she had seemed so tired all the time.

"When will he come home?" I asked. "I miss him."

"I miss him too, Ganesh." Amma's voice sounded more tired than ever. "I wish he was home now. We do not know how long it will take for him to be released. We will make an offering at the temple today. We will ask Sri Ganesha to help free Appa from the camp."

At home, Amma sent me to pick some bananas and a coconut from our trees. Mangos were not ready yet. She found some fresh chillies and the bit of new cloth she was going to sew into a school bag for me. We put the fruit and the chillies in the centre of the cloth and Amma tied it carefully with some colored hair ribbon she had in the sideboard.

As we left home to take the offering to the shrine, the Catholic rosary was being broadcast over the loudspeakers in the next street. I decided to pray to the Catholic god as well, but once I had done so, I was afraid perhaps Sri Ganesha would be jealous and refuse to answer our prayers for Appa. I quickly told him that of course he was true lord of our family, and that the Catholic god was just his assistant.

Amma spent a long time at the temple, praying aloud some of the time and sinking into silence for the rest. I stood and bowed, sat and bowed, squatted and bowed, all the time hoping Sri Ganesha would hear us. At last Amma took my hand and we walked home.

I was careful on my way to school the next day to keep my new shoes from getting dusty. I was still carrying my lunch in the plastic box, and Amma had given me the plastic bag from my shoes to use as a school bag. "We will get you a real bag as soon as Appa returns from Killinochchi," she promised.

When I came home from school, the beggar woman was sitting beside our front gate. She tried to say something to me, but of course I could not understand. I thanked her and asked her if she would like some bananas, but she shook her head and grew more agitated. She was trying very hard to speak, but the more she tried, the less I was able to grasp. Saliva drooled from the side of her mouth and her eyes looked almost mad. I was frightened, and ran into the house.

Amma did not come home. When darkness fell and I turned on the electric bulb, I was very worried. Was this what the beggar woman was trying to tell me? That Amma was working late and would be home after dark? Amma had never left messages with the beggar woman before—there would not have been much value in doing so.

I fell asleep on the mat, but missed having Amma beside me. I woke many times during the night, but I was always alone.

The crows awoke me in the morning, screaming at each other in the mango tree. Still, there was no Amma.

I got myself ready for school, hoping Amma had just gone out for a few moments, that she had been home after all and would soon reappear, but she did not. I packed the last of the dal into my plastic box, slicked down my hair with water from the bucket, and went to school.

All day I worried. If only Amma would meet me at the gates, if only she would be home when I got there, if only . . .

She was not at the gates and not at home. Darkness fell again and once more I slept by myself on the mat.

In the morning there was no more dal and no rice. I had nothing to take for my lunch at school except the two bananas I found that were ripe. The road seemed longer than it had ever been before, and the people I passed all seemed to be secretly watching me. The morning was already hot, and the monsoon was a long way off. Dust rose with each step I took. It didn't seem to matter any more if my new shoes got dirty, and I scuffed my way along, studying the little puffs that exploded out from under my feet with each step. The sounds of voices and traffic blended together into a steady background roar.

When I reached the school gates I was surprised to find I had been crying. My face was wet, and I knew without looking in a mirror that the tears would be mixed with dust. I quickly wiped away the moisture, but I could still feel the eyes of the older boys following me as I entered the grounds and headed for the primary school. I took a moment by the water pump to wash my face and hands, then went to sit on the concrete block near the swings.

My teacher, Miss Navaratnam, was standing in the doorway of my classroom, looking in my direction. She seemed to be puzzled. A few seconds later she was striding across the playground to me. I sat still, looking at the ground. Maybe she was going to deal with one of the other pupils, but no, she came right over to me and sat down beside me on the block. It was a strange thing for her to do; I had never seen her—or any other teacher—sit down in the play area before.

"Ganesh," she said quietly, "is something wrong? You've been crying." How did she know that? I had washed my face.

I didn't answer her at first. I was going to shake my head no, but I waited too long. I felt the tears running down my cheeks again; there was a burning in my eyes. Miss Navaratnam put her arm around my shoulders and pulled me closer to her.

"Tell me, Ganesh. What is wrong? Is it about your father? Have you had bad news?"

I couldn't speak. I just shook my head. She continued to question me in her quiet way; she asked about my school friends, my health, and then about Amma. I nodded.

"Is your mother unwell?"

At last I could talk. "No, Miss. She has gone. I do not know where she is. She has not been home for two nights now." Then I confessed. "I am afraid."

"Oh, Ganesh. I am so sorry. Who is staying with you?"

I just shook my head again. My nose was running and I stared at the patterns the drops were making in the dust at my feet.

"No one is staying with you? You have been alone for two nights? Ganesh, you can tell me about this. You could have told me yesterday."

"I am sorry, Miss."

"No, no. You do not have to be sorry. It is not your fault. But we must do something about this. You can not go on living by yourself in the house. We must find your mother." She stood up, and I raised my face to look at her. I almost thought she was ready to go with me immediately to search for Amma.

Miss Navaratnam held out her hand and I took it. She called out to one of the other primary teachers to look after her class for a few minutes and then she and I walked together to the main office building. I had never been here before, and the first thing I noticed was how cool it was. All the windows were open in the entrance hall and the portico shaded the doorways. Trees along the outside of the building made deep shade. The floors were polished, dark green like pond water.

In the main office, Miss Navaratnam told one of the women that we had come to see the principal. This alarmed me. I was afraid I was in trouble for staying alone in my house, that the principal would be angry with me, perhaps even expel me from school.

A voice from one of the open office doors called out. "Come in, please, Miss Navaratnam." We crossed the office and entered the principal's private office. A huge wooden desk, its polished surface gleaming red-brown in the dim light, almost filled the room. There were piles of papers spread across it and a small electric lamp with a green shade. A pen set, made of what looked to me like pure gold, sat on the left side.

"Please, sit down," said the principal, pointing to the chairs in front of the desk. "What is the reason for your visit? And who is this young man?"

Miss Navaratnam sat down, but I stayed standing, as close to her as I could get without climbing onto her lap. Again she put her arm around me.

"This is Ganesh Sugananthan," she told the principal. His eyes opened wider and he looked at me carefully. "His mother has disappeared, and you already know that his father has been arrested and interned. Ganesh has been alone at home for the past two nights."

A thought appeared to strike her. "Ganesh, have you eaten anything?" I shook my head.

"We'll get you some food very soon. Principal, I think we need to do something to protect this child. He is a good pupil, doing well in second primary. How can we help?"

The thought of food filled my head. I was so very hungry. I almost didn't hear the principal speaking. He reached for a paper on the corner of his desk.

"We have a new group of sponsorship agreements this morning, Miss Navaratnam," he went on. "Let me see. Yes, this is one of our Old Boys who has left Sri Lanka and lives now in Australia." He looked at me. "Ganesh, an Old Boy is what we call ourselves after we finish school. Our Old Boys are now grown up men and they live in many different places, here in Sri Lanka and all over the world. They are very generous in helping the school. You maybe noticed that all the new hardware in the technology laboratory was paid for by our Old Boys in Canada and America." I hadn't noticed, but I nodded just the same.

"Many of our Old Boys, and many other kind people who know about our school, sponsor some of the boys who are at the school now. Sponsoring means they pay for the boys' school fees, for their food and uniforms, for their medical care and even for their games and activities. The same thing happens at the girls' school where your mother works." I looked up in surprise. He knew that my mother worked in the school across the street. Did he know where she was now?

He wasn't saying. "Ganesh, until your mother and father come home to look after you, I think you will live here at the school, in the hostel. You know that many of the older boys come here from the camps and the outer towns. They live in the school, and we take care of them using the money that our sponsors send. We will be glad to have you stay with us until we find your parents."

He looked at Miss Navaratnam. "I will handle the paperwork to gain guardianship for the time being. Can you do your usual inquiring about this new missing one?"

Miss Navaratnam seemed to understand this strange question, because she answered, "Of course. Thank you, principal. I'll take Ganesh to the dining hall right now and get him some breakfast."

The words were welcome news. As we walked together along the path from the administration building to the dining hall, I could hear the cries of some of the older boys on the cricket pitch. I wondered which of them lived at the school. I had never seen the place where the pupils lived; I thought everyone went home after class each day, just as I had always done.

After I had greedily eaten a bowl of rice with potato curry and roti and sambol, Miss Navaratnam took me to see the building where the boys lived. It was right next to the primary school playground, where my friends and I spent our games times, but I had never wondered about it before. I thought it was part of the main office building. We met the hostel master, who was busy sweeping the concrete floor, and Miss Navaratnam introduced us.

"Well, Ganesh, welcome," said the hostel master. "You will be the youngest boy in the dormitories, but we will look after you. Don't worry about anything. Do you have any special things you want to bring from home to keep near you?"

I didn't have much; even my bag was gone. I thought about the picture of Sri Ganesha that hung over the sideboard, but I wasn't sure if it would be allowed here—the school was run by the Anglican Church of Ceylon. Besides, maybe it was better for Sri Ganesha to keep watch over our house while everyone was away. I looked at the master and shook my head.

"Well, that keeps things simple. Let's find you a good bed and a clean mosquito net." He led me to a big open room that was filled with dozens of beds. These beds were the strangest sleeping places I had ever seen. They were raised up off the floor, and they were set up in twos, with one bed perched up on top of the other. It was as if the bottom bed had a ceiling over it, and the boy on the top bed was lying on the roof. How did anyone sleep in these beds, especially the top one, without worrying about falling out? There was a small railing around the edge of the bed, but I didn't think it would stop someone from rolling over onto the concrete floor.

"Here's an empty bed," said the hostel master, pointing to a bottom bed. "We'll rig up a mosquito net this afternoon so you don't get bitten in the night. There's more dengue fever in Northern Province again, and we don't want to take any chances."

"Thank you, Uncle," I said.

Miss Navaratnam also thanked the hostel master and told him we had to go back to class. He smiled at me. "I'll see you this afternoon, then, Ganesh. Do you know where to go for lunch?"

"I'll take him," said Miss Navaratnam. "And I'll bring him to you after class, if that is all right." The hostel master nodded.

"See you later, Ganesh."

All that morning, as we recited our lessons or worked in our scribblers, I tried to make sense of what was happening. Amma and Appa were gone, and now I was living at the school until they came back. I was happy that the principal and Miss Navaratnam both talked about finding Amma. Maybe that would be soon, and I could go home again. Still, it was reassuring to know there would be food for me here, and the hostel master seemed like a kind man.

Miss Navaratnam did not call on me in class to answer any questions, and I was grateful.

At lunch time, she walked with me to the dining hall, where a huge, noisy crowd of older boys was pushing and pulling at each other. Three busy-looking women were putting out large pots of rice and curry on a table, and the boys eventually started to line up and take a bowl from a stack at the end. As the boys filed down one side of the long table, the women spooned rice and curry into their bowls and they went to sit at the tables that filled the hall. Miss Navaratnam picked up a bowl and took me behind the table, where the women were standing.

"This is a new boarder," she told them. "He's younger than the usual group, so I will ask you to keep an eye on him during meals and make sure he gets something to eat. He will be shy at first." I was looking at the floor when she said this, as if to demonstrate the truth of her words.

The first woman spoke. "Of course, Miss. We'll take good care of him at mealtimes. He won't be hard to spot in this crowd." She smiled at me and I couldn't help smiling back, just a little.

"Thank you, Auntie," I said.

"And he's polite," said the woman. "Maybe we can find a little treat for him after he finishes his rice. I think we have some boiled eggs. We'll get a little extra nutrition into him."

Miss Navaratnam turned to the crowd of boys in the dining hall, all of them busily chattering away as they gobbled their food. She clapped her hands several times until they all fell silent and looked at her.

"Boys," she said firmly. "This is Ganesh. He's a new boarder, and as you can see, he's younger than you. I want you all to make sure he is welcomed, and to show him what to do without waiting for him to ask. Jananan, you're a head boy. I'm putting you in special charge. Please let me know if there are any difficulties." The boy named Jananan stood up and nodded. He was not much taller than me, kind of stocky, with very dark skin and bright teeth that flashed when he grinned at me. He had a kind expression, and I felt better already.

"Thank you, boys. Please continue with your lunch."

Jananan came over to me and led me to a space at a table, not far from where he was sitting. He smiled warmly at me, and I felt much better. Maybe this would be all right after all.

The other boys at my table were loud and cheerful. They were stuffing handfuls of rice into their mouths as they talked, and little grains were flying everywhere. No one seemed to be too concerned about manners. They weren't even using their finger tips to pick up the food, but were scooping it up with their hands. I looked around for the water bucket, but didn't see anything to wash my hands in. Maybe I would have to lick them clean after lunch. I had heard that some families had taken on the English custom of eating with forks and spoons, but no one at my table—or anywhere in the hall—had forgotten the Sri Lankan method of eating with the fingers. Or, in several cases, the fist.

One of the dining hall aunties brought me a boiled egg, with the shell already peeled off, and put it in my bowl. I wasn't sure what to do; no one else had an egg. I was afraid they would be angry at me for this special treatment, but the boy next to me said, "Go on. Eat it. It's your welcome gift—you won't get another if you don't eat it." I did, and the boys at my table all clapped their hands.

After lunch, Jananan had to go to cricket practice, so he asked one of the other boys to take me to the washing sink, and I got my hands clean. Then I wandered back to the primary school for afternoon classes.

The hostel was busy when I finished classes for the day. The boys were packing clothes that had been laundered and arranging their mosquito nets. Then everyone headed out to the cricket grounds to watch a game between the senior boys' teams. Dinner, study hall, a game of catch in the playground, then showers in the shower room, with everyone sliding around on the soapy floor and falling in a pile of laughing boys. There was no time to stop and feel lonely, or to worry about Appa or Amma, until I was lying in this strange bed, staring into the darkness.

The next day after classes, I asked for permission to go home and fetch something. I went to the cupboard in the corner of our house and got one of my mother's scarves, a dark blue one that looked like silk but was probably just thin cotton. This I took back to my bed in the hostel and put under my cover, so I would have something of Amma to keep me company during the night.

All the boys were good to me, just as Miss Navaratnam had asked. Jananan or one of the others always showed me what I needed to know. The hostel master made sure I had clean clothes to wear. The boy in the bunk above me helped me to straighten my bed each morning and arrange my mosquito net each night. I was lonely and worried, but life was comfortable—perhaps more comfortable than it would have been at home.

I had always felt that school was a safe place, and the other pupils, as well as my teacher and the principal, seemed to be proof of that, but one day we were all shaken awake by a loud explosion. A bomb had gone off just outside the school gates. A passing automobile was damaged and three of the boys from our school were badly injured. It was lucky the blast had happened so early in the morning. An hour later the roadway near the gates would have been crowded with children coming to our school and to the girls' school across the way. The three injured boys were all members of the football team, arriving for an early-morning practice.

Of course, we all knew that the school had been almost destroyed in the first uprising, the war that had lasted thirty years. The bicycle shed, which was once a school building, had been left in its bullet-marked and cannon-blasted state, as a sort of memorial, but we were all accustomed to seeing that. It didn't have much impact. This new blast did. Ambulance sirens, police and army vehicles, a mass of curious and frightened pupils, held back by equally alarmed teachers, made a confused tumult at the front of the school. The injured boys were taken away in ambulances and the police ordered everyone else to disperse. The teachers herded us back into the grounds, back to our dormitory.

"Get ready for breakfast," said the hostel master. He looked very upset and we did not dare to ask questions or even talk with each other.

The meal was eaten in painful silence. Instead of one teacher on supervision, there were five. When we had finished breakfast and washed up, we went quietly to class. There was no football practice.

At morning break, I noticed there was a line of army vehicles stopped in front of the school, and several soldiers were standing outside the main office building. Miss Navaratnam came over and chased us away from the fence, telling us not to stare at the soldiers or the trucks. There was a grim expression on her face instead of her usual smile.

The soldiers were there all day, and they were still standing outside the school gates when we were called in for bed. Some of them must have remained on duty all night, because they were at the main office building as we walked to the dining hall for breakfast.

The day went slowly, with no one feeling much like playing or even talking. After lunch, the older pupils were all called to the assembly hall. We primary boys had our usual classes, but I knew I could find out afterward what had happened in the assembly.

"The principal and some of the teachers were at the front, on the platform. There were two soldiers with them. The principal said we should not be afraid; the soldiers were going to protect us. The three boys who were injured will live, but they may have some permanent injuries."

Another boy chimed in. "The principal says if we see anything unusual, we must tell a teacher right away. You know, like strange people around the school compound or in the street outside."

"There are always strange people in the street. Most of them are soldiers."

"Shh! Don't talk like that. We might get in trouble if we insult the army."

"I didn't mean they were strange, just that they were strange—like we don't know their names or where they come from."

"It doesn't matter what you meant. It matters what you said. We all must be careful about our talking."

The hostel master came into the dormitory at that point and we all stood guiltily around. "What are you boys up to? You should be out on the cricket ground practising or something." We filed out to get some of the equipment from the sports room.

I was still thinking about the need to be careful, to watch what we said. As I sat under the papaya trees on the edge of the cricket ground, watching the older boys playing a half-hearted game, I wondered if anything I had said had made Appa and Amma go away. My mind kept circling back to that morning at the string hopper man's stand. Who was the man who had spoken to me, and what had he done to make so much trouble for all of us?

"Hey, Ganesh! Are you coming? It's time for dinner." I couldn't remember how long I had been sitting thinking, and I suddenly realized my face was wet with tears. For the first time in days I really missed Appa and Amma. I quickly wiped my eyes and stood to follow the others to the dining hall.

That night as we lay in our beds, the others began to talk quietly. Sometimes it was difficult to hear exactly what they were saying. Most of the time they spoke in Tamil, but a couple of times the talk switched to English. I didn't know much of the language, but the tone of voice was clear.

"The soldiers beat my father until his ribs were broken. They thought he was with the rebellion."

"My older brother ran away after the army came for my father."

"Our house was burned because the army wanted the land."

Then Jananan spoke softly. "I hate them all," he said. I had never heard him say anything bad about anything. Jananan always seemed so full of kindness. If I had had an older brother, I would have wanted him to be just like Jananan. Everyone fell silent.

Jananan continued. "I hate the army and I hate the rebels. They are all devils." No one spoke. I was waiting for Jananan to explain what he meant, but he sighed loudly and rolled over in his bed. "Let's go to sleep now," he said. No one argued. I lay awake in the darkness for a very long time, wondering about Jananan.

At morning break the next day, Miss Navaratnam asked me to come with her to a quiet corner of the playground. "I have something for you, Ganesh," she said, smiling at me. She handed me an envelope with a big red cross printed on it. "Go ahead, open it."

Inside was a tiny scrap of paper, covered on both sides with Tamil writing. I looked at Miss Navaratnam, and she nodded at me. "You know how to read, Ganesh. Read it."

The first words stopped my breath: "My son." I turned the paper over quickly and looked at the signature. It was from Amma.

Some of the writing was hard for me to read, but I understood most of it. "I am in a camp in Killinochchi. There are many other women here, and we are getting food from the government. I am hoping to come home soon. I know that you are living at school, and this makes me feel very happy. Remember to study hard and be brave. Listen to your teacher and trust the principal. Appa and I love you and I think of you all the time."

I could not hold back the tears. I felt happy to think Amma might be coming home soon, but loneliness was flooding back into my heart. Miss Navaratnam put her arm around me and hugged me close.

"It's all right, Ganesh," she said gently. "You have a right to feel sad. You miss your Amma and Appa. Maybe they will be back sooner than you think, though, and you will be able to go home."

I slid the note back in the envelope and put it in my pocket. "*Nandri*, Miss. Thank you."

"Why don't you go and play for a little while, Ganesh?" She smiled and wiped my eyes with the silky edge of her sari. I couldn't believe she would do that for me, but it made me feel much better. I nodded and walked off to the swings.

After class, I was wandering around the school compound, near the main gates, and I passed the open doors of the church. I had never been inside the church before, but today I was drawn toward it by the sound of singing. I climbed the stone steps and stood uncertainly under the front portico, then slipped quietly into the cool interior. The ceiling was high above me and straight ahead was a window made of colored glass, pieced together to make a picture of a man with several children standing around him. The singing was coming from near the front, on the right-hand side.

I walked as quietly as I could up the aisle on the right side. There were many plaques on the wall, but they were all written in English and I couldn't read them. I was afraid they might be warning signs, that I shouldn't be there, but still I went on until I reached the front.

There was a small group of boys there, and just as I came up, they stopped singing. A teacher whom I did not recognize was there, too, seated at a piano keyboard. She looked at me, and all the boys turned to stare as well.

"Hello," the teacher said in English. She smiled at me.

"Hello," I replied, then switched to Tamil. "I heard the singing. I came to see . . ." I couldn't think of any excuses, so I just stopped talking.

"Do you like to sing?" asked the teacher. I didn't know what to say. I liked to hear the singing, but I didn't really know how to sing myself. I had never done any singing except in class, and then I tried to keep myself as quiet as possible.

"I like to listen," I replied finally.

"Well, then, sit down and listen. Maybe later you will want to join with us." The boys all turned back to her as I sat on one of the long benches. She played a few notes on the piano and the boys started to sing again.

I don't know how long I was there, but when I came out, it was time for dinner and Jananan was looking for me.

"There you are, Ganesh. It's time to eat. I was getting worried about you. What were you doing?"

"Listening to some boys singing in the church. I like to listen."

"That was the junior choir. In another two years you can join if you want. Come on, now. We don't want to miss dinner." He ran toward the dining hall and I followed as fast as I could. We joined the line for food.

As I lay awake in bed that night, I thought I could hear someone singing in the distance, but it must have been my imagination. It was not yet curfew, but no one would risk being outside even an hour beforehand.

One day the soldiers were gone from the main office building and the front gates. There had been no disturbances in Jaffna for a month, but the curfew was still in force. The guards still stood at the corner of the street, holding their guns, but there were not as many army vehicles on the road.

I was going regularly to the junior choir practices to listen to the singing, and the teacher didn't seem to mind. The boys liked having an audience, even one as small as me. Jananan came and sat with me once, but he didn't seem to like it as much as I did, and returned to his cricket practice after a few minutes. I was disappointed. I liked having him nearby, like a protective older brother. In fact that was how I was beginning to see him.

There was a small graveyard next door to the school, where many of the former principals were buried, along with priests who had served at the church. Some of the names were English, some Tamil. The graves bore dates stretching back into the 1800s. It was hard to imagine a time that long ago. What was Jaffna like then?

It was a poya day, and there were no classes. We had spent the entire afternoon playing football and cricket. I wasn't much use in either of these sports, but the other boarders put up with me because Jananan told them to. There had been a lot of traffic on the road all day, mostly military trucks full of soldiers. Maybe they were going to temple.

After dinner no one had enough energy to go back to the football grounds, and I drifted off to play in the sand near the big scoreboard at the end of the senior sports area. No one had used the scoreboard for many years, but once boys would have been up inside it, changing the numbers by hand as the cricket game or football match wore on. The doors were locked.

Sometimes it was really lonely being the youngest boarder. No one wanted to play toy cars with me in the sand, especially since there were no toy cars, just pieces of wood I pretended were cars. Jananan would occasionally drift over to watch me for a few minutes, but he never joined in. I didn't ask him to. On this occasion he was nowhere to be seen.

The hostel master called me in for bed. The other boys were still at the canteen, because they had got some money to spend on the poya day. I brushed my teeth in the empty washroom, arranged my mosquito net and climbed into bed. I was growing accustomed to sleeping up off the floor. When the other boys returned to the dormitory, they made a lot of noise, and I almost got out of bed to join them in their toothbrushing. Instead, I rolled over and pretended I was asleep.

Jananan came over to my bed when he was finished brushing. "Goodnight, little friend," he said softly, then he was gone without waiting for a reply.

When I woke up, everything was quiet. The light of the full moon filled the room, and I could see that everyone was asleep. But no, not everyone. Someone was standing in the shadow beside the windows, looking out into the schoolyard. He moved silently to the outside door and opened it slowly.

The moonlight hit his face and I recognized Jananan. What was he doing leaving the dormitory after curfew? I thought perhaps he was sleepwalking, but he looked around as if he was checking for watchers. He moved out of my sight into the night.

Cautiously I got out of bed and went to the door. I could see Jananan slipping along under the tamarind trees beside the primary school, staying out of the light. He did not look back. I felt a mixture of fear and curiosity, and at first the fear won out. I stood frozen in the doorway, hoping Jananan would turn around and come back. When he did not, I found myself sliding out into the night, under the trees, heading in the direction he had gone.

I found him crouched in the shrubbery, next to the graveyard wall. He was looking into the graveyard, and my eyes followed his direction.

I pulled in my breath. There was a woman in the graveyard, glowing in a strange white light. I almost cried out, but choked back the dry fear and stared. The woman glided soundlessly across the graveyard toward the road and suddenly a man stepped out from the trees near the wall. He was dressed in army uniform, but the woman showed no alarm and walked steadily toward him. He held out his hand and she reached for it. In that instant I recognized Miss Navaratnam; it was her ghost I was seeing. Some sound must have escaped my lips, because Jananan whirled around and looked straight at me. He signalled me to stay quiet and scuttled over, keeping low to the ground.

"Ganesh! What are you doing?" he hissed. "You should be in bed."

"I woke up. I saw you go out, and I wanted to come with you. What is happening? Why are you here? What is my teacher doing in the graveyard?"

Jananan pulled me back towards the dormitory. "Come on," he said. "I'll tell you when we get back to the room."

Although I was eaten with curiosity about Miss Navaratnam and the soldier, it was a relief to be returning to the dormitory. I did not know what happened to boys who disobeyed the curfew, and I was terrified of finding out, for Jananan's sake as well as my own. I was afraid that if I got into trouble, it would mean my mother and father would not be let go from the camps, that Jananan and I would be expelled from school, maybe even sent to prison. My heart was thundering in my chest when we gained the outside door of the dormitory. I half expected to find the hostel master standing waiting for us, but there was no one in the open doorway.

When we had crept back into the dormitory, Jananan led me to the far end, to the small room where the linens were stored. We went inside and shut the door. It was completely black, and all I could hear was Jananan's breathing. At last he spoke.

"She goes there almost every night," he said. "She meets that soldier. Sometimes they just talk; sometimes he puts his arms around her. I can't always see very well. Tonight the moon made it easy, but most nights I can't tell what they are doing. But they can't see me, either. Ganesh, you almost got us caught tonight." I shifted uneasily in the dark.

"But," I asked, "Why doesn't she get in trouble? She is not supposed to be out after the curfew. He's a soldier—doesn't he have to make her stay inside in the night time?"

Jananan did not answer for a while. "I don't know," he admitted. "Maybe she has special permission. What does she have to do with a soldier? I've been trying to understand for a couple of weeks now, since I found out she was going to the graveyard."

"How did you find out?"

"An owl told me."

"What?"

"I heard an owl crying. It was hooting in the trees. I thought maybe I could see it. I've never seen an owl before. Only it wasn't an owl. It was someone in the graveyard. Then I saw Miss Navaratnam come out from the gateway on the other side of the graveyard. I could see through the part of the wall that had fallen down. They didn't know I was there because I was staying quiet, trying not to scare the owl."

Jananan fell silent for a few minutes. When he spoke again, his voice was filled with a hollow-sounding weariness. "I wish I had never gone to look for that owl," he said. "I wish I had never seen Miss Navaratnam in the graveyard with that soldier. I used to like her. She was always good to me."

"You don't like her any more?"

"I hate anyone who is in the army, or who helps the army. Just as much as I hate the rebels."

"Why, Jananan? What did they do to you?"

"To me? To all of us, Ganesh. Don't you know why so many boys are boarders? Half of us have no one to look after us. Our parents are in prison, in the camps, or dead. What about your family?"

I explained what had happened in the market, and how the army had beaten Appa and taken him away, how Amma disappeared and was now in a camp.

"You're lucky. You know where your parents are. Some of the boys have no idea what happened to their families."

"You? What happened to your family, Jananan?"

"The army killed my father. He was in the field and they just shot him. He wasn't running away or anything. One of the neighbors saw. My mother and my little sister were waiting for a bus, and a car bomb went off. The rebels. I'm the only one left."

"That's why I'm here. The principal finds people in other countries to help us with food and school. When he told me I would be a head boy, I was afraid, but he told me that the other boys needed someone who understood what they had to face. I promised I would do my best to look out for everyone, and now the boys are like my family. You, Ganesh. You're my little brother. We'd better go back to bed."

My admiration for Jananan was immense, but I found it hard to understand what Miss Navaratnam had been doing in the graveyard. No matter how I tried to explain it, it did not make sense. I slept through every night for the next couple of weeks, but in the morning the sight of my teacher brought all the questions bubbling up again.

One night I woke up suddenly with a sense that someone was moving past my bed. It was completely dark, with no moon and no lights in the school compound. As my eyes adjusted to the blackness, I heard the door to the outside slowly opening. It had to be Jananan. I undid my mosquito net and crept out of bed to follow.

There was just enough light to see him sliding through the shadows to the graveyard wall. If I had not known he was there I would not have noticed him. Again he headed into the hibiscus bushes where the wall had fallen or been knocked down. I knew that Miss Navaratnam must be in the graveyard again.

My bare feet made no sound on the concrete of the walkway as I moved from pillar to pillar in the colonnade. Jananan was now completely invisible again, an ink stain in the black foliage. I could see no one in the graveyard, but there were certainly voices, a man's and a woman's. Keeping low to the ground, I crossed quickly to the bushes and bumped into Jananan as he crouched in the opening of the wall.

I caught him off-guard and he squealed. Instantly the man's voice called out in Tamil, "Who is there?" Loud footsteps were coming across the graveyard towards us and I could make out the shape of someone tall taking long strides. In a moment he was on us, and Jananan squealed again.

"Run," he said. "Go quickly back to bed." There was a sound of thrashing in the shrubbery and I felt a hand grab at my shoulder and slide off again. Even though no one was holding me, I was too paralysed to run away as Jananan had told me. I couldn't even make a sound.

The man had gone after Jananan instead. "Let me go! Please!" Jananan's voice was frightened. My eyes had adjusted to the darkness now and I could see the man was a soldier. He had Jananan by the arm. Jananan was twisting and kicking, and eventually the soldier lifted him right off the ground and wrapped his arms around Jananan's chest.

"Jananan? What are you doing here?" It was Miss Navaratnam's voice. I had not seen her come up to the wall. Jananan did not answer.

"I suppose you could ask me the same question, though, couldn't you?" she continued. The she saw me. "What, there are two of you? Who else is there?" She peered closely at me. "Ah, no. Not you, Ganesh! Now what? Please, Ranjan. Let the boy down. Jananan, I will take you and Ganesh back to the dormitory. In the morning we will all three of us go to the Principal. You will not be in trouble. Everything will be explained then. In the meanwhile, it is very late and you boys should have been asleep long ago."

Miss Navaratnam walked back to the hostel with us and made certain we were inside and the door was closed. I heard her footsteps moving away from the building and caught a hint of her voice in the far darkness.

"Jananan, are we going to be expelled? Where will we go?"

"No, Ganesh," he replied hesitantly. "I think we're all right. Miss Navaratnam said she would explain everything and that we would not be in trouble. You go to sleep now." He fastened my mosquito net and went softly back to his own bed.

I lay there for several minutes, thinking and worrying, but I could not resist sleep for long. My dreams, though, centred on soldiers grabbing me, holding me, locking me away. I awoke in the morning unrefreshed, unready to face whatever the day was going to bring.

Nothing seemed any different. We went to the dining hall for breakfast, we collected our school things, we went out the door to go to class. Miss Navaratnam was waiting.

"Jananan, Ganesh, come with me, please. Do not worry. You are not in trouble. We need to speak with the principal about what happened last night." Despite Miss Navaratnam's reassuring words and tone, I had a deep feeling of dread, and looking at Jananan's expression told me he was frightened too.

We crossed the cool green foyer of the main office building and found the principal in his office, sipping on a tumbler of milky tea as he read through a sheaf of papers.

"Come in, come in," he called, and Miss Navaratnam shepherded us in ahead of her.

"Principal," she began, "these two boys are troubled by what they saw last night next to their dormitory. I will let you determine how much explanation you want to provide them, but I think perhaps we should be open about the situation. I believe they can both be trusted to keep it quiet."

I was surprised and puzzled by the fact that Miss Navaratnam did not mention that we had been out of the dormitory, that we had been spying on her and the soldier, that she had been in the graveyard, not the school yard.

"The boys know that I was meeting Captain de Silva after curfew. Captain de Silva actually caught and held Jananan for a few minutes, but the boy is not hurt." She looked quickly at Jananan for confirmation, and he shook his head.

The principal studied us for several moments. "You do not think Ganesh is too young to be included in this? He is only seven if I remember correctly—primary two?"

"I leave that to your judgment, Principal. He is a bright boy and has already been through many things children his age should not have to endure."

The principal sighed. He looked at me and smiled. "Ganesh, if you wish to stay, you are welcome. If you would rather go to your class, you may go." I wanted very much to leave the room, to escape back to the usual morning routine, but I was reluctant to leave Jananan. I had by now realized that it was because of my following him last night that he was sitting in the principal's office this morning. I looked at him for direction, but he was staring straight ahead with an empty expression. I could not catch his eye.

"Very well. Miss Navaratnam, why don't you tell the boys who Captain de Silva is?"

She looked at Jananan, then and me. There was a slight smile on her face, but her voice was serious. "Captain de Silva is an officer in the Sri Lankan Army. He is based here in Jaffna, at the headquarters on Hospital Street. His job is to communicate with the Tamil people and to make sure the army command knows about any problems we are having. He is also my fiancé."

At this, Jananan looked up in surprise. I did not know what "fiancé" meant.

"That means I am going to marry him," Miss Navaratnam went on. "We are keeping that information secret right now, because it might upset some of the parents of our pupils here at the school to know that I was marrying a Singhalese. Captain de Silva is a good man, boys. Ganesh, it was Captain de Silva who arranged to get the message from your mother."

She paused and looked at Jananan. I followed her glance and realized that Jananan's face was wet with tears. "Jananan," Miss Navaratnam said, "what is wrong?"

Jananan sucked in his breath and ran his hand across his nose. He said nothing.

I do not know why, but I also began to cry. It hurt to see Jananan so upset, but my tears were coming from somewhere else, a part of me that I could not identify. I wanted so much to roll back time, to go home, to see Amma and Appa again. My thoughts kept drifting back to that day with the string hopper man, and I felt again a rush of shame and sorrow.

Suddenly Jananan stood up and rushed out of the office. The principal looked startled, but did not say anything. Miss Navaratnam made a small movement, as if she might get up and run after him, but she, too, remained silent.

At last the principal spoke to me. "Ganesh, I know this has been difficult for you to understand. You will have questions. Why don't you go and see if Jananan is all right, and then you and he can come back here later—today, tomorrow, whenever you want—and I will try and answer those questions." He pulled a paper handkerchief out of his desk drawer and handed it to me. I wiped my face and walked out of the office, looking for Jananan.

I found him behind the dining hall, sitting with his back to the school, leaning against a scrawny young tamarind tree. There was nothing I could think of to say, so I just sat down on the ground beside him. We must have stayed like that for half an hour or more.

At last he spoke to me. "Hi, Ganesh."

"Hi."

"I don't understand how she can marry someone from the army. He's Singhalese. He might even be the soldier that killed my father."

"Miss Navaratnam said he was a good man. A good man wouldn't do that."

"She's going to marry him. She won't say anything bad about him, even if it is the truth. I hate them; I hate them all." He made a kind of choking sound and looked down at the ground. I didn't know what to say. Miss Navaratnam had always been kind to me, but so had Jananan. I didn't want to choose between the two; I wanted to keep them both close to me.

We sat.

I do not know how long we had been there, but when I looked up again there was another boy sitting with us. He looked a little bit older than Jananan, and he wasn't wearing a school uniform.

Jananan looked up and saw the boy too. For a long time they stared at each other. The strange boy looked very sad, and so did Jananan.

"Who are you?" he asked the boy.

The boy did not answer. He continued to look at Jananan; he stared so long that I began to grow uncomfortable, but Jananan did not seem worried.

Finally the boy spoke, and his voice was filled with the same sadness as his eyes. "I can help, if you want," he said.

Jananan looked puzzled at this, and the sadness on his face was replaced with curiosity. "How?"

"I can take away the pain," the boy said.

"I'm not hurt."

"Yes, you are. I can make it go away."

Jananan's expression changed. He was confused, I thought, just like I was. Doubt slid across his face, to be replaced by something I recognized as hope. This boy was both familiar and mysterious. I was certain I had never seen him before, and yet at the same time I felt that I knew him from somewhere. Perhaps Jananan was feeling the same. In any case, I could tell he was really interested now. He leaned toward the boy. I found myself leaning with him. "Show me," he said.

The boy reached up and touched Jananan once on the forehead. Jananan jerked back, then straightened. "Where are they?" he said softly. This was a strange question. The boy only looked into Jananan's eyes with that same sad, remote look. Jananan slumped, and I thought maybe he was going to cry, but instead he simply smiled and whispered, "Thank you."

Then the boy turned to me. I wasn't sure what was happening, and he didn't ask me. He just reached out and touched my forehead. I could barely feel his fingers, but there was a sense of calm that came over me. The confusion I had felt seconds before was wiped away, but my body seemed heavier than before. To move would require more effort than I thought I could possibly summon.

The strange boy stood up and smiled gently. He turned and walked away. Jananan and I sat immobile, watching him go, unable to even speak until after the boy had disappeared around the corner of the dining hall.

Jananan was the first to stand up. "Come with me, Ganesh," he said. "I must find Miss Navaratnam."

She was in class, working with a small group of my fellow pupils. When we came into the room she looked quickly at us, an expression of concern on her face. Jananan walked right over to her, and I followed dumbly.

"Miss," he said, "I am sorry for running out. I am sorry for everything."

"Oh, Jananan," she replied. "You do not need to apologize. I know everything was very difficult for you. I only hope you will understand some day."

They smiled at each other, and Jananan turned and left the classroom. I went to my seat and took out the reading book. I felt more at ease than I had since Appa was taken away. The feeling that everything was going to work out properly filled my heart.

The next day there was great excitement in the streets around the school. People were streaming past the gates on foot, on bicycles, even in taxis.

"What is happening?" I asked one of the day boys as he came through the entrance. He didn't know—only that crowds were heading to Old Park, just to the east of the school.

As more and more of the day boys arrived, I caught snatches of animated conversation, with frequent mention of Killinochchi and Trincomalee. Several times parents came into the school yard and called to their boys, taking them back out into the street and heading east.

The principal and two of the teachers emerged from the main office building and headed for the gates. An army truck loaded with young soldiers drove past, slowed to a crawl by the crowds. More soldiers passed on foot. The people paid them no attention.

I felt a hand on my shoulder and turned to see Jananan and two of the other boarders. "What's going on?" he asked.

I shrugged. "Lots of people going past on the road."

"That I can see," he laughed. "Where are they going?"

"Old Park. I don't know why."

The principal came back into the school yard. Several more teachers were with him, and they all seemed to be talking at once. He pointed to two of them and they nodded, then turned and went out into the street, following the crowds. I realized that many of the older boys were slipping out of the gates and joining the procession. Loudspeakers somewhere in the neighborhood were broadcasting Hindu prayers.

Jananan turned to the two boys who were with him. "I'm going to see what's happening," he said. "You coming?" They nodded, looking nervously around at the teachers.

"I'm coming, too," I chimed in.

We got as far as the security guard's booth at the gate. "Where are you boys going?" The principal and two of the teachers were looking right at us.

Jananan didn't hesitate. "To see what's happening, sir."

"I don't want you leaving the school by yourselves," said the principal. Jananan looked deflated. "I'll come with you." Jananan glanced up in amazement. The principal was grinning like a young boy. "Let's go and see."

On the way, the principal told the four of us to stay with him no matter what. "You are boarders, and I'm completely responsible for you. Promise you won't go running off." We promised.

"We've been receiving reports for three days now," the principal said. "This same thing has been happening all over the country. In Colombo and Galle first, then in Kandy and several of the hill towns, and now in the north. If the stories are true, something astonishing is going on." He was moving so quickly that we had some difficulty keeping up with him. It was easier to walk right behind him, letting him plough a passage through the crowds, but he wanted us where he could see us, and this meant he had to stop every dozen paces or so and pull all of us together again. I was reminded of the ducks at the reservoir, how the mother would herd her ducklings into a group before taking to the water.

"There are rumors about a boy who can cure illnesses, who can bring peace instead of war," the principal said over his shoulder. I stopped walking. Jananan had also come to an abrupt halt. We looked at each other. Jananan's mouth was open, and perhaps mine was too. He looked stunned.

"Come on, boys," the principal urged. "We're almost at the Old Park."

The crowds were jostling us from all sides, and we moved into a tighter formation around the principal. Jananan grabbed my wrist and held on.

Many of the very old buildings in the park had been demolished a long time ago, but the foundations were still in evidence and the fountain still sprayed up from the well. The people in the crowds now seemed to be going in both directions, heading to the north end of the park and away from it. Those we met seemed calmer and happier than those who were walking with us. There were many soldiers, but they, too, seemed to be caught up in the movement of the masses.

Almost without warning, we were in front of him. I felt Jananan's hand clutch my wrist more tightly, and I looked up to see the same boy we had met yesterday. He was sitting on a bench under a tamarind tree, and people were coming up to him, presenting gifts of fruit and flowers. He touched each person's forehead gently, nodding gravely each time.

"Is he a god?" I whispered to Jananan. "Why are people making offerings?"

"I don't know, Ganesh. Is he the same boy?" I nodded.

People were pushing past us, placing their plates of mangoes and pineapples, their bananas and oranges on the ground beside the bench. Soldiers were bringing lotus flowers. There were hundreds of flowers piled there, and two small mountains of fruit. The smell was delicious.

One of the boys with us, Edgar, stepped forward and stood in front of the boy on the bench. The boy reached out and touched Edgar, and Edgar turned back to us, smiling. Then the other boy who had come with us followed and he too came away smiling. The principal hesitated only for a few more seconds before he also stepped forward, bowed and was touched.

We walked back to school in silence. No one questioned Jananan or me. We had not stepped forward, but the boy on the bench had looked at each of us and given a tiny smile. The smile did nothing to change the deep sadness in his eyes, but it made me feel as if somehow he remembered us, in spite of the hundreds, perhaps thousands, of others he had seen since yesterday.

On the way back we passed many of the boys and teachers from our school, all heading to the Old Park, along with pupils from the girls' school across the road. Everyone was mingled together with the crowds of ordinary people and soldiers from Jaffna.

As we sat on my bed in the hostel, Jananan and I spoke about the way our feelings had changed since the boy had touched us.

"I'm not afraid any more," I said, filled with a new confidence. "I want to go and find my Amma and Appa."

"I'll go with you. I don't feel angry like I did before. I just want to help." This was a surprising claim in one respect. I would never have said Jananan was angry before; he was always so kind to everyone.

The boy was gone the next morning. It seemed as if everyone in the school had gone to see him, including Miss Navaratnam. She said that this same event had been repeated all over the world, and that many, many people had already seen the boy. This was hard to believe, unless the boy truly was a god. Still, there was no denying that people—boys and teachers—in the school had been changed. There was still the same rough play, but no one was getting hurt. Boys were careful not to push things too far. In class, pupils were more attentive and teachers all stopped twisting ears when we gave the wrong answer to a question. Everyone seemed to smile more.

I did not need to go looking for Amma and Appa. Amma was the first to come home, arriving on an army bus from the camp in Killinochchi. When I came out of class that very afternoon, she was standing in the primary play area with the principal. I cried out and ran to her, hugging her as if I would never release her from my arms. She fell to her knees and put her arms around me. I buried my face in her hair and closed my eyes. She smelled so good, so fresh. I knew without being told that she had seen the boy. There was something reflecting in her eyes, and a serenity about her movements that bore witness.

When I opened my eyes and looked over her shoulder, Jananan was standing there. He looked confused and hesitant. I released my grip on Amma and ran over to him, pulling him to Amma.

"This is my friend," I said, then corrected myself. "This is my big brother, Jananan. He has looked after me ever since you went away."

Jananan looked shyly at Amma. To his obvious surprise, she wrapped her arms around us both and hugged us close.

"Let's go home," she said. "All three of us. I think Appa will be back soon. We must get the house ready and make some dinner."

The house was surprisingly clean. The picture of Sri Ganesha, the elephant god, the Overcomer of Obstacles, looked steadily down on our one big room, the space he had protected all these months while we were away. There was rice and curry in the cupboard and the propane tank was full.

Amma was right. Appa came home a day later. He did not want to talk about what had happened, and we did not urge him to tell.

Now, thirteen years after the boy came to Jaffna, I am in my final year at the University of Jaffna, studying agricultural technology. I hope to help develop crops that will provide better nutrition, now that so much of the population does not eat animal protein.

My big brother Jananan also attended Jaffna University, and graduated in business studies with high honors. Amma and Appa are very proud of us both. Jananan is working in Colombo for the government finance ministry, but he comes home every month on the poya day. We all go to the temple to offer prayers for his mother and father, then we share dinner. He works four days a week, and often is able to stay for the weekend as well.

Sri Lanka seems to be full of children. For some reason we are all growing up much more slowly, so even secondary school pupils look like they have just started their studies. No one understands why this is so, but it has happened all over the world, everywhere the boy was seen.

Was the boy a god? He certainly made many miracles, but now he has been gone for ten years. There have been no more appearances, not even rumors of appearances. It no longer matters. When he came to Colombo and the other cities in our land, the powerful people, the government leaders and the wealthy, pushed their way to the front of the crowds. I guess they had heard about the boy's powers, about his deeds in other parts of the world, and wanted some of that healing for themselves. It turned out well for all of us. Our leaders changed overnight. Corruption is now a thing of the past; the anger and the fear between the different communities in our country have been softened, almost eliminated. Everyone has a place to live, food to eat. Children are all in school.

Miss Navaratnam? She married Captain de Silva and moved to Colombo. Jananan sometimes visits them when they all have time off.

Appa still works at the school. He is now head groundskeeper, with three other men to help him. Amma runs the kitchen at the girls' school. The principal at school is still the principal and still watching over all the pupils.

And I am happy.

7.

VANCOUVER

Dear Daniel,

Further to our conversation this morning, I think it might be helpful to put in writing some of the reasoning behind my advice. Please do not misconstrue my intentions; as your doctoral supervisor and—I hope—as your friend, I wish only success for you. I apologize for using the word "obsession" in relation to your work, but while I realize that you have strong personal reasons for your proposed choice of research topic, I must continue to urge you to reconsider.

These are rich times to be engaged in sociological studies. Your master's work on the shifting relationships in Sinaloa society, precipitated largely by the collapse of much of the drug trade in Mexico, has been widely acclaimed within the department and beyond the bounds of the University of British Columbia. You have been rightly lauded as a brilliant analyst and a writer of clarity and eloquence; this combination is not frequently observed in postgraduate students in sociology.

Nonetheless I feel your proposed investigation to the nature of "the boy" (this so-called "El Niño") who is widely credited by the public with having a role in the massive evolutionary leap in human genetics would be a mistake. One has only to look at the example of Dr Wolfgang Drossler to see where this can (and in all probability will) lead. When Dr Drossler published his studies on the flood of refugees migrating away from the rising sea levels in the Bangladesh lowlands, and their successful integration into Indian society in West Bengal, he made the fatal error of reporting the local stories about the boy without questioning them. Note that he did not claim the reports were true; he merely referred to them without attempting to explain or debunk them. If you have forgotten the savage attacks on his professional integrity, you might want to review a couple of the online journals: *Contemporary Sociology* would be a good place to start, with last March's issue being particularly full of vituperative responses. I cannot in all conscience wish a similar fate on you. Dr Drossler was, according to my sources, first in line to succeed Dr Martina Schenkel as Dean of Arts and Sciences at the University of Munich. Now even his position as Head of Social Sciences is being questioned and the journals won't touch his papers. Remember Sayres's Law? "Academic politics is the most vicious and bitter form of politics, because the stakes are so low." Do not for a moment think that any indiscretion in choice of topic will not be used against you.

Of course, Daniel, I realize that you have a great deal of primary source material to work with, since your own parents claim to have not only seen but also interacted with this mysterious boy. I do not doubt for an instant the honesty of their assertions, but I suggest to you that the academic community in general will tend to explain away your parents' (and everyone else's) perceptions of this boy as a side effect of the mutation process. In other words, people honestly believe the boy is real, when he is simply a widespread hallucination that accompanies the genetic shift.

By the way, I hope you do not take offence at the term "mutation," which I use in its strictest scientific sense. I am aware that many people object to being referred to as "mutants" and I try to avoid the label as much as possible. The word mutation, though, seems to have been accepted when discussing the process that you and so many millions of others have undergone. Evolutionary biologists are having seizures over the possibility that mutation can occur after conception; let us leave them to solve the biological problem. We have enough on our sociological plates at the moment.

So, let us first of all look at the available empirical evidence for the existence of this boy. We have the unshakeable sworn testimony of millions of eye-witnesses. This is very powerful, but there is one major flaw: all of those millions have undergone the evolutionary mutation. We have no—I stress no—testimony whatsoever from eye-witnesses who did not show the mutation. There is no one on record anywhere on earth who saw the boy without being affected genetically by the encounter.

The corollary of this is that we have no physical evidence at all. It is hardly credible that if the boy existed, there would have been no photographs, no video recording, no trace of his DNA, nothing. Millions of people saw him, and most of those millions were equipped with mobile devices with which they could have captured photos. No one—absolutely no one in all those millions—thought to do so. The journalists and videographers who flocked to scenes of his appearances came away with nothing to show except reports of the crowds. The only journalists who actually claimed to have seen the boy underwent the mutation. The same is true of the police, civil guards, military personnel and other emergency workers who attended the crowds.

There is the problem of his ubiquity. Over the course of the twelve or thirteen years he was reportedly working his alleged miracles, the United Nations estimates that eight hundred million people underwent the mutation. One need not be a mathematical genius to note that even if the boy were busy twenty-four hours every day for those dozen years, he would have to be processing an impossible number of people every minute. Most people relate their experiences as occurring almost in slow motion, as if the boy were focused entirely on them, at least for a few seconds. The numbers do not work out.

In addition, there are reports of the boy appearing in different places at the same time. Either one accepts that there were several of these children at work (which might account for the eight hundred million figure), or one admits the extreme unlikelihood of the reports being true. How is it possible that the boy is in Cambodia in the morning and in the afternoon he is half a world away in Peru?

Daniel, you know that my husband is from the Kitsumkalum Reserve, far to the north of here near Terrace, and that I grew up in Terrace itself. Both my husband's family and my own have members who have undergone the change. They all state that when the boy appeared in Terrace for those few hours, he was seen by thousands of people, including my brother and my in-laws. We believe the information our relatives give us, but no one else in the scientific community will. Your own transformation has been studied in incredible depth, has it not? Have any of the researchers studying you ever admitted the possibility of supernatural causes?

Then there is the question of the boy's description. He has been assigned to just about every ethnic group on the face of the earth. He is Scandinavian and Chinese, First Nations and Ethiopian, Arab and Indian. No one has ever heard him speaking a language other than the one the listener understands best. There are reports, as you well know, of different people in the same crowd hearing the boy speak in different languages at the same time. Surely that suggests the boy himself is a function of the observer's perceptions, rather than a concrete reality. Some observers have even insisted there was a girl, not a boy.

There seem to be only two elements on which all the reports agree. The first is the expression in his eyes: everyone describes an intense sadness. May I suggest this is a reflection of the unhappiness many of these people must themselves have been feeling? After all, in many instances this boy has popped up like a *deus ex machina* when some crisis or other arose—the food riots in North India come to mind immediately, and the civil wars in East Africa. Even in your own case, your parents must have felt enormous grief at the prospect of losing their only child. It is hardly likely they would envision a laughing boy under such circumstances.

The second element on which all the reports more or less concur is the age of the boy (or girl). No one puts his age at less than ten or over fourteen. There is a greater degree of consistency in this aspect than in any other, apart from the eyes. This of course, is problematic. Even given the slowing of maturation that occurs in mutated children, where puberty is delayed until age seventeen or eighteen, and where skeletal and muscular growth proceeds evenly over an extended period, the boy is remarkably slow to develop. From the first recorded appearances to the final encounters in Morocco we have a span of twelve years. Your parents and those other first families in Finland and Korea all estimated his age as twelve. The Moroccans put him between eleven and thirteen. This freezing of time as it relates to the boy's physical development again points to his not being a real person.

The pattern of his appearances is erratic. He shows up during major crises, like the Central African pandemic fourteen years ago, or the mass exodus of climate refugees from the Mekong Delta, each accompanied by enormous social upheaval and suffering. He also shows up in moments of personal crisis, such as the one your parents endured. And he appears when there seems to be no particular impetus at all, like his arrival in my home town. That being said, he fails to materialize in other times of great suffering—Hurricane Issachar nine years ago, which devastated so much of the Caribbean apparently did not trouble his radar. The randomness of his appearances speaks against any kind of purposeful reasoning.

Finally, the very fact that you yourself have the mutation, and were so intensely studied as a child and teenager, may seem like an advantage, but again it will more likely be used against you if you choose this path of research. You will be accused of scientific blindness, superstition based on your own hallucinations (or those of your parents), or even mental instability. The few social scientists who have also undergone the mutation will come to your defence, but they themselves are already isolated within academia.

Occam's razor, Daniel. The simplest explanation is the most likely to be true. I realize that this principle is not a valid scientific proof, but it is useful in setting up theories. The simplest explanation for the boy is the one science has proposed: he is a hallucination generated by the same forces that produce the mutation, and at the same instant.

Well, now that I have outlined the rationale for abandoning the research topic you propose, let me make a few suggestions for alternatives. I am not in any way trying to manoeuvre you into any of these choices, simply offering up some starting points for you to consider, in the hope that your own thought processes will take you in a direction that you find challenging and engaging.

The slowing of physical and to some extent social maturation has been extremely well documented, not just in your own case, but in thousands of others. No one seems to have a generally-accepted theory as to what evolutionary advantage might derive from this drawing out of the process, leaving the field ripe for investigation. If, as I suspect, there might be some social—as opposed to biological—advantage, this would be right within our purview. We have the example of island species that lower their reproductive rates so as not to outpace the ability of their limited environment to support them, and I suppose it is possible that this slow maturation in mutated humans is a form of birth control. There may be examples of mutated parents who have given birth to more than two children, but so far no one has reported this. Having only one or two children is obviously better for the environment, but is it a biological advantage for the parents? Biology dictates that the more children one has, the greater one's chances of passing on one's genes. Socially, however, smaller family size perhaps may make a lot of sense. This could be an interesting investigation.

Does this slowing of maturation have implications for education? No one at this juncture seems to have a clear answer to that question. Certainly children with the mutation have an easier time of academic learning. They seem free from learning disabilities of any type, and their intelligence in all aspects, including kinaesthetic and musical, is generally above average. Some exhibit a slight delay in interpersonal intelligence, but that gap closes by the end of secondary school. In your own case you seem not to have encountered any difficulties in your academic progress and I know you relate well to others. As more and more of these children enter the school systems, will we need to adjust our pedagogy, and if so, how?

Your master's work on the rearranging of the social hierarchy in Sinaloa State, Mexico, leads into many other possible areas. We know that the mutation seems to prevent people from becoming addicted to alcohol, nicotine and other drugs, and to "cure" such addictions in those who suffered from them before undergoing mutation. It also, for some reason, seems to make it difficult, if not impossible, for mutated people to assimilate animal protein. Mutated humans avoid meat, eggs and dairy products—they are vegan by nature. There are already enough mutated humans to have had an impact on the world's farming industries, with many regions now reducing the size of their animal herds and flocks. You may not have noticed, but prices for chicken here in Vancouver have fluctuated wildly over the past three years, with gluts and scarcities roiling the markets. There is an obvious biological advantage to this, since the supply of plant foods will tend to be greater than the supply of animal foods. Raising crops is economically easier than raising animals. The social dislocation caused by this trend is worth investigating—not only beef farmers will be affected, but all the peripheral suppliers and processors as well. What happens to one's local butcher, for example, or those who transport cattle and hogs?

We are seeing less need for other professions as well: the drop in the crime rate is reducing the need for police; the powerful increase in mutated humans' immune systems is leaving health care workers with more free time. How many other professions and occupations will be impacted? It is still early in this new era for humanity, but perhaps we will even see the day when conflict of many types, local and international, will be minimized. Perhaps you might investigate the options in a world where traditional labor models are being displaced.

There is always the option of death. Dr Jakob Baaksfeld at the University of Witwatersrand in Johannesburg has already done valuable preliminary research in the process of dying as it occurs with mutated humans. The mutation affected a significant population of older persons worldwide (let us leave the investigation of the mechanisms of this to the geneticists and other bioscience enthusiasts) and it appears that the mutation does not extend the average lifespan. The clinical observations of death in this population are well known: the sudden onset of great fatigue—what the dying often call "weariness;" the strange narrowing of the peripheral vision, causing the person to focus intently on a very limited field; the mysterious perception of imaginary fragrances, usually vanilla or cinnamon, which no other people in the room can sense; and the final silence and physical relaxation, accompanied by the trademark slight smile and the closing of the eyes. All these have been reported worldwide. As sociologists we are less concerned with the symptoms of death than we are with attitudes toward it. No one seems to have undertaken any serious study of how this "new" way of dying has affected those attitudes. If death no longer is a painful and unpredictable process, do people approach it with less anxiety? Are funerary practices changing in any way?

Daniel, I realize that you may feel this memo has taken on the length of an undergraduate essay (and may have as many fallacies), but I am hopeful it will help to convince you to focus your research on sociology rather than the supernatural. I do not see any way to investigate "the boy" without succumbing to the temptation to normalize the paranormal, and in the process jeopardizing your credibility as a doctoral candidate.

Please consider all these points carefully, and then let's get together—perhaps on Tuesday next week, and discuss the next steps. I'm looking forward to hearing about your decision, whatever it may be.

With warmest regards,
Marianna da Cunha Ph. D.
Head, Department of Sociology
University of British Columbia

8.

NEW YORK

EVEN AS A BABY Calvin was different. I had taken maternity leave from my work at First Congregational Parish so that I could be the perfect mother. If Calvin needed anything, I would be ready and willing. Instead, Calvin was quiet, almost solemn. He rarely cried. He placed no demands on me that I couldn't immediately fulfill. Richard and I could take him in his carrier wherever we went and he would make no fuss. I am sure he would have slept peacefully through a church board meeting; I once joked that I had known several board members to do so as well. The joke is not funny.

The initial ease of motherhood with Calvin made me overconfident. When the problems came, they struck me out of the blue and I was thrown off balance. Perhaps if he had had a more normal infancy, made more demands, things would have turned out differently, but I suspect it would have made no difference. I would never have been ready to deal with my son; no amount of preparation would have been enough.

Looking back, I can see the signs as clearly as if Calvin had painted them in big red letters on the wall, but at the time I was blind. Richard was more attuned to the strangeness of our child than I was, but he was no more able to face the problems. I saw only the sweet-tempered, placid child with big eyes, straight blond hair and a fear of conflict. Calvin looked angelic. At three, he had an open, innocent expression, a trusting look in his grey eyes. There was a light dusting of freckles across his nose that gave him a sunny appearance quite at odds with his inner reality. A dozen years later not much had changed. His last school photo, looking out at me from its spot on the end table, still has that sweetness, only now with a subtly haunted overlay.

Richard and I both loved Calvin with an intensity that was almost like an ache. We made sure that the first words he heard from us when he awoke in the morning were, "I love you." We spoke those same words every night as we tucked him into bed. He heard them many times in between.

There is a grim irony in our naming him Calvin. The choice was driven by the fact that both of us liked this name, not by any theological considerations: Calvinism, predestination, austerity. Perhaps our child's destiny was already written in infancy and we were powerless to change it. He certainly didn't have much in common with that original Calvin, often stereotyped as stern and unbending in his faith. Our Calvin was only too ready to bend.

I had met Richard when we attended New York University, where we were both in the School of Business. At the time he was attached to another woman, and we never became more than casual acquaintances. He finished his business degree and went into what was then called investment banking, while I drifted out of business and into philosophy and then theology, eventually getting what I felt was a "call" to serve God and the church. I had rather forgotten Richard when we met up again at a class reunion in Brooklyn.

At that party Richard was very attentive to me and I was frankly flattered by his flirting. One thing led to another and eventually we found ourselves living together in a small apartment right in Manhattan. No view of Central Park for us, of course, but things were comfortable and we were close to all the conveniences.

When I was ordained I was settled in a suburban parish in East Brunswick, New Jersey. Despite the loosening of the "moral" standards that had been ongoing since the beginning of the century, we felt it would be prudent to formalize the relationship, and so I started my ministry in East Brunswick as a married woman. This was a few years before the church union movement swept the mainline Protestant denominations in the United States and we became part of the Uniting Church of Christ in America, the UCCA (which Harris often called the "Yuck-Ah").

Harris, or as he insisted on being called, Doctor Harris McVey, was at the same time an inspiration and a thorn in my side. He lived three doors away from us in East Brunswick, but he was pastor of a small storefront church in downtown Newark. I learned later that his doctorate came from a rabidly fundamentalist Bible college somewhere in Kentucky, and that he knew very little about anything other than the text of the Old and New Testaments, with a fierce emphasis on the Old. He was a man of medium build, mouse-blond hair and brown eyes. His chin and eyes were a little too small and his nose and ears a little too large, giving him a faintly rodent-like appearance.

Harris disapproved of many things, although his disdain was never bitter. He opposed the idea of women in ministry, although even the right wing of Christianity had long accepted such a modernization. He never used the title "Reverend" with my name; it was always "Mrs Edwards" or occasionally "Sister" Edwards. Richard preferred to avoid him as much as he could, although Harris always showed a clear respect for Richard.

Harris had no use for demythologizing the scriptures: "After all, Mrs Edwards, if God is not supernatural, what need do we have of Him? The universe is already filled to the brim with natural things." He pronounced every word of the Bible to be the literal truth, except for those passages which he himself declared to be symbolic (John 15:5: "I am the vine, ye *are* the branches" was clearly Jesus speaking in symbols, because it was ridiculous to think of the Lord as a plant, but Genesis 1 was to be accepted verbatim as the scientific truth). Long after most of his right-leaning fellow evangelicals had moved past Creationism (or Creation science, as they preferred to call it), Harris clung to the theory that dinosaurs had walked the earth in Adam's day, and had missed the boat in Noah's great flood. When every state in the union had legalized same-sex marriage, Harris still resisted it. He wasn't all that keen on interfaith unions, but at least he accepted them as legitimate. Harris was against Islam, Judaism and most Christian denominations, and Hinduism and Buddhism were beyond the pale, but he was open and friendly with Jews and Muslims, even with liberal Christians. He frowned at "spiritual" practices, and believed—or claimed to—that good works were essential to salvation.

Harris, in other words, was the opposite of everything I stood for and respected, and yet I could not help engaging in conversation with him when we met on the sidewalk. The conversations almost always became debates.

I am not sure why Calvin was so drawn to Harris, but he was.

The problems with our son began even before he could talk. As he grew, we could not let him see any videos or hear any stories where someone—a person or an animal—was hurt or even upset. Calvin would start to cry and ask why the fox was chasing the rabbit or the boxers were hitting each other. Richard and I had to make sure we never raised our voices with Calvin or each other.

"Maybe we should be training him to deal with this, instead of avoiding the whole thing," Richard kept suggesting. I suspected he was right, but I had no idea how to go about hardening Calvin without breaking him in pieces. Just how fragile our son was, in terms of his ability to deal with others' pain, was a question to which I had no answers.

"He'll grow out of it," my mother declared. "Wait until he's exposed to other children. They'll teach him how to handle the problem."

We put him in nursery school, but Calvin did not grow out of his extreme sensitivity. If anything, it became worse, and we would often pick him up from his afternoon sessions only to find him in tears, sometimes hysterical, because someone had been angry or sad.

"Perhaps you might try some sessions of therapy," suggested the director of the nursery school. "We don't have the expertise to give him the guidance he seems to require."

Richard and I took him to a psychologist in Newark who specialized in treating emotional dysfunction in children. It took us several sessions before he would believe that Calvin had not been abused or traumatized by some terrible event in his early years.

"No, no," we kept saying. "Nothing bad has ever happened to him. He just takes everyone else's pain so seriously—far more seriously than the victims themselves in most cases."

It was on one of these trips into Newark for therapy that we encountered Harris in his work environment. As we were leaving Newark Penn Station, there he was, squatting on the sidewalk in the bright sunlight, talking with a homeless young man. Calvin ran up to them before I could grab his hand and started to chatter.

"Doctor Harris! We're going to see that man again. What are you doing here?"

Harris smiled at him and glanced up at me as I approached. "I'm just talking with my friend here. Dustin, this is Calvin. Calvin, meet Dustin." Harris waved his arm towards me. "And this is Calvin's mother, Mrs Edwards."

"Hello, Dustin," I said, noting that he was about twenty-five or so years old and smelled pretty bad, even from several feet back. Dustin didn't really acknowledge me; he just grunted and continued to focus on Harris.

Harris went back to his conversation and I tugged Calvin away. He resisted for a few moments, looking back at Harris and Dustin, and then we were around the corner and on our way up to the office.

The meeting had an effect on Calvin. Every time we went into Newark after that he was on the alert for Harris. We saw him only once more on the streets, leading a woman by the hand. She was obviously under the influence of alcohol or drugs; Harris quietly said hello to us and smiled widely at Calvin, but he didn't introduce the woman. I was relieved. It was hard enough dealing with Calvin without having to explain that she was hurting herself.

After a year of therapy, Calvin, who was now four years old, had made essentially no progress in overcoming his hypersensitivity. The therapist was at least honest about this. "I'm going to have to admit defeat, Mrs Edwards," he intoned. "I'm washing my hands of this case. I don't really have anyone to recommend to replace me, but you might try Columbia University." I was more shocked by his careless phrasing—"washing my hands of this case," as if Calvin were some piece of filth—than I was surprised by the failure of the treatments.

So we were once more adrift. Three additional therapists eventually came to the same conclusion as the first had, although they phrased it less crudely. The times when Calvin was smiling grew fewer and farther apart. Each episode of upset lasted much longer than each period of calm. Richard was beside himself. Our conversations distilled down into questions:

"What are we going to do about him?"

"When will he outgrow this stuff?'

"Is there anybody in the family who has ever had a situation like this?"

Bringing Calvin to church or Sunday school was out of the question. There was too much violence in the scripture readings, the Easter story was sure to set off a round of hysteria, and the image of Christ on the Cross that hung in the hall would give him nightmares for a week. I could not imagine what the story of the massacre of the holy innocents, the slaughter by King Herod of all the baby boys in Bethlehem, would have done. Richard and Calvin wandered off to the park or down to the ocean on Sunday mornings.

We took him once to the Museum of Natural History in Manhattan, to see the passenger pigeons recently brought back, through advanced cloning technology, from their long extinction. He was fascinated by the beautiful blue-grey and pinkish-brown birds, perched together in the large open aviary, and I was moved by the fact that such a resurrection of a species was feasible even after more than a century of absence. When the museum interpreter began to explain the reasons the pigeons became extinct in the first place, the descriptions of slaughter were too much. We quickly led Calvin away, but he cried for hours afterward.

One day I was walking Calvin home from kindergarten when the unthinkable happened. A squirrel ran across the road just ahead of where we were walking. Traffic was heavy in both directions and the animal did not make it safely through. A car ran over the squirrel's back legs, crushing them, and the squirrel, in obvious agony, struggled a couple of yards further, dragging its useless back legs and hips, until another passing car ended its suffering. I was horrified by this sudden scene, but Calvin was catatonic. He didn't cry or say anything; he stood with his mouth open and his eyes starting out of his head in panic. He couldn't tear himself away from the lifeless body of the squirrel, reduced from a lively little bundle of fur to a bloody stain on the pavement.

It was several seconds before I could move myself. "Come on, Calvin. Let's go home." I could feel the weakness in my own voice as I spoke. I wasn't sure that I wouldn't vomit or even faint. Calvin didn't budge. In the end, I picked him up and carried him home.

For hours that evening we tried to get Calvin, as Richard put it, to snap out of it, but his trance-like state continued. He wouldn't fall asleep and wouldn't respond to anything. We ended up taking him to the emergency department at the Children's Hospital of New Jersey, where the doctor on duty gave him a sedative and sent us home.

The next day Calvin seemed no better, and I stayed home with him, sitting next to his bed and talking non-stop in a soft voice. There was no response, and I am sure anyone observing us would have thought me insane. I think maybe I was. We went back to emergency several more times, hoping that the hospital would admit Calvin, but each time we were sent home with another dose of sedative. I made an appointment with a specialist in New York for the following week.

Two days later, there was a knock at the door and I opened it to see Harris standing there. "Good morning, Mrs Edwards. I was just talking with Mr Edwards. He says that your little boy is not doing well. Do you mind if I come in and say hello to him?"

I almost shut the door in Harris's face, but for some reason I stood aside and gestured for him to come in. Was this some sort of morbid curiosity on Harris's part, or did he think maybe he could pull off a faith healing?

Harris followed me into Calvin's room and leaned over the bed, looking intently at Calvin's face. He stroked Calvin's hair gently. "Mrs Edwards, may I say a prayer for him?"

I was speechless with shock and guilt. In the time since Calvin had seen the squirrel die, I had not once prayed for God's help. I hadn't even thought about it. It took Harris to bring me back to the ground of my belief, or what I claimed was my belief. I nodded. "Of course."

"O Lord," Harris began, "You see the suffering of this child. In your mercy, heavenly Father, bring him comfort and let him find happiness again. Let his parents rest easily in the knowledge that their son is restored to them. In Jesus' name we ask it. Amen."

I echoed the amen and looked quickly at Calvin, half expecting him to rise from his bed like Jairus's daughter in the New Testament story of Jesus bringing the dead girl back to life. Calvin didn't stir a muscle and his eyes remained shut.

"I hope he will be back to normal soon, Mrs Edwards. Thank you for letting me see him." Harris let himself out.

It was another day before Calvin opened his eyes. Whether the sedatives had caused his long sleep or whether it was still an effect of seeing the squirrel, we never knew. He never spoke again of the incident and of course we were not about to remind him.

He did speak of Harris, though. "Why did Doctor Harris come to see me?" he asked a couple of weeks later.

"When do you mean?" I said, although I knew.

"When I was asleep. He came to see me and said some words to God. Why did he come?

I wish I knew. "He came because he heard you were feeling bad. He wanted to see if he could make you feel better."

"I feel better, Mommy. I'm okay, right?"

"Yes, Sweetheart. You are more than okay. I love you." I hugged him close, thinking that in truth Calvin was not okay.

Calvin's connection with Harris remained strong, and I was more than a little bit jealous at times. Harris seemed to be completely at ease with Calvin, something that was certainly not true for any other adult in Calvin's life, Richard and me included. Harris had a way with my son that I could only envy. With no children of his own, no family at all that I knew of, Harris was able to reach Calvin on a level that I could not even dream of.

Most of the times when I heard Calvin laughing were times when Harris was with him.

Then Harris was gone. His house went up for sale and he simply vanished without saying goodbye to us or to Calvin. I didn't know whether he was still working out of his storefront in Newark; I didn't know where the storefront was or what it was called, and I wasn't about to go prowling around that part of Newark seeking him. Still, his disappearance was felt by Calvin and by me.

By the time he was ten, Calvin had begun asking theological questions for which I had no satisfactory answers:

"Why did God make a world where people get hurt? Where they die? How come God made animals that have to eat other animals? Doesn't God care about the animals that get eaten?"

Calvin stopped eating meat and fish. He couldn't bear the thought that the chicken or cow had died so he could have dinner. His distress over this forced Richard and me to go on a meat-free diet as well. It wasn't much longer when Calvin gave up eggs, and then he learned at school what happened to dairy cattle and he went off cheese and milk. I was growing more desperate for ways to make sure he was getting a balanced diet. Luckily I came across an English-language Jain cookbook on a website, and I ordered it. Of course I had already gone through a number of vegan recipes, but the Jain book seemed to offer a proactive aspect. I was afraid it would only be a matter of time before Calvin would start to wonder about killing plants so he could eat, and the Jain cookbook had a whole section on how to prepare plant foods without killing the plant. I would be ready with the arguments when Calvin asked the questions, but he never reached that point in his thinking.

When Calvin started high school we moved to Brooklyn, to a townhouse on Albemarle Road. Four local Uniting Church congregations had been combined into a single charge, and I was called to minister there. Richard was working in Manhattan for the National Bank of America, one of the new institutions formed from the remains of the unregulated banks that went under two decades ago.

The church was in serious decline, of course. Not just the UCCA, but all churches—all religions for that matter—were increasingly seen as irrelevant, even here in America. Many of our UCCA congregations had in fact become "house churches" which met in someone's living room or basement. For a while, the more fundamentalist denominations had resisted this trend, but even they were now facing a loss of membership and financial support. Catholic churches were being sold off along with all the others.

We in the mainline churches responded first by combining resources—sharing sanctuaries, services, offices. Then we began to amalgamate more formally. The negotiations that led to the UCCA went on for almost a decade before the final charter was signed by all six denominations. The Episcopalians split over the issue, with the more Anglo-Catholic elements separating to join with the Roman Catholics and the other eighty percent becoming part of the UCCA.

The bleeding continued. We tried updating the services, enlivening the music, bringing in more media and in some eyes rendering our services no more than cheap entertainment. We told ourselves that quality of membership was more important than quantity, dancing blindly around the thought that we had neither.

We demythologized the message. The Bible speaks in parables we said. It is a record of humanity's increasing understanding of the nature of God. The resurrection, the incarnation, the redemption from sin—all were myths, stories that contained a moral, but not necessarily a literal, truth. The Swiss theologian Karl Barth, writing more than a century ago, had resisted this trend, which he called the heresy of modernism. We try to control God by making the revelation of the word fit our logical, scientific understanding. Along the way, we lose sight of the very real fact that the appeal of Christianity, of religion in general, is its supernatural. Harris had been right about this. Our classic American novelist and poet, John Updike, shared the position. In *Seven Stanzas at Easter*, he warns that the rational explanations for the biblical narrative become a mockery of God. Yet that is exactly what we did: downplayed the miraculous because we were embarrassed by its lack of scientific, logical rigor. The sheep drifted further from the shepherd.

So now we have gone from slow decline to free-fall. With the ongoing consolidation, the UCCA offices were all centralized here in New York.

Richard and I had been praying that when Calvin entered his teens, the hysteria and pain he struggled with would subside, if only a little, but we were disappointed. Instead, his questions became more and more directed at us personally.

"Dad," he would say, "how can you work for the bank, knowing that the profits it makes come from other people's work?" Calvin was not only an obsessive environmentalist, he was becoming a socialist, an advocate of the same communal ideals that marked the early church and that have been discredited so many times since in the history of economics: the failed kibbutzim of Israel as much as the failed communes of Soviet Russia.

To me, the age-old question: "Mom, how can God be all-knowing, all-powerful, all-loving and still allow the kind of suffering that goes on? How can he have created a world, maybe even a whole universe, where billions of creatures die in pain and fear every day? How could he create so much evil?"

Calvin wasn't buying the argument that God didn't create evil, that sin was an invention of Satan or of human weakness. "But if everything was created by God, then God must have created the conditions that allowed Satan or humans to be evil. He must have seen where his ideas would lead, or he wouldn't have been all-knowing. Or he wasn't all-powerful; he couldn't stop evil from growing. Or he just doesn't care; he doesn't love the world the way Jesus claimed."

We in the church, of course, have no answers to these arguments, and we fall back on the same old weary excuses and devices. "Calvin, we don't understand how the mind of God works. What seems to us to be God's lack of knowledge, or power, or love, may be part of a larger, necessary plan or pattern that we are still unable to see. Once we meet God face to face, as Saint Paul says, we will understand the point of it all."

"But Mom, if God loves us, why would he put us through all that? Would you make me suffer so much pain, even die, just so I could learn a lesson? What kind of lesson are we supposed to learn from all this suffering?"

"Calvin, it's a mystery. That's why we call it faith, not certainty. We just have to trust in the ultimate goodness of God." I found myself groping in the dark for some way of reassuring my son, but all the while I felt the floor giving way under me and the walls closing in.

In his mid-teens, Calvin's bleak outlook became almost constant. He stopped asking the questions, and I am ashamed to say that this was relief in a way. I was fearful of his dark moods but glad that the burden on my own beliefs was lifted a little.

School never came easily to Calvin. He got through the elementary years by regurgitating what he was expected to learn, but in high school he floundered, then drifted. He seemed to have no friends, no interests outside of his own thoughts. He eventually stopped reading, stopped watching television, stopped going out unless we dragged him with us. He didn't complain about anything, but he showed no desire to participate in the world around him. He dreaded any competitive activities; the only sport he ever took an interest in was swimming, and even that he would do only if he wasn't competing against someone else.

Was he bullied at school? He denied it several times and we stopped asking. There was no hint that he was picked on, and his teachers were concerned more with what one of them termed his "self-enclosure" than with any obvious negative attitude from others. Some of his teachers wondered aloud to us about drug abuse, but Richard and I were both completely sure Calvin had never experimented. He probably would not know where to look.

It was a week after his sixteenth birthday that I got the text. I was at a meeting at the central office in Manhattan and I almost didn't bother to read it when the tone sounded, but I pulled the phone out and saw that it was from Calvin. It was rare for him to message us, and curiosity pushed me to go out into the corridor and check. I froze.

"Mom," it read. "Don't come in the basement when you get home. Call 911."

For a few seconds I couldn't move, couldn't even see. The world around me flashed red and black and I thought I was going to pass out. Then I did as Calvin said. I called 911 and gave them the address, told them to break down the doors if they had to. I called Richard as I raced to the subway.

"Richard! Come home right away. There's something wrong with Calvin.

"I don't know what. He texted me, said don't come in the basement. Call 911.

"Of course I did. Please hurry." I shut off the phone before he could ask any more and raced down the escalator to the platform. There was a crowd waiting for the train, but I pushed my way through to the front.

It took a lifetime to get home. When I ran up the street from the Flatbush subway station, the EMS people were already there, with a police car and an ambulance. The front door of the townhouse was open; Calvin must have left it unlocked.

I raced up the steps and into the front hall. A police woman was standing there, and I halted. She must have seen the fear on my face. Her own expression reflected the anxiety in my heart.

"Are you his mother?" she asked. I felt the blood draining away. I nodded.

"Is he okay? He texted me; don't go in the basement. I told the 911 person."

"Ma'am, come and sit down." She led me to the living room and eased me into a chair. I knew what was coming, but tried frantically to hide from the words.

"Ma'am, we were too late. Your boy hanged himself."

I tried to cry out, but couldn't breathe. I don't think I lost consciousness, but there was a pause in time; the world stopped spinning and the sun stuck motionless in the sky. Richard was beside me.

"Jill," he said. "Oh, Jill. What will we do?"

I had no words of comfort—not for Richard, not for myself. A sudden thought stabbed through me: what if I had taken a cab? What if I hadn't stood on the subway platform, waiting, waiting? At each stop on the line urging people to hurry out of the car, hurry in so the doors could close and we could be on our way again. Could I have reached home in time to stop Calvin?

Where was God? I screamed the question inside my skull. Why had God allowed this? What kind of loving being . . . I had to stop myself. Calvin's questions. The ones I had never been able to answer for him.

Harris was at the funeral service. I don't know how he learned of Calvin's death. He had no words of advice, no answers to any questions, but he came. He held my hand for a minute, said, "I'm so sorry, Jill. Calvin was a good boy." It was the first time Harris had ever called me anything other than "Mrs Edwards". I was afraid he would see Calvin's suicide as a sin, that he would blame my son for weakness, but instead he just looked sadly into my eyes and said again, "I'm so sorry."

Harris came with us to the cemetery and stood quietly beside Richard as the casket was lowered into the grave. His head was bowed and he was whispering a prayer as we each took a small handful of earth and threw it onto the coffin. We turned and headed back to the cars as the cemetery workers moved in to complete the interment.

"If I can be of any help," Harris said, "please call." He handed Richard a business card, which Richard glanced at and slid into his pocket.

"Thank you for coming, Harris," I said. "Calvin always liked you."

"I thought well of him, too. I hope you find peace." Harris walked away to the bus stop and Richard and I helped my mother and his parents into the limousine to return to the funeral home where we could catch the bus home.

Months of emptiness, of feeling that nothing was worth doing, nothing worth saying, nothing even worth thinking. I tried to keep working, but the days crawled by in meaninglessness. Like Jesus on the cross, I called out to God, "Why have you forsaken me?" Did Calvin cry the same words, or had he long before written God off as unresponsive?

My mother called almost every day to ask how I was doing. I always told her, "It's difficult, Mom. I can't stop thinking about him." She would reply with "I love you, Jill," and remind me that she was thinking about us. "I'll call tomorrow, Jill. Feel better, Honey."

Richard and I passed each other wordlessly at home. He would touch my hand, or I would lean against him as we sat on the sofa together, but we rarely spoke. What was there to say? Eventually Richard began to turn on the wall television as we sat, but I didn't pay much attention. Some island nation in the Pacific was being evacuated to New Zealand because of rising ocean levels. The Democrats were poised to sweep the election in California. It was Richard who got our meals, and urged me to eat. I imagine I must have seemed to him like some sort of zombie, a walking corpse that was feeding, not on his brains, but on his soul.

I couldn't understand how my husband, Calvin's father, could continue to function in the world. I still don't know how he did it; he was strong, but not stronger than me—at least I had never thought of him as stronger. Still, while I sank deeper into myself, Richard began making the effort to pull out of the swamp we lay in. He ran music through the sound system. It wasn't upbeat music, but it wasn't a dirge, either. It was intended, I guess, to be soothing, but it didn't help me.

I was no longer able to minister to my congregations, and I was given a position in the head office, developing weekly liturgies for house churches and the dwindling number of congregations. It is lonely work, and I get no feedback about the results of my efforts. I am not sure that I care.

I can't remember the exact moment when we became aware of the boy. The media began to carry stories about a strange boy who was causing a stir somewhere in Asia or Africa, and then he was all over the news. People at the office could speak of nothing else some days.

The evangelical churches were the first to suggest that this boy was the precursor to the second coming of Christ, sort of a latter-day John the Baptist. Some even went further and hinted that perhaps this was Christ himself, curing the sick, giving sight to the blind, comforting the afflicted. As the boy materialized in China, in Indonesia, in New Zealand, excitement mounted in our fading churches; maybe the long-awaited Kingdom was at hand.

There were no reports of the boy appearing anywhere in America, although he had been seen in Canada and the Caribbean. The evangelicals began to pray that he would arrive on our shores soon.

That seemed to be the signal. Suddenly one evening, there was Harris, the same Doctor Harris McVey, on our screen, speaking earnestly about this boy. The interviewer asked him his opinion of the theory that the boy was the second Incarnation.

"Not a chance," Harris said calmly. "He is a trick of Satan. In the Book of Revelation we read, 'He deceiveth them that dwell on the earth by the means of those miracles which he had power to do.' This boy seems to cure the sick and strengthen the weak, but what message does he bring? Does he preach the gospel of Jesus Christ? Does he condemn evil and call people to repent before they are cured? No—he just goes ahead and cures their physical ills. At best, he is a tool of the devil; at worst, he is the devil in disguise. Why else would he have appeared in China and not America?"

I couldn't believe my ears. I had always known Harris could be opinionated, but he had been kind to Calvin, and to Richard and me. He worked among the poor of Newark. Now here he was on television, sounding like a chauvinistic bigot. With a disgusted cluck, Richard flicked off the channel.

The boy, as we all know, soon appeared in America as well, in Oregon and Missouri first, then in many places. Harris continued to speak out against him, urging people not to go to the boy's healing sessions. Richard had begun to follow the controversy, and found out that the rest of the world, the part that hadn't been preoccupied with Calvin, had known all this for three years already.

The boy came to New York. Word spread rapidly that he was in Ferry Point Park in the Bronx, and crowds were converging on the place in spite of all Harris's warnings. I was at the office, my eyes glazing over with a dusty piece of prayer I was trying to compose for house church use, when Richard walked in.

"Come on, Jill. We're going to the Bronx."

On the way there by cab, Richard told me the boy was known to cure pain; Richard wanted his pain cured. He was prepared to suspend disbelief and beg for healing. He wanted us to be at peace.

Peace was not a word one could apply to Ferry Point Park that afternoon. The park itself is a derelict stretch of land at the north end of the

Bronx-Whitestone Bridge. It looks, at the best of times, like an abandoned landfill site. The trees are scrubby bushes, mostly new growth rising up after Hurricane Travis four years ago, one of those superstorms that have done so much damage to our stretch of the coast. With what must have been tens of thousands of people coming and going, it lost all resemblance to a natural area. The heat, noise and litter were oppressive. New Yorkers of every description were loudly being New Yorkers: aggressive, argumentative, in a hurry.

Richard paid the cab driver and took my hand. We followed the crowds, coughing in the foul air and blinking in the sun. I had left my sunglasses at the office, and the glare was painful.

After all the media reports, the boy was a disappointment. He was small, no more than twelve years old, and seemed vaguely Asian. He did not look the least bit like Calvin, and I realized with a biting pang of sorrow that I was hoping for some hint of my son.

Without a word, Richard moved toward him, gently pulling me by the hand. Standing directly in front of the boy, I saw the depth of sorrow in his eyes, reflecting the grief I felt myself. There was a faint smile on his lips, but it did nothing to soften the ache in those eyes.

Richard leaned toward him and the boy reached out and touched Richard on the forehead. I felt my husband's hand tighten on mine and he stepped to one side so the boy could reach me. The boy looked directly into my eyes; I shook my head and stepped back without his touch on my forehead. The next people took my place.

Richard did not notice that I had refused the touch. He would not have understood, would have urged me back, would have perhaps even begged me to accept.

I could not.

The pain was my connection to my son. Grief tied me to him as tightly as love, and I could not let that bond break. There was a ragged, Calvin-shaped emptiness in my heart, a space that only sorrow could fill. Without sorrow, what would be left? The Canadian novelist Yann Martel once wrote that "in the end, the whole of life becomes an act of letting go" and I suppose he is right, but I could not let Calvin go. I still cannot.

By the time I told Richard what I had done, the boy was gone from New York. He appeared that same evening in Maryland and the next day in western Pennsylvania. Richard wanted to try and catch up with him, but I refused.

It was a shock to see Harris on television again, recanting his earlier condemnation of the boy. "I went to Ferry Point," he told the interviewer. "I meant to confront this boy, to show people the true face behind the benign mask. Instead, I felt him reaching into my heart, even as his fingers touched my forehead. This was my own moment on the road to Damascus."

The interviewer clearly did not catch Harris's allusion to Saint Paul's conversion. From his expression, it seemed as if he were trying to remember whether Damascus was in New Jersey. Harris continued. "It was as the Bible says: the scales fell from my eyes and I beheld the truth. Wherefore by their fruits ye shall know them. I am sorry it took me so long to understand."

Richard stays with me. He looks after me as gently and untiringly as a parent would. I am grateful, but also resentful. Richard stays with me because it is the right thing to do, and he is no more capable of making an anti-social decision than an ant or a bee. The boy has done that to him. He is at peace, but it is a soulless peace.

Maybe that is as close as we'll ever get to the answer, Calvin, to your question about why God allows pain. It makes us human—it distinguishes us from the insects. It is a holy agony. Without the capacity for making bad decisions, even evil ones, we have no capacity for making good choices.

Richard would disagree, of course. He speaks gently of his own sadness, but he accepts that Calvin made his decision. He is certain that if Calvin had known how much his action would make us suffer, Calvin would have chosen differently. This is true, I know; Calvin would have been horrified at the pain he has caused.

How much pain am I causing Richard? I have the power to stop, but I have chosen not to use it. What does that make me? I am soaked, drowning in self-pity, perhaps, but I cannot pull away.

I am useless to the church now. My prayers are hollow, my meditations not worth putting on paper. Richard does everything to bring me round, but I am deaf and blind. He should leave, save himself, but I know he won't. I turn Jesus' cry around: "My God, why have I forsaken you?" There is no answer.

I long to believe that there is a heaven, that there really exists a place in an afterlife where Calvin's spirit waits patiently for my arrival, but the belief will not come. There is nothing but darkness.

So many people's hearts raced to the hope that the boy would bring us to God, to a new Eden. That he was preparing us for the reign of the Lord.

For me, there is only this broken world, a world without God and without hope.

9.

FLORENCE

I SAW ADRIANA TODAY. Or at least I thought I did. I made a fool of myself.

I was sitting by the window in that small restaurant in the Piazza Santa Croce, the one that makes the wonderful artichoke salad, watching the people strolling through the square in front of the church. Some youngsters were trying to climb up onto the statue of Dante Alighieri, and the usual crowd of musicians and other performers were plying their trade around the edges of the piazza.

She walked into my field of vision from the west, as if she had been shopping in the old city. Her elegant stride, her perfect clothing, her simple, natural beauty—just as she always appeared. I felt my breath catch, and I jumped up, knocking over my chair and almost tipping the table. The bowl rocked back and forth several times before settling.

By then, I realized she could not possibly be Adriana. She looked like the Adriana of forty years ago, the Adriana I had fallen in love with, but she was not Adriana. As she melted into the crowd in the square, I reached down and righted the chair. I sat down again.

My heart was thudding heavily in my chest and I felt slightly dizzy. The waiter came up to me, and at first I could not understand what he was saying.

"*Signor*, are you all right? Can I get you anything?"

"Oh, no, Enzo. I'm fine. I just saw someone in the piazza. I thought I recognized her, but I was mistaken. I'm sorry to worry you."

"*Bene, signor*. If you need anything, I am nearby."

Damn it. I have tried to avoid thinking about Adriana, and of course it is impossible to recall Adriana without bringing up the memory of Marco as well. The two of them are entwined in my heart more intensely than they were ever entwined in reality.

Adriana Moretti. I fell in love with her when I was twenty, and I've never fallen out of love with her, not even after all these years. Her absence has only made my image of her more beautiful, more charming, more inaccessible. When she walked out of my life, I was devastated. That, you understand, is why I have struggled so hard to lock out the memories, and why I was so shocked to see the woman today.

Marco Salotti. My best friend in childhood and youth. He and I grew up together, on the same street here in Florence. His family was originally from Venice, but they came here long before the sea began reclaiming Venice in earnest. Marco too walked out of my life, and I feel the loss. It is painful to remember him, but even so I find myself smiling at the recollection of our friendship.

And the third member of the trio: me, Vittorio Costa. Marco always called me Vito; he was in too much of a hurry to pronounce four syllables, and after all, two syllables were all he had to his own name. I was, and still am, cautious by nature, where Marco was reckless. I was, and still am, more than a little shy in company, where Adriana could converse easily with anyone. So here I am, growing old in Florence, and today I find myself at last wondering what became of Marco and Adriana. Do they ever think of me? How did they move on with their lives?

As I said, Adriana was beautiful. She came to Florence from Milan, and I always imagined that she had breathed in the sense of fashion, the grace of movement and the simple elegance for which Milan is known. Her dark hair was usually swept up in a style that hearkened back to the time of Garibaldi. She could have been the model for many of the marble busts in the Galleria dell'Academia, where my office is today. Her skin was flawless, as if it, too, were modelled on those alabaster portraits in the gallery. She used little make-up; she needed none. No matter what she wore, it always seemed to have come from the fashion runways of Milan, and yet she herself was always the very antithesis of the robotic mannequins that stalked those runways. Her lips wore a smile as lightly as the water wore sunbeams. She treated everyone as if she wanted to be in their company. I never heard her say an unkind word to anyone—except me, and I surely deserved it.

Marco, too, was beautiful. The neighbor women along our street exclaimed constantly over his good looks; his long eyelashes were wasted on a boy, they said. His hair was such a dark shade of brown that it appeared black. His facial features were perfectly balanced; everything was the right size—his ears, his nose, his jaw. His teeth were straight and dazzlingly white against the deep red of his lips. I know all these details because I heard them discussed so frequently on the steps of nearby houses. Marco had the serene confidence of someone who has known all his life that he was attractive.

People told me I was handsome, too, but they never meant I was as perfect as Marco. In my teens I was spotted with acne, an affliction that never touched Marco. I was shorter in the legs than Marco, too, making him a good four or five centimetres taller. I wore a dental appliance for three years, and still my teeth were never as perfect as his.

Marco never dwelt on his perfection. He was as careless of his good looks as he was of everything else, but his carelessness was in itself beautiful. He could wear anything and make it look stylish. When we were in secondary school, other boys studied his outfits and copied them, always without the same success Marco had.

He was loyal. Never once did he leave me out of anything, although he could easily have joined any group in the school had he so chosen. No matter what activity he was invited to, he asked me along, and I was usually only too pleased to accept. This got me into difficulties on more than one occasion.

He found an inflatable dinghy once; God knows where. Nothing would do but that we should try it out.

"Come on, Vito! Help me blow it up all the way. We need to go for a sail on the river."

"How can we go for a sail? There's no sail on this thing."

"We'll just have to paddle it."

"Marco, there are no paddles, either."

"We'll use our hands." Marco always had an answer for everything, it seemed.

We took turns puffing into the raft until Marco declared it seaworthy. Neither of us had any concept of what "seaworthy" might entail, but when we pushed our craft down the weed-grown bank and into the Arno, it bobbed cheerfully enough on the surface. Marco was first in, and his weight depressed the floor of the dinghy so that one side came up out of the water.

"I'm not sure about this, Marco," I said, instantly regretting the whining tone of my own voice.

"Come on, Vito. Just jump in. It's easy."

Although I had already had enough experience to realize that when Marco said something was easy, he didn't mean it would be easy for me, still I jumped off from the bank and into the dinghy. It rocked unsteadily and I fell over in a heap, making water slosh up over the side and soaking us both.

"Good work, Vito. Columbus would be proud." All I could do in response was to sit myself upright and stare foolishly at Marco.

"Okay, let's go!" he said, and began paddling furiously with his left hand. I copied him, using my right hand on the other side of the dinghy.

Marco had failed to take into consideration that neither of us possessed very large hands, and our fingers were not webbed. Once we were out from the bank, the current grabbed our boat and we found ourselves drifting downstream toward the centre of the city.

"Paddle, Vito!"

"I'm paddling! How do you steer this back to shore?"

"We have to paddle harder. Toward the bank."

Paddling harder, it appeared, meant paddling faster and splashing more furiously. Soon we were completely drenched and further from the bank than ever. We were heading toward one of the weirs that had been installed after the great floods of the last century. The river slipped over this little dam in a pale sheet of silver.

"Marco!" I screamed, "We're going over the dam! We'll drown!"

For once Marco didn't contradict me or tell me I was worrying needlessly. He kept splashing ferociously, producing a shimmering wall of spray that must have looked supremely impressive from the shore.

When we reached the weir, though, we didn't plunge over to our murky graves. Instead, the dinghy bumped stupidly up against the concrete and lodged there, our bodies pushing the floor down enough to stop us from sailing across the barrier.

"Hey. No problem," shouted Marco. He began to pull us along the edge of the weir until we reached the bank. He clambered out onto solid ground and held the dinghy until I could also make landfall. Then he released our ship and we watched as it slid over the weir and went twirling downstream. We stood, soaking wet, until it vanished from sight, then squelched our way back upstream and home.

Marco was the best soccer player in the school, and even the older boys were always asking him to come to the pitch with them and play. He loved the game, but would only play if I were on his team. While I wasn't a bad player, I wasn't in the same category as Marco, but the other boys always put up with me so they could have him take part. Many times I tried to tell him it was all right to play without me, that I would come along and just watch, but he was insistent: "It's more fun if you play, too, Vito." That's what I mean by Marco being loyal. Sometimes I wished he wasn't quite as eager to have me join in, but most of the time I was grateful.

Once we went on our own to the old city, to the Duomo, the Basilica di Santa Maria del Fiore, our huge cathedral. I wanted to see the paintings inside, and Marco wanted to look at the dome, which was said to be one of the largest in all Italy. When we got to the main entrance, though, we found we would have to pay to go inside.

"Whoever heard of paying to go to church? It was free a couple of years ago," said Marco in disgust. "Jesus said to let the little children come to him. We're little children. We should get in for free."

"We're not so little," I reminded him. "We're thirteen years old."

"So? Can we vote?" He grinned at me. "Come on, Vito." He pulled me toward the entrance.

The security guard was watching the tourists as they paid their fees and trooped into the Basilica. Marco marched right up to the line and I followed. When we were almost at the desk, Marco started waving at someone inside the cathedral and yelling, "Hey, Mama! Papa! We're out here! Wait for us!"

The security guard looked quickly in the direction Marco was waving and Marco made a dash for the inside of the church, tugging me along. We heard the guard shouting at us, but within seconds we were hidden among the tourists. I had never before been inside the building, although I had seen it many times from the piazza. The outer walls were decorated with hundreds of statues of saints and other carvings, and the stone of the walls was laid in different colored marble bands. Inside, though, it was a new world for me. The walls and ceiling were covered with paintings, paintings so huge I couldn't imagine how anyone could have executed them. The colors had faded slightly, but I could picture them when they were fresh, with all the vibrant tones of the renaissance palette. It was mesmerizing.

"Hey, Vito! Come on! Let's climb up into the dome and get a closer look."

I do not like heights. I feared them as a child and the fear has never left me. Marco was urging me to come with him up the dome stairway, which looked to me far more fragile and precarious than it really was.

"I don't think so, Marco. I don't like climbing that high."

"Come on, Vito. It will be fun. We'll see everything from up there."

I didn't want to see anything from up there, but he was already pulling me toward the base of the stairway. Then he got another surprise. There was an extra fee to climb into the dome. I felt a surge of relief.

The relief was short-lived, though, as Marco ran towards the stairs and raced upward. The attendant shouted after him, but did not follow. I stayed on the ground.

It was a long time before Marco came back down. "Vito, you would have loved it. The pictures are so big. Everyone down here looks so small." A security guard was coming toward us. "Let's go," Marco said, heading back toward the entrance. At the last moment, we realized we had to exit through a different door than the one through which we had entered, but soon we were out in the piazza again and I could breathe more easily.

There was one skill I had that Marco lacked. I could draw. When we were twelve, I had made portraits of every student in our class, and done them well enough to ensure my popularity for the year. Marco bragged that I was one of the great artists of Florence, and although I was embarrassed by his claims, I didn't try to stop him from spreading the word. I knew even then that I wanted to follow in the magnificent artistic tradition of my city, and I took every opportunity I could to study the works of my predecessors.

Florence, of course, is one vast art gallery, thanks to the efforts of the Medici and other noble families of the past. The Galleria dell'Accademia, where I work today, would be a leading art museum in almost any other city on earth. In Florence, it is just one of many, although it houses Michelangelo's famous statue of David. The piazzas are full of works by famous sculptors; our churches are decorated by the great masters of the renaissance. New trends in architecture, new techniques in painting, new ways of imagining the world, all had their start here in our city. As a young boy, I was acutely conscious of all this; I could hardly wait to take my place in the pantheon.

We went with our class, Marco and I, to visit the Palazzo Vecchio, Florence's city hall, and the piazza in front, which boasts a host of statues, including a rather poor copy of Michelangelo's *David*. The Loggia dei Lanzi, on one side of the piazza, has a whole gallery of statuary by sculptors such as Flaminio Vacca and Cellini. Even Marco was impressed, and we wandered around the piazza almost in silence, taking in all the famous and not-so-famous works. There was even an exhibition of modern sculpture under a nylon awning at one end of the piazza.

I had brought my sketch pad, and sat for half an hour drawing the huge *Fountain of Neptune* by Bartolomeo Ammannati while Marco and my other classmates walked from one side of the piazza to the other, checking every so often to see how far I had progressed with my drawing. Even the teacher came by several times to see my work, and to smile encouragingly at me.

After school, Marco and I went to his house. His mother and father were both still at work and his older sister wouldn't be home for another couple of hours.

"Let's play an art game," suggested Marco.

"What kind of art game?" I had never heard of art games, and was surprised that Marco had.

"You turn and face the wall, and I will become a work of art. Then you turn around. You have to guess which work."

"Okay," I said. This would be easy, since Marco would only remember two or three of the more recognizable pieces. "How long do I have to stare at the wall?"

"Until I say ready." I could hear him scuffling about, and it sounded as if he had opened a cupboard door and shut it again. It was several minutes before he spoke again.

"All right, Vito. Turn around."

What a shock. Marco had stripped off his clothes, and was wearing nothing but his socks and a bicycle helmet. In his left hand, held high in front of him, he clasped his shorts, and in his right hand, straight down at his side, he had a short plastic sword. He looked ridiculous. I think that at that age I was persuaded that sculpture should be dignified, something worthy of permanence, and Marco was anything but. He was an affront to my aesthetic sense.

"What are you doing, Marco?"

"I'm a statue. Which one?"

I recognized Benvenuto Cellini's *Perseus with the Head of Medusa*. At least Marco had been paying attention in the Loggia dei Lanzi. "It's the Cellini statue," I said. "The one of Perseus with Medusa's head."

"Hey, that's right!" He looked at me. "Now it's your turn."

"Marco, you goof. This is a stupid game. I don't want to play. Let's do something else. Maybe go kick the soccer ball." Marco would usually light up at that suggestion, but he seemed disappointed.

"I thought you'd like the statue. You spent a lot of time drawing that other one at the Palazzo today."

"Yeah, well, I'd rather draw a statue than be one. Let's go outside. Get dressed." We never played that game again, or even mentioned it.

My drawing skill became useful the summer we were fourteen. Soon after classes let out for the holiday, I went with Marco to stay with his grandmother in Venice. She didn't live in the main part of Venice, on San Marco Island, but on a smaller island, Burano, even further out in the Adriatic, where she ran a small shop selling the lace items she and several of her friends created. The place is under water now, but in those days it was still a thriving tourist area, with narrow canals weaving among brightly-colored houses and shops. Each of the canals had a wide pedestrian walkway bordering it on both sides, and as in Venice itself, there was no motorized traffic. We arrived on the water taxi, pulling up to the landing and clambering ashore near the big red brick church.

I was impressed. Marco's nonna greeted us with a huge plate of seafood pasta, the most delicious I had ever tasted. Of course, after the change, I couldn't eat such a dish today, but at the time it was wonderful. Nonna's guest room was upstairs, overly-large, with two beds, a spacious wardrobe and a window that looked out over the canal that bisected the town. I spent as little time as possible stashing my clothes in drawers or on hangers, pausing by the window every few moments to look out on the scene below. Marco had told me to bring all my art materials, because I would want to sketch and maybe even paint, and he was certainly right about that. His grandmother had set a table at the foot of my bed, where I could spread out my art papers. I had a portable drawing board with me so I could sketch anywhere.

After we had settled in a bit, we went off to explore the island. Marco had been there many times, and led me down the central canal, stopping at a gelateria to purchase some refreshment. I got my usual, cappuccino, but it somehow tasted better in Burano than in Florence. Marco wanted me to try the crema, his favorite, but I saved that for the next time.

"Notice anything interesting about the church, Vito?"

"Not really. It's just an old brick building. Why? What's different about it?"

Marco led me around to the waterfront side of the building and pointed to the bell tower, the campanile. "Just like Pisa, eh?"

It was true. The tower leaned off centre—not as dramatically as Pisa's famous tower, but enough to be noticeable. "I'm coming back here to sketch that later," I promised.

A couple of doors down from Marco's grandmother lived another Marco, a year or two older than us. As the sea level rose and Venice was increasingly threatened with flooding, a lot of families took to naming their sons Marco, after the patron saint of the city, hoping for divine intervention. No response from Heaven ever came, but there is a whole generation of Marcos to mark the effort. This Marco, whom I called Marco Burano to distinguish him from my friend, worked part-time in a café down by the docks. A couple of hours before noon each day he would mount his skateboard and weave his way through the pedestrians to the café to set up for lunch. He didn't work evenings, so we got a chance to spend a lot of time with him.

Marco—my Marco—was determined to master the skateboard. He didn't seem to have much interest in riding when we were back home, skateboards being very much out of style in Florence, but suddenly it became a matter of utmost importance here on the island. He begged Marco Burano to let him use it.

"This isn't a good place to learn, Marco. The sidewalks are too crowded. There's a park down near where I work. We'll go there."

This was a good decision. There was more room and the pedestrian traffic was thinner. I took my drawing board to sketch the church tower, and the two Marcos set about training sessions on the skateboard. I didn't expect it would take long for Marco to learn, and I was right. Within a half hour, Marco was zipping around the small park as if he had been born on a skateboard, Marco Burano shouting cries of encouragement. Marco learned a couple of maneuvers and ended the session well pleased with himself.

We began going to Marco Burano's café in the mornings to borrow his skateboard. I tried it a couple of times, but I couldn't begin to equal Marco's ease. He spent his time rolling around the park while I drew the town, the trees, the boats on the Adriatic. I wanted especially to sketch the people who occasionally meandered along the pathways, but they didn't stay in one place long enough to allow this.

Eventually I had sketched everything there was to sketch in the park, and decided to move into the main part of town to draw the canal, the shops, the brightly-painted houses and the crowds of people on the sidewalks. Marco went as usual to the café to borrow the skateboard, and I expected he would spend a couple of hours in the park before coming home for lunch. Instead, he showed up on the board while I was sitting on a low bench by the canal, drawing one of the footbridges that spanned the waterway. There was a street stand nearby, selling Venetian pancakes, and Marco bought a cinnamon crepe which he offered to share with me. It smelled great, but I was busy with my drawing and shook my head.

Marco was bored. He finished his snack and set about rolling back and forth on the skateboard, dodging in between the pedestrians on the walkway. He skated down to the bridge and back, then raced down to the church. I looked up to see where he had gone and saw him returning up the sidewalk. On the way he had to swerve sharply to avoid a little girl who ran in front of him. He lost his balance and the board went shooting off from under him and landed in the canal with a soft splash.

"Oh, shit!" I heard him say, and he ran to the edge of the water. Instead of floating, the board had sunk out of sight. I jumped up and went over to stare into the murky waters of the canal with him.

"Marco Burano is going to kill me, Vito. How deep do you think the water is?" I looked at him helplessly and shrugged.

"I'm going in. I've got to find the board before Marco Burano finishes work." Marco took off his leather sandals and slid down the edge of the canal into the water. It was up to his armpits. "It doesn't smell too good. The bottom feels all mucky." He began walking slowly and carefully around. I could tell he was feeling with his foot, hoping to encounter the skateboard.

A small crowd of tourists gathered, gawking at this Italian kid bathing in the cloudy water of the canal. I could hear them talking behind me and across the canal, in Italian, English and a couple of other languages I didn't recognize. Someone called out to Marco to ask if he was all right. He nodded grimly and continued his sweep of the canal floor.

After about fifteen minutes, he stopped his search and looked at me. "I don't get it, Vito. Where could the damn thing have gone? I've covered the bottom of the canal for thirty metres in both directions. It has to be here somewhere." I had a brief vision of some fish picking it up and carrying it away, but realized this wasn't at all likely. Marco hauled himself up out of the water and sat dejectedly on the edge of the canal, dripping stinking water down the wall.

"I'm in for it now, Vito. Marco Burano isn't going to let me off easily. He'll make a big fuss with Nonna and she'll be embarrassed in front of all the neighbors. I'd buy him a new board, but I don't have enough money and I can't ask Nonna to pay. Besides, I don't know where I'd even get one of those things."

"We saw some sporting goods stores on San Marco when we were there," I reminded him. "Maybe they have skateboards. They'd at least know where to get them. And we can put our money together to pay for it."

"Thanks, Vito, but you and I together just have enough cash to take the boat back to San Marco. We don't have enough money to buy anything there."

While we were discussing all these possibilities, I hadn't noticed people looking at my drawings of the bridge. I had left one sketch on top of my board, a portrait of a young woman who was sitting on the bench a couple of metres away from me as I pencilled in the scene. That same young woman was staring at the drawing and speaking to the young man beside her. I walked over and picked up the board and the drawings.

The young man spoke to me in English. I had studied the language in school, of course, but I wasn't all that confident. Still, I understood enough to know that he wanted the drawing and would pay for it. He wanted to know how much it was, and switched into Italian. "Quanto costa?"

I had to think quickly. How much could I get for one of my drawings? "Due euro, per favore, signor."

The man reached into his pocket and took out a wallet. He handed me a ten-euro note. I tried to explain that I didn't have any change, but he didn't seem to understand. He waved me away, gave the sketch to the woman, and walked away with her. I was left with a ten-euro note and a stack of paper.

"Marco," I said excitedly, "I think we can get some money." I quickly composed a sign in Italian and English offering portrait sketches for ten euros.

"Here, Marco. Hold this up so people can see." He looked a bit surprised, but did as he was told. I rushed off a quick drawing of him to use as a sample, and he held that, too. The canal water continued to drip off of him, but he didn't complain. We were both excited.

Our first customer arrived within minutes, a woman about my mother's age. She was Italian, from Bologna, her first time in Venice, she wanted a souvenir, she liked the sketch I had done of Marco, could I put the bridge in the background. She talked a lot. Behind her back, Marco was rolling his eyes. I tried not to look at him in case I began to laugh.

"Yes, signora. I can do that. Please sit here on the bench." While I drew the portrait, Marco ran down to the café to tell Marco Burano what had happened. I considered this a good move; Marco Burano could hardly stage a temper tantrum or become violent in front of his employer.

I can draw fairly quickly; the portrait was done to the lady's satisfaction in less than fifteen minutes, and I had another ten euros in my pocket.

Marco came back, still wet from his canal search. "Marco Burano says no big deal. If we give him the money, he can buy another board."

"How much?"

"One hundred euros."

"Holy! Who knew those things were that expensive?" In fact, we found out when we got back to Florence, that was almost twice what Marco Burano probably paid for his board.

It took a while for our next customers to show up, a young Danish couple who wanted both their portraits in the same drawing. Twenty euros. They gave me a five euro tip as well.

And that was it for the day. No one else wanted their portrait done. We had forty-five euros, which we handed over to Marco Burano when he arrived. We promised the other fifty-five euros as soon as we had them.

It took three more days, and I was growing weary of waiting by the canal for a tourist to stop and ask for a portrait. The days were even more boring for Marco. He longed to be going somewhere, but he was feeling guilty and didn't want to leave me waiting alone for a commission. Besides, I needed someone to hold the signs.

This experience taught me one important lesson, however. I could make money from art. I hadn't exactly abandoned my earlier dream of becoming one of the great Florentine artists, but as I grew up, doubts crept in. I didn't know anyone who worked as an artist. Even my art teacher at school had to hold down a job to finance her painting.

That was how, in my senior year of secondary school, I came to apply at the Accademia in Florence. I wanted to learn the techniques that had made Michelangelo and the others famous. I wanted to make great art, to receive commissions to paint murals and canvases.

Marco was more realistic. He wanted to study hotel management, perhaps even to go to school in Switzerland, where the world's greatest hoteliers had learned their trade. He would have to work for a while to earn the money to go abroad, but in the meanwhile he enrolled in a private hospitality college here in Florence. The certificate probably wouldn't be worth much, but it would prepare him for the more rigorous Swiss school and allow him to earn some cash while he studied.

We stayed close. Both of us were still living at home in our old neighborhood, and although we had different schedules, we found time almost every day for a game of soccer or a run by the river.

In my third year at the Accademia, everything changed. It was one of those still, crystalline afternoons near the end of September, when the narcotic heat of summer has almost come to an end and the rain has held off for a week. I was sitting in one of the staircases of the Accademia di Belle Arti, chewing on a piece of sausage and bread, when she came up the steps toward me. I don't think she even noticed I was there, but I certainly noticed her.

Adriana had a way of moving that seemed fluid, like a leopard slipping through the grass. She was dressed in a plain shirt of very pale blue and close-fitting blue jeans. In her right hand she carried a very large portfolio, so deep she had to bend her elbow and hunch up her shoulder to keep the bottom of the case from dragging on the stairs. She was with another girl, smiling and speaking quietly. I had never seen a more beautiful woman; she put all the paintings in Florence in shadow.

As she passed, I caught the fragrance of some unknown flower. I quickly stuffed the rest of my lunch into my backpack and stood up to follow, to find out where she went. It wasn't difficult. She turned into the first doorway on the second floor, the graphic design studio.

As a senior student I was permitted to observe classes in all departments, and I went in and sat down in one of the chairs at the side. Adriana—I didn't know her name until later—sat with her friend and opened her portfolio, spreading the textured art papers and a small tablet onto the table in front of her.

Much as I tried not to stare, I found it difficult to take my eyes off her. Throughout the class, no matter how often I glanced at other students and their work, no matter how I attempted to attend to the instructor, I found myself looking steadily at Adriana. This was a completely new situation for me. I had never felt much need for a girlfriend; I had always been content with my group of male and female friends—and that's all the girls were to me—and of course, with Marco's companionship. Now I wanted more than anything to get to know this woman.

Oh yes, I knew that this was not love; it was nothing more than lust, but the lust was not particularly sexual—not at this point, anyway. I was absolutely enthralled with her beauty, which I was taking in through the eyes of an artist. I visualized myself painting her, making her the centre of my oeuvre, like Rembrandt had done with Saskia, like Dante had done in verse with Beatrice. Together we would storm the art world.

Near the end of the class, she looked directly at me and smiled. I felt myself flushing red, and smiled back, then tried to appear nonchalant. I scanned the room again, pretending to be interested in other students' efforts.

I left before the class was dismissed, and immediately regretted the decision. I couldn't very well hang around outside, waiting for her to emerge, and I cursed myself for missing the opportunity to remark on her work, to start a small conversation that might lead to more.

The next day, though, I positioned myself again on the staircase, hoping she might once more pass by. She did not. I repeated the attempt the following day, missing one of my own classes to do so. This time I was lucky; she came up the steps as she had done two days earlier, and I looked directly into her eyes and smiled.

"Ciao," I said. "I saw your work in the graphic design class. It is very good."

She was startled, I could see. She was trying to quickly identify me, but not having much success. I felt myself shrink a little.

"I'm Vittorio," I said hastily. "Third year, painting. I sat in on your class two days ago. Your design work caught my eye. Good use of color; excellent composition. Your pieces are very effective."

"Thank you, Vittorio. I am just beginning, but I hope I'll be able to find a position in advertizing eventually. But now I'd better hurry. I don't want to be late."

"Can we meet, afterward?" I was shocked at my own boldness. "We could have coffee."

"I can't today. Maybe we could get together next week? I'm in this class on Tuesdays, Thursdays and Fridays. I'll see you then? I must go now. Ciao!" She was gone up the stairs and into the studio. I resisted the urge to follow her and sit in on the class again.

"Idiot!" I said to myself. "You didn't even ask her name."

The following day, I waited again on the staircase, and as she came up I greeted her and found out her name was Adriana. We agreed to meet after her class on Tuesday.

I spent all of Saturday with Marco. He had the day off work and we went to watch a soccer match, Florence against a team from Ravenna. We came back to his house and ate pasta his mother had left for us; then we sat and watched television, some American movie with Italian subtitles. It grew late and I walked home in the dark. I hadn't mentioned Adriana to Marco, and I wondered why.

Coffee with Adriana became a regular event on Tuesdays and Fridays. I soon discovered that she was as kind and polite as she was beautiful. It was as if the exterior and interior were perfectly aligned. She moved and spoke with profound confidence, but there was always a sense that behind the confidence there was a hint of self-doubt. It showed when she talked about her work.

"I wish I could draw as quickly and accurately as you can, Vito. It takes me hours to get the human figure right, and hours more to put the right expression on someone's face. I am capable of composition, and the instructor praises my use of color, but the details of life drawing escape me."

"It will come with practice, Adriana. If you like, I can help you with some suggestions."

This led to extra time together, with me as the smitten instructor, guiding her hand as she pencilled in various features. It gave me a chance to move very close to her, to breathe in the fragrance of her hair, to touch her arm as she drew. In fact, she was progressing very rapidly in her skills. I was afraid she would decide she no longer needed any coaching, but she showed no sign of wanting to discontinue our sessions. This gave me hope.

I suppose other boys might have pushed a little faster, a little harder, but I was finding it difficult to move our relationship beyond the level of fellow artists and casual friends. Certainly Adriana didn't seem to think we were anything more than schoolmates. I lay awake at night wondering how I could broach the possibility of declaring my feelings without risking losing her friendship completely. The thought of being rejected haunted me; I could not bear the idea that she might not want to be with me, and yet I could not bring myself to tell her that I wanted her.

Adriana was relaxed. She flirted openly with me, and when we parted, she always pulled my head down and kissed me on both cheeks. If we chanced to pass in the corridor of the Accademia, she would call out to me and wave, and whenever I saw her I would smile and mouth a kiss. That was as far as it went for several weeks.

We were sitting with our cappuccinos at a small terrace near the school one day when Marco walked by. For one shameful moment I wanted to let him keep walking, but I said to Adriana, "That's my friend, Marco." I called out to him, and he turned, surprised to see me.

Naturally, he came over to the table and I introduced him to Adriana. He sat down without waiting for an invitation, and I found myself pinched with a brief spasm of resentment. I wanted Adriana to myself. Luckily this feeling did not last; Marco asked the waiter to bring another cappuccino and before long all three of us were in conversation as if we had all been together for years. I had to credit Marco for his ability to fit right in to any situation.

This group of three coffee break became a regular twice a week event. All of us had two hours free on Mondays and Wednesdays, and we used the time to sit together, sipping coffee on cool days or spooning gelato during the warm days that lingered through October that year.

I had the brilliant idea of doing a series of paintings for my portfolio, paintings based on one of Shakespeare's Italian plays. I considered *Romeo and Juliet*, then *The Merchant of Venice* and *Julius Caesar*, before settling on *The Taming of the Shrew*. I felt this work had been less thoroughly interpreted in Italy, and would provide some dramatic compositions. It also had a happy ending, which appealed to me. I was going through a stage where I wanted my art to be uplifting, not depressing.

Of course, this would require someone to pose for me, and I had already planned to ask Adriana to model. When I suggested she take on the part of Katherina, she agreed, and urged me to invite Marco to play Petrucchio. He was willing, and we began spending Sunday evenings at my flat, where I would sketch in the outlines and then make a color study for the final painting.

This project took several months, and I had studies for almost every scene in the play. My plan was to winnow these down to five or six to add to my portfolio as finished paintings.

After the sessions we would usually go out to a café for a glass of wine and often something to eat as well. I found myself hoping that Marco would excuse himself before Adriana took a taxi home, but he always seemed to hang around to say goodbye. I wondered if I should just tell him straight out that I'd like some private time with Adriana, but I worried that he might be offended and decide not to complete the painting sessions. We seemed not to be on the same easy terms as we had been as boys.

Adriana was pleasant with Marco, especially when he flirted with her. He would tease her about her character as Katherina, complaining about her temper and her biting tongue. Adriana would retaliate by calling him a reprobate, an unreliable suitor, a wife beater. It was fortunate that no one overhead these exchanges.

I hit upon the idea of doing the final six paintings one character at a time. This would allow me to paint Marco into each scene and then invite Adriana for a separate set of sessions, where we could become closer. This went smoothly for the first of the three sessions with Marco, and then Adriana asked if she could come and watch me at work. I couldn't think of a good reason to refuse, and so we were once again a threesome. I was hoping that Marco wouldn't want to watch me painting Adriana into her scenes.

The project went badly. Technique was not an issue; I could paint, I could draw, I could arrange a composition on the canvas. What I couldn't seem to do with these dozen paintings was to breathe any kind of life into them. They were photographs, cleverly posed, but posed nonetheless. By the time I began the third one, I was in despair over the series, ruing the choices I had made and doubting my own ability as an artist. The pictures were flat, boring. I hated them.

Marco thought the paintings were amazing. He marvelled at the detail, at the perfect likenesses of Adriana and himself, at the way the colors imitated the fall of the light on fabric and skin. He was no artist, of course, so he could not see the fatal lack that so troubled me.

Adriana knew. She was evasive in her praise, rendering it something other than praise. Finally she just came out and said it. "Vito, you can do better. Why not try another subject? Maybe Shakespeare has been dead too long."

Although her comment hurt, I was glad she said it out loud. She was only speaking the thoughts that gripped my own brain, and she was offering another possibility.

For many days I ran over in my mind all the possibilities that I might pursue in creating my portfolio. My graduation would depend on being able to demonstrate a mastery of the skills; I was confident that even these lifeless portraits would show forth my ability to draw, to use color, to apply with expertise the techniques of my art, but I wanted more. I wanted to be a great painter, not a technician, and this would require me to rise above the mere application of the lessons I had been taught.

I thought long about Adriana's suggestion. I wasn't sure I had enough time to restart my portfolio, but I could at least try a couple of additional paintings to include with the failed pieces. Adriana agreed to model for another portrait, and we set up a time for her to join me in the studio at the Accademia. All I needed to do was contrive a theme, a pose, a story to go with the painting.

This, of course, was the problem. I could draw, I could paint, but I wasn't a story-teller. Finally I just decided to let Adriana pose herself, tell her own story.

She was happy to do this. She sat on the block, turned partly away from me, looking up and into the distance. The pose was strangely familiar, but I couldn't place it.

"Adriana, tell me what's happening right now. What's the story that leads up to this moment in your pose?"

She didn't know. "It's just the way I feel, Vito. I can't concentrate, so I'm staring into space."

The look was beautiful, even for Adriana. There was a softness, a gentleness in her position; she was almost like a figure in a dream sequence. Her long dark hair was free and fell loose around her shoulders. She had only a tiny bit of makeup on, and even this was unnecessary. Her eyes were clear but distant, and her mouth held just a hint of a smile, as if she were deciding whether to be content with life or disappointed. One hand was in her lap, the other lay flat on the block beside her; her left arm was straight, giving a slight lift to her shoulder. She was wearing a simple gown, pale blue with tiny yellow flowers along the neckline. The sleeves were short and undecorated. The only jewellery was a pair of Venetian crystal earrings, glinting softly in the natural light of the studio.

I started work at once, drawing the image onto the gesso-primed canvas. As I have mentioned before, I can draw quickly, and the basic outline was in place within minutes. Soon I was working the color study, choosing just the right shades from the palette and brushing the paint tentatively onto the drawing. Adriana sat stoically through it all, frozen in place, barely moving her eyelids. That absent expression never left her face and her eyes remained focused in the distance. We did not speak. Finally I picked up my camera.

"I'm just going to take some photos to use as reference, Adriana. Then you can break the pose and relax."

When I had done, we took a break and went for coffee in the small café around the corner.

"Thank you for doing this, Adriana. I can't afford to hire a professional model, as you know, and besides, there are no professionals who are as beautiful as you."

She laughed quietly and took another sip of her coffee. She smiled over the edge of the cup and looked into my eyes. "Flatterer," she said. "Words are worth more than cash, though."

"Adriana," I began, but she put out a hand and touched my wrist.

"Not now, Vito," she said. "Let's finish the coffee."

I was puzzled and hurt, and I imagine my expression showed this. I wasn't even sure what I was going to say, but there was obviously something Adriana was not yet ready to hear. I was quietly cursing my shyness, wishing I could be as confident as Marco would have been in my place. He would have simply confessed his love to Adriana and let the pieces fall if necessary. I knew that the pieces would be fragments of me, and I wasn't prepared to let them fall.

We finished in a sort of stilted politeness, and I walked Adriana back to the Accademia. She went to prepare for her next class and I went back to the studio to work on the painting. Suddenly, though, the canvas seemed barren; the drawing and its touches of color held no promise of any future meaning. I sat down heavily on the floor and looked at the portrait in despair. I must have sat there for an hour or so, long enough for the light to fade and the room to be cloaked in shadows, before I stood up and left the studio.

Even days later, I couldn't make the portrait work. I covered it with a cloth and put it aside. Marco was my next hope; maybe I could do something with his portrait that I couldn't do with Adriana's. Maybe I was so taken with her beauty that I couldn't capture enough of it on the canvas. I called Marco and he readily agreed to come and sit for a portrait the next day.

I made a good beginning. He was standing beside the block, with one arm leaning on it and the other resting lightly at his side. I had forgotten just how good-looking Marco was; his facial features were perfectly formed, and he was well-built, slender but not too thin. There was a light stubble across his chin, his hair was just slightly ruffled. He looked like a farm boy, or perhaps a hunter—someone used to the outdoors and comfortable with physical work. He was looking straight at me, his dark eyes locked on mine.

There was no hint of a smile, just a purposeful look that suggested he was about to undertake some daunting task.

Again the drawing went quickly and again I got the color study done without incident. Again I caught his expression on camera. Just as we were about to finish, the studio door opened and Adriana walked in. When she saw Marco, she stopped, a stricken expression on her face. She looked as if she would like to turn and run from the room, but instead, she came over and kissed him on the cheek, then did the same to me.

"Nice to see you again, Marco," she said, flashing him a smile. "I've missed you since you started working in Montecatini." As part of his hotel management course, Marco was doing shifts at one of the hotels in the spa town.

"I'm staying at the hotel," he explained. "Today is my day off, and Vito asked me to come and pose, so here I am."

Adriana was looking about the room; I knew she was wondering about her own portrait. "I'm still working on it," I told her. "It's not ready for display yet."

A brief shadow of disappointment passed over her features, but she smiled brightly. She suggested we all go for coffee when Marco and I were finished, and we settled in at a table at the little café on the Piazza Santa Croce. Migrant workers from Sénégal and Guinée hawking counterfeit goods, elderly Roma women begging for coins, teenagers clad in hoodies and jeans, fashionably-styled young women and the omnipresent pigeons made a lively scene, but I was more interested in speaking with Adriana alone. At last Marco said he had to go to his parents' house for a visit and dinner, then back to Montecatini so he could work the early shift in the morning. He clapped me on the shoulder and leaned in to give Adriana a hug. She reached up and touched his cheek, a look of such longing on her face that I could not ignore it or explain it away. I felt something inside my chest shrink, and I struggled to keep my expression neutral.

I walked Adriana back to her flat in silence; she did not invite me in, but put her arm on my shoulder and kissed my cheek. All the way back to my street I could smell the faint fragrance of her perfume, a haunting presence that left me feeling sadder than ever.

I worked fitfully on the portraits, but nothing would come right. The lines were perfect, the composition was balanced, the colors were muted and real, but the whole was less than the sum of its parts. Neither Adriana nor Marco lived on their canvas. I began once again to rethink my career choice.

One afternoon when I had tried in vain to work some spark of energy into Adriana's portrait, I thought for a second that I saw Marco pass the studio door. Knowing this was impossible, or at least very unlikely, I went back to my labor.

A short while later, Adriana came into my studio. She was crying; her eyes were wet with tears and she almost stumbled as she walked toward me. I jumped up and helped her to a seat.

"What's wrong? Are you hurt?"

She looked at me, uncomprehending. She made no sound, but the tears continued, one by one, to run down her cheeks. She shook her head. "It's Marco," she said simply.

I knew. I had known for weeks, months. She was in love with Marco, not me. I was too slow, too hesitant. I had lost her, and it was my own fault. For long minutes I was mute, unable to open my mouth, unable to even think of anything to say. I put my arm around her, and she leaned into me. I reached across to the table for a tissue and handed it to her.

"Vito," she said quietly. "I've been such a fool. I built such a dream world, and now it has all dissolved. I just didn't know. I didn't see any of it. I'm so sorry."

I couldn't bear to see her so full of grief. "Adriana, it's all right. I understand." The words were coming to me. "I love you, Adriana; I hoped you might come to love me too, but I want you to be happy. If you and Marco want to be together, you have my blessing. I'll tell him the same."

Adriana turned sharply and looked at me, her eyes flashing with sudden anger. I was taken aback. What had I misjudged?

"Vito," she almost spat at me. She jumped up and faced me. "You're just as stupid as I am! Stupid, blind, stupid!" Her face was contorted, her eyes red, but even in her sudden rage, she was beautiful.

I had never heard her speak like this; I had no response. For a few seconds she stood looking down at me; I suppose the look on my face must have been one of shock and confusion. Certainly that was what I was feeling. Adriana's voice softened, then, as if she were melting.

"Vito, Marco doesn't love me. He just told me so. Marco is in love with you, has been for years. How could you not have known?" She turned and walked out of the studio.

I was stunned. How indeed could I not have known? Marco had never said anything, never done anything to show his feelings toward me. He was my best friend; that was all. I couldn't understand where Adriana had got such an idea.

Marco was standing in the doorway. "Ciao, Vito," he said sadly. "Adriana must have told you. I'm sorry. Sorry for everything. I'll go now."

I didn't try to stop him. I should have, I knew. Maybe there was no way to save our friendship, maybe he was as hurt as Adriana had been, but I should have tried. I should have told him that nothing needed to change, even though we both knew that everything had changed. Above all, I should have told him that I loved him. Adriana was right. I was blind and stupid. Now I had lost her and Marco both. I felt the tears coming and made no effort to resist. I leaned on the table and sobbed until I was exhausted. I had never been so empty.

Adriana's failed portrait was propped up on the easel, mocking me with its flatness. I picked up my brush and began to place tiny strokes of color, working from the eyes to the rest of the face, then to the body. I was hardly aware of what I was doing, but I kept at it until the light faded and I could not see to continue.

I must have fallen asleep in the studio. The night watchman came and woke me, asking if I needed anything. I shook my head and went out into the cool night. I was overcome with the dread that I would not see Adriana or Marco again, that they were gone forever.

I began again the next morning, working at the portrait with an intensity that I had never been able to summon before. Instead of the long, broad brush strokes I usually employed, I was working in minute dabs of paint, each tiny touch of the soft bristles adding only a milligram of paint to the canvas. It was as if something was guiding my hand, choosing the colors for me, showing me where to touch the canvas. I worked all day, without a model, calling up the memory of Adriana in my imagination and painting what I remembered, not what I saw.

By late afternoon I was faint from hunger and thirst, my arms ached from the sheer physical demands of painting, and I was unsteady on my feet. Finally I admitted that I needed to stop for the day, but I went back to it the next day and the next until at last the portrait was done, and it was good. In fact, it was better than good; I knew I had a masterpiece, a portrait in a new style, one that I could present as the best I was capable of achieving.

I went home, ate and slept. The next morning I rose early and returned to the studio, where I restarted the portrait of Marco, working from memory and using the same tiny strokes and careful technique. I took no breaks for lunch, rarely even pausing to drink the bottle of water I had brought from home. By late afternoon three days later, again, I had a finished work of art, and it was the equal of Adriana's portrait.

In both paintings I had captured something fleeting, a look of grief that gave a depth to the eyes and a paleness to the cheeks. In both the lips seemed almost to tremble with restrained sadness. Adriana was looking away, up and into the unknown, while Marco was staring straight into the viewer's own eyes, into the unknown sorrows of the viewer's own life.

Then I took up the brushes again and reworked two of *The Taming of the Shrew* portraits. It was a kind of magic; the pictures of Adriana and Marco together held a subtle paradox—one got the sense that they were attracted to each other but separated by some unseen barrier. If you ask me today how I achieved this effect, I would be unable to explain.

The teachers on the graduation jury were stunned, and one even asked me to swear the work was my own. I offered to let them watch me complete another painting, and they accepted. Before I had even finished, though, they were urging me to submit the portraits, all four of them, into the Biennale, which had been moved from Venice to Verona because of the flooding. There was some quick discussion about whether portraiture, in the formal style, was too "traditional" for the Biennale, but ultimately everyone agreed that I should enter. The Biennale was an exhibition of modern works of art, and I had developed a modern form of portraiture.

At home, I began to second-guess myself. Would it be ethical to exhibit the paintings without the models' consent? I wondered whether the judges would even consider work from a painter who had yet to graduate from the school of art. In the end I realized that the models were as fictional as Shakespeare's characters—I had painted them from my imagination, not from life; the opinion of the judges did not matter to me. I would exhibit.

The paintings went ahead of me to Verona, and when I caught up with them they had already been mounted and labelled as paintings of Romeo and Juliet, the lovers who had made Verona famous. My immediate reaction was to object to this incorrect identification, but I recognized that the expressions on the faces were tragic, not comedic. *Romeo and Juliet* was a far better fit than *The Taming of the Shrew*. I left the labels.

The critics flocked to the paintings, along with the general public. The judges awarded me two medals, and I was besieged on all sides by people who wanted to know the techniques I had employed. Representatives of the São Paulo Biennale in Brazil and the San Francisco Museum of Modern Art in America asked me to lend the paintings. In the end I fled back to Florence, leaving the Biennale curators to deal with the return of the paintings.

The paintings now hang in the Galleria d'Arte Moderna in Rome, where they continue to attract visitors after all these years. I wonder if Adriana and Marco have ever seen them, and if so, what they thought about them. I have never gone to visit.

On the strength of those four paintings, I was given a number of commissions, which I began to work on immediately. The results were competent, pleasing even, but not ground-breaking. The life that breathed out from my portraits of Marco and Adriana was muted in each of my subsequent works and the critics soon lost interest. I became a sought-after portraitist to the wealthy of Italy, of which there was an abundant population. Just having a work by Vittorio Costa was enough; the paintings did not need to be good.

I had money and I had contacts. What I lacked was personal happiness. There was a constant nagging insecurity, a sense that I was incomplete and would perhaps always be incomplete. When I was asked to take a teaching position at my old school, the Accademia in Florence, I accepted, just so I would have a base from which to work. Eventually I was also granted a curatorial position at the Galleria next door.

I forced myself not to think of Adriana or Marco. At first this was difficult; even reminding myself to think of something else inevitably made me conjure up memories of my two lost loves. Eventually, though, they faded from my conscious mind and I was able to go for weeks without recalling either of them; their very images in my mind began to blur.

Still, there was an emptiness to my life that I could not ease. My commissions led to invitations to openings, to art lectures, and even to many house parties, where I was the quiet guest in the corner. I met many very attractive young women who wanted to model for me, but I always ended up comparing them to Adriana and they always fell short of that ideal.

As an artist I was pathetically unaware of what was happening in the wider world. My painting consumed my working hours, and my leisure time was filled with thoughts of the next project. It wasn't until the entire world had come to hear about the boy that I noticed the reports.

This boy had already been seen in many parts of the world, starting in Africa, it was said, and then appearing in places all across Asia. He was healing all sorts of diseases, physical and mental, if one were to believe the increasingly far-fetched tales we were getting. He was credited even with stopping armed conflict, bringing peace to the troubled region of East Africa.

Now he was appearing in Europe; he had been in Vienna and then in Belgrade, then in a host of other places throughout the southeastern parts of the continent. People were flocking to him, crowding in to be cured of their ills. I was not really much interested in joining the throngs, but when rumors began to run through the streets that the boy was in Florence, my curiosity was piqued. I thought perhaps he would make a good subject for a painting—the miraculous boy, the healer of the multitudes. I at least wanted to see what he looked like.

And so I found myself swept along with the crowds, jostling together in the narrow streets of the old city until we crossed the old rail yards and poured into the Via Frusa, then into the Stadio Ridolfi. The stadium had an air of carnival, with people of all ages laughing and shouting, some dancing to tunes played on accordions. No one seemed in a hurry to come or go, but the numbers filling the stadium were increasing steadily. It took me almost an hour to work my way through the wall of humanity to face the boy.

I stopped, dumbfounded. The boy was Marco! At least, he was a perfect double for a younger Marco, with dark hair slightly long and a little bit wavy, those same deep, dark eyes, the perfect jaw line and long lashes. He looked sad, though, in a way I had never seen Marco look until that final day in the studio. I thought I was going to faint, but the boy looked straight into my eyes and I nodded. He reached out and touched my forehead, his fingers cool and light on my skin.

The thudding of my heart slowed; the dizziness was replaced with a profound sense of calm. "Grazie," I murmured. I don't think he heard me; he was already reaching out to others as the crowd pressed in on him. I stood immobile for a while, watching him, convincing myself that he was not the boy I had grown up with. Of course he wasn't; I knew that, believed that, and yet I was almost hypnotized by the resemblance.

When I got home again, I sat for long hours in darkness, wondering, wondering. There was a peace, but there was also a host of questions. At last I fell asleep, still in my chair.

They say the boy cures all diseases of the body and mind, but I would ask whether he cures the afflictions of the soul. Does he heal grief? It is true that I have never been ill since that day, that I have grown forty years older without a decrease in energy. But it is equally true that I still feel regret, and a sense of loss. I have been able, for the most part, to suppress these feelings, until something brings them to the surface again, as inexorably as lava flowing from a volcano.

I have not created a single painting in decades now. Whatever talent I had withered away after my meeting with the boy. This seems to be true for everyone—the only worthwhile works of art and literature, the only really fine musical compositions these days are coming from those artists who have never met the boy. Maybe the arts, the whole realm of imagination and creativity, demand some kind of suffering. Works like Michelangelo's *Pietà*, Dante's *Divina Commedia*, Verdi's *Aïda*, do not come from contented spirits. While I would not describe myself as "content" I have lost any urge to create great paintings.

Instead, in my posts as associate director of the Galleria and instructor at the Accademia, I curate. My role has become that of protector and preserver, passing on knowledge and skills to generations that increasingly are unable to use them. Although the boy has been gone now for over thirty years, his legacy endures. Some people say it is nothing more than a genetic mutation, and I do not understand enough biology to doubt that, but others insist the boy brought healing to humanity just in the nick of time. No matter who is right about its origins, the change is passed down from parent to child, apparently even if only one parent carries the genes. Each generation gives rise to more and more people with the new strengths—and the new loss. The genius of men and women today goes into restoring the natural environment and preserving our history. The present is consumed with the future and with the past.

I wonder why I have never tried to find Adriana or Marco. Just as I cannot explain why I did not run after Adriana that ill-starred day, or why I never told either of them how much I loved them, so I cannot explain, or even understand, why I have made no effort to reunite with either. I do not know why neither of them has communicated with me. Instead, I grow old without aging, alone but not lonely. Do I thank the boy or curse him for this gift?

Perhaps I will try now to reach out. The shock of seeing the young woman yesterday in the Piazza Santa Croce reminds me of a grief I have buried too long. It might bring me some further measure of peace if I can learn that Adriana has made a happy life for herself, if Marco has found someone to share his days, if they have each found another love as great as that which once bound the three of us together.

10.

TORONTO

And so it all comes to an end. When the fatigue hit me yesterday afternoon, I knew it wasn't just the tennis game that had worn me out. This tiredness was much more pervasive, reaching into every fibre of my body, every cell. At eighty-seven years old I cannot complain about life being too short, although I would certainly like to go on. Some of us still last more than a century, but I will not last much more than another day or so. That is how the pattern goes, after all.

My wife, Jessica, is bustling around the apartment, while I sit here in this recliner and watch with weary eyes. Already I am losing much of my peripheral vision, so I know that time is running short. Jessie is busy making coffee and getting some slices of cake onto plates. The family has been summoned to attend and must be shown proper hospitality. I know that this is Jessie's way of distracting herself from what is really happening, and I am happy that she has something to take her mind off my dying.

Dying is not so bad, you know. It isn't focusing my mind the way it is said to do. There is no pain and no real fear. I am a bit curious, although I confess I really don't have much faith in a life after death. Still, I wonder what it will be like to leave this world behind.

The outside door opens and my daughter, our only child, Anna, is coming towards me, her arms outstretched. I feel my face lighting up. She gives me a warm hug that lingers just a little longer than usual, then she steps back and looks at me.

"How was tennis yesterday, Papa?" she asks. She is sounding very upbeat, but there is a bit of strain in her voice, and her face does not look at all upbeat.

"It was good," I reply, "until it wasn't. I got very tired. You know what that means. Your mother must have told you, right?"

She nods. Her eyes are wet, but she will not cry. My son-in-law Eric and my grandson Zachary come in from the hallway. They have been to the bakery downstairs and have brought some fancy pastries. Zachary strides over and gives me a hug, just as warm as his mother's. He is all of twenty-four years old now, almost grown up. He is tall and thin, a perfect candidate for the basketball team, although his sport is actually swimming. He has reddish-blond hair and the most striking green eyes, both of which characteristics he gets from his paternal grandmother. I could pick him up and swing him around, a game he loved, until he was twelve, but I would need a crane to lift him now. I love this boy more than I can say.

Eric comes over and puts his hand on my shoulder. "We came as soon as we heard, Papa Dan," he says. He's never been able to call me "Dad" or "Papa," and "Papa Dan" is as good as it gets. I smile at him and say thank you. Like Anna, he carries the mutated genes, thanks to a mother who was touched by the boy long ago in Toronto. He has been a devoted husband and father and a wonderful son-in-law.

Jessica has switched on the wall panel for the communicorder. The green light is on, so I know it is in translation mode. I recognize Rachel's house in Bangalore. One of my great-nieces, Rachel's granddaughter Rohini, is speaking in Hindi, and the English subtitles are running across the screen. The early versions of the communicorders needed to be programmed for the language we wanted translated, but these days the machine can identify most of the world's major tongues automatically and do the translation almost instantaneously. Now the face of my brother-in-law fills the screen. Navin speaks English, but he and Rachel use Hindi at home and it is the first language of the girls, my two nieces, and of their children. Rachel hopes to keep all the varied parts of the family heritage alive.

Rachel is not home, but Rohini is calling her on the mobile to relay the news of my condition. Rachel will call as soon as she gets back from her meeting.

Rachel and her family will not be joining us. The journey from India takes too long now that air travel has been so widely restricted. High-speed trains and jet-thrust ships still would need almost a week to get them to Toronto. We will say our goodbyes electronically. Jessica closes the session.

I have lost track of Eric. Ah, there he is, in the kitchen. He's slicing fruit and arranging it on a plate. I have to turn my head completely to see what he's doing. There is darkness along the outer edges of my view. For several long minutes I wonder what the scent is, and then I recognize the fragrance of cinnamon. I have studied enough about the dying process to remember that this is one of several smells that seem to accompany the end of life. I like cinnamon, so the aroma is comforting.

My body is worn, exhausted, but my mind is busy. In earlier times, people used to say that in the moment of dying your entire life flashes before you, sort of a time-lapse recording of all you have been and done. I don't know if that is still true—or if it ever was. I haven't heard anyone make the comment in many years. My thoughts drift from the present to the past and back again.

I think about my parents, waiting in that long-ago hospital room for their little boy to die. My mother is sitting beside the bed, her head bowed. I can't imagine the anguish it must bring to lose a child. I think about that other boy, El Niño, the one with the miraculous touch, who came into our lives at that critical point and restored me to life.

I think about my childhood, so free from anxiety and pain. How lucky I was, compared to most of my contemporaries. Although it took me longer than my friends to grow up, I was never bullied or left out of things. I had my bar-mitzvah at thirteen and a great crowd of friends turned out for the celebration. Zachary, like most kids these days, didn't have his bar-mitzvah until he was eighteen—the tradition changing with the times. This change didn't occur overnight. There were endless discussions in the community about changing the age for the ceremony, but eventually people just ignored the arguments and waited. By the time Zachary's turn came the question had more or less been decided.

I think about my time in university in Vancouver, earning my doctorate in sociology. People told me there was no future in sociology, that, like economics, it was destined to become a discredited discipline, but in fact it was about to come into real prominence as the world adjusted to the rapid changes the evolutionary tsunami was unleashing. I was advised to study engineering, biology, ecology, anything except a social science. I'm glad I didn't listen.

I think about meeting Jessica, after my return to Toronto. She was working in early childhood education, and I was introduced to her at a party by my sister, who knew her through other friends. She was between attachments, she said, by way of conversation. "The guy was like a barnacle, he was so attached. He just wasn't attached to me," she added. We got along from the outset. She was funny, open-minded, full of life. Within a week we were calling daily, and I knew that she was the one. She was a little more cautious, naturally, but I won her over and we have never looked back.

I think about those early years together, living in the apartment in Toronto, where Jessica took the subway every day to the preschool at the bottom of University Avenue. Most of her charges lived in the neighboring condominium towers, but some were brought in from farther afield by parents who worked in the area. I did a lot of my consulting work from home, but traveled every so often to Ottawa or Edmonton or some other city for a face-to-face meeting with my clients. I learned to cook so that Jessica would come home to a decent meal every night. It was difficult for me to prepare any kind of meat dish, though, and eventually Jessica simply chose to follow a vegetarian diet like mine.

We were busy, but even before our daughter was born, Jessica had transitioned to a four-day work week, like almost everyone in the country. Now she works two days a week in administration, claiming she doesn't want to retire although she has the option. Many people who do not have the mutation find it too tiring to keep working as they approach their eighties, but Jessica seems as fit as ever.

I remember Anna's birth. Everything went smoothly at first; labor was not overly-long and Anna was brought neatly into the world, wrapped in a blanket and handed to me. Jessica does not have the mutation, so there was always the danger of complications, but we were not worried. The birth had proceeded fairly easily and the baby was healthy-looking and beautiful. Within minutes, though, Jessica was moaning in pain. The obstetrician quickly checked her over and discovered a ruptured artery. The haemorrhage was severe, and it took almost three quarters of an hour to repair. By then Jessica had lost a great quantity of blood, and despite the transfusions she was given she looked pale and utterly exhausted. I was terribly frightened by the whole experience, but Jessica gradually recovered and returned home to us. Still she and I were never able to have another baby, so our daughter grew up—slowly, as I had done—as an only child.

I think about Anna's childhood. In her generation there were more and more children with the mutation, so she fit in better with her peers than I had with mine. Almost half the children were growing up at the slower pace, and no one thought it unusual. Of course, by the time Zachary was born, almost all children were carrying the genes. Anna was an exceptionally easy youngster. She was always playful and eager to go places.

She almost never got upset, and then only with good reason. She learned quickly and collected new skills and ideas like a squirrel gathers acorns. She loved going to High Park, the Islands, the Leslie Street Spit—anywhere she could see birds and small animals. We didn't miss a single tree-planting day for eight years.

I adore my daughter, and we had a special bond in our genes. It was up to us, she said, to take care of her mother whenever Jessica fell ill with some virus. "We don't get sick, Papa, so we have to look after Mama. That's our job." We moved from the Toronto apartment to a townhouse in Richmond Hill when Anna started school. Anna and Eric still live there; although the town is much smaller than it was in her childhood, it still has the subway link to Toronto and the surrounding parklands and farms are Anna's ideal environment.

For my doctorate I ended up studying alterations in forms of governance, and I traveled to the small island republic of Mauritius in the Indian Ocean, where almost the entire population had undergone the genetic shift. Mauritius was experimenting with direct decision-making, as opposed to parliamentary democracy. Instead of electing representatives to a governing body, Mauritians were drawing names randomly from a national roster, like we once did for jury selection at trials in Canadian courts. The people chosen were named to the assembly for a five-year term. Some of them were less capable, but by and large the assembly came up with good policies, which were presented to the public and widely discussed. Usually modifications were made as a result of these consultations. Then people voted electronically to accept or reject the proposals. In the two years I was there, not a single proposal was defeated, although almost all of them were amended on their way to acceptance. The wisdom of crowds, they used to say.

When Canada began investigating the possibility of similar structures here, I was ideally placed to consult. The arguments were civil but profound: how could we adopt a system that had worked, as far as we could tell, only in a small, relatively heterogeneous society like Mauritius. Canada was a vast land with wide variations in its traditions, two official languages and a host of Indigenous communities. We managed to get pilot projects going in several Manitoba First Nations reserves, and the success of these experiments led to Portage-la-Prairie and five other Manitoba towns trying the same ideas. As you know, much of the world is now governed this way. Zachary has already served his term as a city councillor in Richmond Hill, the only member of the family so far to have his name drawn in the lottery. I am proud of my role in developing the new constitution and having it adopted across the land.

There was an old witticism about a Chinese curse: "May you live in interesting times." I have to say that my life has been lived in such times. Now, as it draws to a close, I am grateful; I do not feel cursed.

My thoughts are interrupted. Eric is talking to me, and I am momentarily flustered at not noticing.

"Papa Dan, are you comfortable? Is there anything I can do?" I am comfortable. Everyone is already doing what needs to be done. I smile and shake my head.

My main occupation has been sociology, the sociology of governance, but my true calling has been the mystery of the boy. I have spent countless hours researching his appearances, traveling to the places he once visited, interviewing the witnesses. I have almost three thousand of these interviews on record, and they are remarkably consistent.

Those who have met him say, with very few exceptions, that the boy is young, about twelve (today we might think he was older). His clothing is simple and completely unremarkable; he seems to wear whatever the local style is. He has dark hair and very dark eyes. His skin is an intermediate color, not really light, not really dark. He smiles, but his eyes have a look of deep sadness. He speaks many languages but uses few words. He is quiet and his touch is light.

Witnesses report feeling as if they are immersed in calm, in relief, in a sense of security and well-being. He appears as if out of nowhere and vanishes the same way, often reappearing in another place far away. People describe him as magical.

That's the sticking point, even today, for those who doubt. There are too many coincidences, too many contradictions, too many impossibilities. To speak about the boy, all these years after his final appearances, is to shut down conversation; an embarrassed pause ensues. No one wants to reopen the arguments. Conflict is a source of great discomfort for us.

Someone once advised me to apply Occam's razor to the mystery. The simplest explanation is most probably the correct explanation. By "simplest explanation" people invariably meant the theory that the boy is an illusion generated as part of the sudden evolutionary shift in human populations, a sort of mass hallucination.

I have come to the conclusion, however, that there is an even simpler explanation. When literally millions of people all report the same thing, when they describe the boy in the same terms, surely the logical explanation is that they are telling the truth. We know that those who claim to have met the boy are almost totally incapable of lying about anything else, and they are steadfast in their stories. I believe what my mother repeatedly told me about her own experience, and I believe the people I have interviewed since.

It was the boy who changed us. The benefits flowed from his fingers, not from random chance.

He gave us peace instead of conflict. He gave us health instead of sickness. He gave us food instead of hunger, water instead of thirst. He brought us trust instead of suspicion, hope instead of fear. We have long periods of leisure instead of constant stress. Our age-old problems with crime have all but vanished.

Yes, we have lost some of our humanity, as the critics have maintained all along. The sense of adventure and uncertainty that accompanied our fears and sorrows was perhaps exciting. Lost love, suffering, war—all the events and feelings that departed from the ordinary—may have inspired great works of art and literature; life is now much more routine and prosaic. Several prominent thinkers who did not undergo the change have argued that what we have lost is in truth greater than what we have gained. They say that humanity without sorrow is humanity that cannot truly appreciate joy, that the good things we seek cannot really exist without their opposites also being possible. Some argue that the loss of diversity in our genes exposes us to catastrophic risks. There is a fringe of thinkers who claim we are in danger from alien invasion, that our pacifist majority won't be able to defend us if we are attacked, but almost everyone dismisses this. The greatest loss has been cultural; there is no new art, no new literature coming out of the changed communities of the world. New inventions, yes, with engineering improving something every day, but no gifts of pure imagination.

Of course, given that my whole life has been possible because of the boy, I think the gain was worth the price. A world where there is enough for everyone, fairly shared, where we work for what we need to be—as Eric puts it—"comfortable" and no more, where we help each other as much as we can; surely this is the world we dreamed of throughout past millennia. Now we have it.

The mutation, we know now, brings with it a limitation of the birth rate. Although there are a few documented cases of mutated people producing three and even four children, they are the rare exceptions. Most families now have only one child, and already in my lifetime the world population has decreased by almost two billion. Population pressure has been the driving force behind all the degradation of the environment and many of the old social ills could also be laid at this same doorstep. The pressure is off at last.

As the population declines, the world is healing itself. Climates are still unstable, of course, but the forests have begun to recover and the air and the oceans are already cleaner. Human settlements are more compact than they were even fifty years ago. Look at how many of the high-rise towers here in Toronto have already been demolished, replaced with low-rise buildings and parkland. We have room, and this seems to bring us closer together in so many ways.

The scent of cinnamon is stronger, and the field of my vision is narrowing still further. Anna has pulled the armchair over and is sitting beside me, and Jessica has at last settled onto the sofa on my other side. Zachary is on the floor beside my feet, his arm resting across my knees. As I die, I am surrounded by love. I can feel it, and I return it. I reach out and take Anna's hand. She squeezes gently.

The communicorder screen lights up again, and it is Rachel. "Hi, Daniel," she says brightly. I am in the direct range of the wall camera, so I smile and look at her face on the screen. "I'm sorry I can't be with you," she continues. "Just know that we love you and hope you are comfortable."

There's that word again. For a brief instant I wonder if perhaps we have become too attached to comfort, too unwilling to face anything that takes us out of the ordinary path. I struggle to refocus on what Rachel is saying, but the words seem to blur and run together. It is a relief when Anna picks up the conversation with her aunt, asking about the girls and the general state of life in India. Rachel rounds off the call by telling me she loves me and wishing everyone well. The screen goes dark.

Life has been good, more than just comfortable. I have a sense of accomplishment, both in my official role as a sociologist of governance and in my unofficial career as researcher of the mystery boy. All my documentation will be passed on to the university in Vancouver, to do with as they wish. Some day maybe a student or professor will continue the study.

I have one regret, though. I have no memory of my own meeting with the boy. He came to my hospital room more than eight decades ago, touched my forehead and my life, then left me. In all the years I have sought his story, he has remained just beyond my grasp. Was he just an illusion, as so many have claimed, or was he real?

And how much does it matter? We have physical and mental well-being, the resolution of conflict, the end of crime and exploitation, the gradual easing of the population pressures, the restoration of a healthy environment. The things that made us unhappy—greed, pride, jealousy, fear, hatred—are gone from the vast majority of human beings, and we don't feel deprived. If we had had the choice, would we have chosen differently?

I feel a slight breeze, as if someone has opened a window and let in the spring air, scented with that ever-present cinnamon. I can hardly see now, except straight ahead. I am so tired. I hear the voices, but I cannot make out the words.

Then, there he is, the boy, El Niño Milagroso, standing right in front of me, outlined against the communicorder screen. Although I have never seen him before, I know him. I cannot tell if he is real, or just an image on the screen itself. Perhaps part of dying is a recurrence of the illusion, but he seems so immediate. I want to reach out and touch him, to take his hand, but I do not move.

He is still young, still the same boy everyone has always described. His dark eyes are looking directly into mine. I do not see sorrow there, though. His gaze is calm, steady. He is smiling, just a little. He holds out his hand toward me. Zachary does not seem to be aware of him; there is no change in the pressure Anna is applying to my hand. Jessica says nothing, but I know she is right beside me.

I feel safe. I close my eyes and inhale the scent of the cinnamon. I know I will not be alone. I smile then, lean forward and fall softly into the warm darkness.

Acknowledgements

My sincere thanks to Ariella Hofmann-Drooker, John McTavish and Marion McTavish, for reading the manuscript in progress and offering encouragement and many valuable suggestions and insightful comments.

Thanks also to Carol Hofmann and Paul Rose for detailed suggestions and for asking questions that made me rethink parts of the story, and to early readers Athena Graves and Quang Tran for their kind words and advice. Tho Buchan helped with the checking of the final manuscript.

I am grateful to Jeyanthan Anandarajan and Chrishanthi Anandarajan, who took me to Sri Lanka and introduced me to an amazing cultural landscape, and who offered helpful advice on the Jaffna section of the novel.

Of course, I owe a debt to the people at Wipf and Stock who took a manuscript and made it into a book, especially Stephanie Hough, Daniel Lanning and Matthew Wimer. Thank you all.

www.ingramcontent.com/pod-product-compliance
Lightning Source LLC
Chambersburg PA
CBHW070629310726
48982CB00001B/223

* 9 7 8 1 5 3 2 6 5 9 7 0 6 *